Welcome Home

Welcome Home

Glenda Poulter

P.D. Publishing, Inc.
Clayton, North Carolina

ISBN-13: 978-1-933720-69-2
ISBN-10: 1-933720-69-7

9 8 7 6 5 4 3 2 1

Cover photo by Glenda Poulter
Cover design by Barb Coles
Edited by: Day Petersen/Verda Foster

Published by:

P.D. Publishing, Inc.
P.O. Box 70
Clayton, NC 27528

http://www.pdpublishing.com

Acknowledgements

There are so many people to thank who helped and/or inspired me to write this novel.

Welcome Home was inspired by some brave souls I knew when I attended high school in the mid '70s. They shall remain nameless to preserve their privacy, but I wish to thank them for their courage to "come out" and face the ridicule of their peers at such a young age and in such an unforgiving time.

I would also like to acknowledge and thank all the teachers I've had over the years, both formal and informal. My Creative Writing and Journalism teacher at Crowley High School in Crowley, TX, thirty-some-odd years ago, Mrs. Joan Leonard, always pushed me to a higher standard. Clarice Dickess, my composition teacher at the University of Alaska, Fairbanks, (during the one time I attempted to achieve a higher education) saw potential in my writing that I denied then and continued to deny for many years. Yet her words of encouragement echoed in my ears and stuck with me even when I wasn't writing.

The members of the lesfic_unbound yahoogroup have taught me more then they'll ever know. The success of the authors has encouraged me; the posted reviews have helped me strive for excellence; the readers' comments have taught me to be open to the opinions of my audience; and the patience of the owner/moderator is unmatched anywhere else. Thank you to all of you!

Also, there is my family – both my "real life" family and my "cyber" family – I would like to thank. Lisa Beemon, my beautiful partner, nagged me to write her a story when I told her back in 2006 my dream was to be a writer. You're holding the result of that nagging in your hands. My daughter Kaycee and her husband Robert and my son Scott believed in me when I told them I was writing a novel. And then there's Donna and Cathy, Barb and Tracey, Marline and Alice, Linda and Sue, and so many more of my online sisters and cheerleaders. I thank you and I love you all!

Last but not least, I would like to thank Linda and Barb for taking a chance on a new writer. I learned so much from my wonderful and patient editors, Day and Verda. Thank you for your help and thank you for making *Welcome Home* so much better than when I first started.

And thank you, readers!

Dedication

Welcome Home is dedicated
to the sweet memory of
my beloved godson,

James Arthur Jenkins
February 16, 1980 – August 9, 2005

and
to the memory of my mother,

Anita May Grimes
August 2, 1937 – April 26, 2007.

I love and miss you both.
Take care of each other up there.
And Mom, quit haunting me!

I also dedicate the book to
the love of my life and my soul mate,

Lisa Kay Beemon.

Thank you!

I stepped back from the sign-in table, pinning my panther shaped nametag to the lapel of my linen blazer. Thirty years. It was hard to believe so much time had passed since high school graduation and the last time I had seen or spoken to most of the people milling around the vestibule and banquet hall. I hadn't attended any of our previous reunions and I wouldn't have been at this one if I hadn't been in town on business.

The reunion committee had put together displays to update us on the activities of our fellow classmates from the class of '76. I wandered among them, stopping at the "In Memoriam" table. It was draped in black and gold, our school colors, but also in this instance, the colors of mourning. Twelve members of the class were already gone. I knew, all too well, about two of them: my good buddy Howie and my dear friend Carolyn. Howie succumbed to AIDS during the early days of the epidemic and Carolyn died by her own hand, a victim of deep depression.

I stared deep into the smiling blue eyes of Howie's senior picture, his spirit still alive on that flat surface. He was the class clown and our school mascot the last two years of high school. He hid his homosexuality well. Only a few of his closest friends knew. Once we graduated, he left town quickly, traveling across the country to the gay mecca of San Francisco. By the mid '80s, he was sick and alone, ostracized by friends and family. At the end, he stayed with me in Atlanta until he died. I spent many hours with him as he wasted away. *"I miss you, bud,"* I mouthed at his picture.

Carolyn's deep sadness wasn't obvious in her senior picture. In it, she fairly glowed. We now knew she was good at hiding her insecurities and unhappiness. Though quiet and sometimes introspective, she always seemed so happy, as if she had all she would ever need. She was intelligent and beautiful and popular, yet she didn't seek or bask in her popularity like some did. In September of 2000, Carolyn took her husband's handgun and ended a life we all thought was charmed. The note she left behind for her husband was simple: "I'm too tired and too sad to go on from here. I love you. Please continue to live, to laugh, to love." We never knew why Carolyn took her life.

I moved on to the "Where Are They Now?" tables. Each member of the class was asked to send in a recent photograph and a short biography. Along with a print of our senior picture, the entries were put into notebooks and scattered about the tables for us to look at. Some of the biographies, the ones the committee found most interesting, were mounted and displayed prominently. I expected the displayed biographies to belong to the reunion committee members or their best friends, so I just glanced at most of them, until one caught my eye.

There I was, my recent photograph and my senior picture enlarged to glossy 8 by 10s, my biography and copies of some of my articles and accompanying photographs displayed on a black background with my name, Shelby Livingston, in large gold letters across the top. I stood there, staring, my mouth hanging open in shock. I couldn't believe they put my life and my work on display.

"What do you think, Shelby?" a voice from my past asked.

I whirled around and stood face to face with the first person who helped me realize I could succeed at anything I put my mind to. She was a student teacher in a couple of my classes my senior year, including Journalism. I privately credited much of my success as a freelance writer and photographer to her. She was now head of the English department at the high school.

"Ms. Gilmore!" Without thinking, I threw my arms around her neck in the hug I always wanted to give her, but didn't dare to, so many years earlier. She returned my hug just as enthusiastically. I felt a bit of my heart melt.

"After all these years, I believe it would be okay to call me Valerie," she said, laughing.

She stood back, still grasping me by the shoulders. We took a long moment to look each other up and down. She was still a beautiful, youthful woman, though I knew she had to be in her mid-fifties. Her smile lit up the room. Her hair, cut short in an attractive style that accented her high cheekbones, was a rich brown with only a few stray silver strands. I wanted to sit and talk for hours but other people vying for her attention suddenly surrounded us. "We'll talk before the evening is over and catch up a bit." She gave my shoulder a squeeze and then turned her attention to the others.

I reluctantly returned to perusing the display of my achievements and shook my head in wonder. Ignored by the popular crowd in high school, I had only a few close friends. After graduation, my friends and I scattered to colleges and towns across the U.S. We seldom came back to our hometown except for family gatherings and special events such as this. To see my accomplishments displayed in such a manner surprised and pleased me in a way I wouldn't have expected.

I was about to move down to the next display when a familiar shock of bright red hair caught my eye. The person I considered one of my best friends for sixteen years of my life and who became my worst enemy during my seventeenth year was headed straight for me. I looked around for a quick escape but there was none.

"Shelby, how are you?" she asked. Naomi's voice was ragged from the effects of too many cigarettes and her skin was rough from working outdoors for long hours without proper protection. "It's been a long time, huh?"

"Yes, Naomi, it has been a long time." Instinctively I was on guard, even though it was over thirty years since she had deeply hurt me and my friends.

"You look good." I couldn't say the same about her, so I just nodded my thanks. "Looks like you're doing well, too," she added, acknowledging the display over my shoulder. "How long are you in town, Shel?" she asked, using the nickname only my closest friends used.

I wanted to tell her she had no right to use it, but I was trying to let the past go and move on, something easier said than done, even after thirty years. "I'm not sure yet, but probably another week or so."

"Can we get together and talk?" she asked, a note of uncertainty in her voice. "Please?"

I looked at her warily, wondering what she wanted. Just then the chimes announcing dinner rang. Without giving Naomi an answer, I followed the rest of the class into the dining room.

The evening passed quickly. People who had little to do with me in high school now wanted to pretend we'd been best friends. It was amazing how a little success and name recognition could change the way people acted. With the exception of Naomi, whom I avoided as much as possible, the few people I'd been close to were not in attendance.

That night, I reflected on the evening.

Valerie Gilmore and I made plans to meet for lunch later the following week. I agreed to call her sometime during the weekend to finalize the details. I was disappointed Melissa and Kara hadn't come to the reunion, but I understood why they chose to stay away. I wondered why Naomi wanted to talk to me. We hadn't spoken in over thirty years, and no matter how hard I tried, I couldn't put the hurt she caused behind me. The banquet hall, though crowded, had felt strangely empty without Howie and Carolyn.

My eyes roamed my bedroom, finally coming to rest on a framed photograph on the bookcase. There we stood, the six of us — Howie, Carolyn, Naomi, Melissa, Kara, and me — arms linked in eternal friendship, ready to conquer the world. The photograph was still clear, as were my memories of that last glorious summer before our disastrous senior year.

Howie had propped himself against the boathouse wall, his long frame stretched against the weathered wood. I leaned back against him, my head against his chest, his arms locked around my waist in a brotherly hug. Naomi stood close, her head against his left shoulder, almost as tall as he, her red hair glowing in the sun. Carolyn stood next to her, a head shorter, a tanned arm stretched in front of the two of them, grasping Howie's elbow and locking them into a tight embrace. To Howie's right, her back against his body, stood Kara, hugging tiny Melissa.

That day was a carbon copy of so many others that summer. We spent the day at the beach just an hour east of our hometown, playing in the surf and building sandcastles. We cooked hot dogs over an open fire and toasted marshmallows for dessert. When we returned home, we decided we didn't want the day to end so we traipsed down to the boathouse to fish for crabs and cast nets for shrimp. My big brother, Kyle, was already there and I asked him to take our picture. I had albums and albums of photographs of my friends and family, but few included me. This photograph was one of my favorites because it showed us all together.

Howie, Naomi, and I knew each other from our earliest days when our mothers got together to visit and let us play. We grew up leaning on, and loving each other. Carolyn joined our group in first grade; two years later, Kara and Melissa completed the Six. From that time on our mothers knew — look for one and it was inevitable they would find the rest.

Except for Howie and Carolyn, we were pretty much considered the outcasts of our high school. Kara and I were unabashedly tomboys at a time when femininity was still highly regarded. Kara and Melissa came from broken homes; something seriously frowned on in our conservative corner of the country, even still in the early twenty-first century. Naomi was loud and arrogant, and committed the cardinal sin of not being beautiful. But we all loved each other and protected each other and kept each other's secrets; at least until that horrible, out of control year that led up to me leaving my beloved hometown and my dear friends the day after graduation.

I turned off the bedside lamp and moved from the bed to the window seat in my darkened bedroom. The ghosts of my youth gathered around me and I could almost hear the giggles that used to resonate through the room. The moon rose, sparkling through the Spanish moss and foliage of the great oak outside my window. The stars glittered in the dark sky, even the smallest ones visible since they didn't have to compete with city lights — one of the benefits of having a house outside of town. The swing hanging from the giant branch that arched over the yard rocked gently in the night breeze.

I hadn't been home since Carolyn's funeral six years earlier. Dad passed away a few years before Carolyn, and since Mom and I weren't close — especially after her behavior when I came out to her, and then during the trial — I hadn't seen any reason to come home. Now Mom was gone, too. I wouldn't have come home now except I was bidding for a permanent position on the city magazine up in Charleston. My job took me all over the world, but I was ready to settle down. At nearly forty-eight years old, the traveling was wearing on me. Maybe if I could stay in one place long enough, I could have a relationship that lasted more than a few months.

I closed my eyes and breathed the night air through the open window. The smells of the salt and the pluff mud, that strange smelling mud that the South Carolina coast is famous for, wafted up from the marsh. The tide was moving in; I could hear the sea grass swish as the water engulfed it. It would be a good night to cast for shrimp. How many nights during that last summer had we braved the mosquitoes and spent long hours on the dock throwing our nets?

Memories I had been running from for thirty years overwhelmed me.

Part One

Chapter One
Late August, 1975

"Shel! Why aren't you ready to go?" Howie's voice boomed up through the branches of the oak tree and into my room. I was curled on the window seat reading and had lost track of time. I was supposed to be ready to go to the beach with the gang half an hour ago.

"I'm coming!" I yelled out the window. "Just give me another minute or two."

My bedroom door burst open and Naomi and Kara bounded in. Kara grabbed my hand and the camera bag and started pulling me toward the door as Naomi grabbed my beach bag.

Kara laughed as she dragged me down the stairs. She was so tan that her skin was nearly the same color as the brown hair pulled through the back of her red and white ball cap.

"Wait. I didn't put suntan lotion in my bag. You may turn as brown as an Indian, but I bake without it," I said. By then we were standing beside Howie's tan, '69 camper van.

"I have suntan lotion." Carolyn was sitting in the seat directly behind Howie's. She wore the white bathing suit and sarong set her parents gave her for her seventeenth birthday. Her long blond hair hung over her shoulders, making her deep tan seem even darker.

My heart jumped when I saw her, just as it always did. I wondered if she realized I secretly had a crush on her. Of course she didn't. Howie had been brave enough to come out to us, but I didn't have his courage. I hadn't told any of my friends I was a lesbian, even though I'd realized it about six months earlier. So, I bit my lower lip and admired Carolyn in silence.

"Let's get this show on the road," Melissa said from the rear of the van. "The day isn't getting any younger."

Kara leaped into the van, joining Melissa on the rear bench. I crawled into the front passenger seat as Naomi folded herself into the seat next to Carolyn. As soon as Howie saw we were all safely in, he sweet-talked the van into starting and we were off.

An hour later, we piled out and raced for the beach at Hunting Island State Park. The lighthouse towered over the park, a once active beacon now a tourist attraction. We raced past it and onto the sand, then wandered down the beach until we rounded a point where few families ventured. We spread our blankets and moved toward the water as one. The day sped by as we played in the surf and soaked up the sun.

By evening, a large group of high school and college students were on the beach. Summer was rapidly coming to a close and we all wanted to make the most of the time that was left before the responsibilities of the school year resumed.

A fire pit was dug and before long a bonfire blazed. As the sun set, couples started breaking off from the crowd, finding secluded areas to cuddle, kiss, and neck.

I leaned back against Howie's knees, my legs stretched in front of me as we talked quietly about school, our jobs, and our dreams. Howie and I had been best friends since before we could walk. We were often considered a couple, which was in Howie's favor since he didn't want anyone else to know he was gay. We looked good together, his tall frame towering over my short, stocky one. Howie wore his ash blond hair long, almost to his shoulders, while my auburn hair was cut as short as I dared. We had a special relationship others thought was romantic, and neither of us tried to explain.

Carolyn was with a small group of kids gathered around the fire. She was popular in a quiet way and the boys all vied for her attention. I watched as she threw her head back in laughter at something someone said. My breath caught in my throat at her beauty and the way her hair sparkled in the firelight.

Naomi's attention was on two horses a couple had ridden up the beach. She was in deep conversation with the riders as she stroked the horses' necks. It amazed me how gentle she was with animals but how brusque and sometimes cruel she could be with people. Naomi's family owned a large horse farm just outside of town, and sometimes I thought Naomi would rather spend time with the horses than with people.

I looked around for Melissa and Kara but didn't see them. They had been best friends since third grade and it wasn't unusual for them to wander off and put their heads together just to talk.

I grabbed my camera from its bag and started wandering through the group, stopping occasionally to take pictures. Naomi turned and smiled at me, one hand on either horse. I snapped her picture and chuckled to think how most of the photos of her were with an animal. I posed the group Carolyn was with, centering her so her hair glowed, backlit by the fire. Howie dozed in his chair, long legs stretched in front of him, hands clasped on his chest. I took his picture from several angles before the flash woke him up and he threatened to throw me and my camera into the ocean.

I set up my tripod to take some timed exposures of the fire and the group. Just as I started taking pictures, I heard a commotion from the far side of the dunes. I could hear Melissa crying and Kara and Naomi yelling.

As I topped the dune, I was shocked to see Naomi and Kara fighting. Melissa was standing to one side, holding her bikini top against her and screaming at them to stop. Howie and some of the other boys arrived and pulled the two girls apart. Naomi's nose was bleeding and Kara would soon have a black eye. I noticed Kara was topless and assumed her top had been pulled off in the fight.

"What the hell is going on here?" boomed Howie, holding Naomi by one arm. Kara picked up her top and tied it on while Melissa stood at her side, her face red and tear streaked.

"None of anyone's business, especially hers!" Kara said, her voice quiet, but husky with anger as she gestured in Naomi's direction.

Now that the fight was over, most of the kids went back to the bonfire, whispering and speculating about what had happened. Soon it was just the six of us. Naomi was shaking with anger and Kara had turned her back on us, gathering Melissa into a hug. Howie stood between Naomi and Kara, using his tank top to stem the flow of blood from Naomi's nose.

"Naomi, Kara, what happened? Why were y'all fighting?" Carolyn's voice was quiet, but stress was evident in the tone. "I've never seen y'all even have a cross word and now you're trying to tear each other apart."

"It was nothing," Kara said, gathering up her blanket and putting a protective arm around Melissa. "We're ready to go home."

"Nothing!" Naomi screamed, trying to lunge past Howie at Kara. She almost knocked him off his feet, but he was able to keep her from attacking again. Kara stepped back, pulling Melissa with her.

"Stop it!" I yelled. "This is ridiculous! Why are y'all acting like this?"

Carolyn stepped in front of Naomi and put a hand on her arm, wordlessly appealing to her. They stood like that until Naomi began to calm down.

"Shel, would you please go get our things?" Carolyn kept her hands on Naomi, never losing eye contact with her as she spoke. "We're all going over to the pavilion to wait for you. Then I think we should find out why this happened before we drive back home."

I quietly went to do Carolyn's bidding. As I approached the fire, I fielded questions from the others gathered there. "I don't know what happened," I repeated over and over. "I don't know why Naomi and Kara were fighting," I said to person after person. The fun had gone out of the evening and almost everyone was packing up to leave. A few stayed behind to put out the fire and clean up.

At the pavilion, Naomi sat with her back to the rest of the group, her elbows resting on the table behind her. Carolyn and Howie sat on either side of her. Kara and Melissa sat further down the table, Melissa's head on Kara's shoulder.

"Okay," Carolyn said. "Let's talk. Kara, Melissa, y'all scoot down here. Naomi, turn around and look at us." When they had complied, she continued, "Naomi, you go first. What did Kara do that made you so terribly angry?"

"I had to go to the bathroom bad, so I decided to take a shortcut over the dunes. I got to the top of that one dune and looked down and, and, and..." Naomi glared at Kara and Melissa. "I can't believe what I saw you two doing!" she screamed at them, lunging across the table.

Howie and Carolyn caught her before she got to them, but Kara and Melissa had already jumped up, overturning the bench, forcing me to my feet as well. Sobs tore from Melissa's body as Kara gathered her into a tight, protective embrace. Howie and I made eye contact as I righted the bench and sat back down. I saw the same shock in his eyes that I knew he must have seen in mine. Our group was seldom angry with one another and never like this.

"Kara," Carolyn was taking charge again, "what's going on? Can you help Naomi understand? Shoot, not just Naomi, but all of us?"

"Melissa and I..." Kara hesitated. She looked down at the petite teen she held close. Their eyes met. It was as though electric sparks flew and each relaxed just a bit. Melissa gave an almost imperceptible nod and Kara continued. "Melissa and I are partners, lovers, girlfriend and girlfriend, whatever you want to call it. Naomi walked up on us kissing."

"Kissing! That's not all you were doing! You two were all over each other! It was disgusting!"

"Why did you attack me, Naomi?" Kara asked, her voice low and husky. "Are you jealous that Melissa loves me or are you jealous because no one will ever love you?"

Naomi growled and started to lunge again, but Howie and Carolyn held her back.

"Kara, there's no reason to be cruel," I said. "But, Naomi, why did you attack her?"

"I don't want nothin' to do with no lesbos!" Naomi yelled. "It's one thing to have to put up with a fag in our presence, but I don't have to put up with dykes, too!"

The rest of us gasped and then held our breath. Howie's face turned red, then white. He dropped his hand from Naomi's shoulder and shook his head. He hadn't said anything since he first broke up the fight at the dunes, and now I could see his heart breaking.

"I think we should head home now," he whispered. I hurried to catch up with him as he strode toward the parking lot, but he shook my hand from his arm.

The drive home was quiet. I had no clue what to say to anyone, but especially not Naomi. I was shocked at how ugly she had been about Kara and Melissa's relationship, more shocked than I was about their relationship itself. I was secretly relieved that it wasn't me coming out to my friends that caused the misery we were all feeling.

Even though it was out of the way, Howie dropped Naomi off first. Carolyn accompanied her to the door and I could see them talking, but couldn't hear what was being said. Naomi was shaking her head violently, her body language obviously mirroring her words of disgust. Carolyn's shoulders slumped in defeat when Naomi shrugged off her hug.

As Carolyn climbed back into the van, I glanced back at her and saw she was as pale as her swimsuit. I reached back and patted her knee and was rewarded with a half smile. I smiled back as Howie maneuvered the van through the silent streets to her house.

I walked Carolyn to her door. "What did Naomi say when y'all were on her porch?"

"She's so upset, so angry. In all the years I've known her, I've never seen her like this. It's kind of scary. I never knew she hated homosexuals so much. She's never said an ugly word about Howie until today."

"Do you think she'll come around?"

"You mean accept Kara and Melissa's relationship? I don't know. I hope so, but I doubt it."

I hugged Carolyn before she went inside. I ached for her. Naomi was her best friend, or had been before tonight. I knew things would never be the same for them, or for any of us, and it saddened me.

Howie took Kara and Melissa home next, dropping them off at Melissa's house. I watched as Kara held the door open for Melissa. She turned, gave us a little wave, and disappeared inside.

When we got to my house, I was reluctant to get out of the van. I knew Howie's parents and little sister were out of town. I didn't want him to go home to be alone with his thoughts and I didn't want to be alone with mine. He leaned across the space between the seats and hugged me. My tears started flowing and soaked the shoulder of his bloody tank top. I looked at him and through my tears started to laugh.

"If your mom sees that shirt, she's going to think you were the one who got into a fight. Why in the world did you put it back on?"

He looked down and grimaced. "Yuck! I put it on without even thinking about how it looks. How am I going to explain this without telling my folks I'm a fag?"

"Don't use that word." I lightly punched him on the shoulder. "You're gay, but you aren't a fag. I can't believe Naomi said that."

He took my hand and kissed my knuckles. We climbed out of the van and walked over to the swing hanging in the oak tree. The swing was wide enough for two people to sit side by side, but I waited until he sat down and then sat between his legs, just the way we had for the past ten years. He shoved off with his feet and then let the swing go to and fro under its own momentum and we relaxed for a few minutes.

"Howie, did you know about Kara and Melissa?"

"No, but I suspected. They always seem to be touching, and they hug each other constantly. And since Melissa and Eric broke up, she hasn't gone out with anyone else. I don't think Kara has ever gone on a date. But I didn't know for sure."

"I must be blind or dense; I had no clue. But you're right about how they always seem to be touching. I'm so used to them being together all the time; I didn't think anything about it."

We sat in silence a few minutes, Howie using his legs to keep the swing going. I rested my head against his chest, wondering if the six of us would ever be the same again. I knew instinctively there was no way we would be, but my heart hoped against hope. I also knew I had to tell Howie my secret.

"Howie, I have something I need to tell you." I felt him chuckle more than I heard him.

"Sugar, if you're going to tell me you're queer, too, I already know."

I fell out of the swing and landed at his feet as I tried to stand up too fast. I looked up at him and he threw his head back in a great belly laugh. I stood up and grabbed the ropes of the swing and held it still so I could look him full in the face.

"What makes you say that?"

"Shel, you've been a tomboy since we were in diapers. And I've only known you to go out with one guy, me."

My tears started falling again. Howie stood up and gathered me to his chest.

"It's true. I am a lesbo, as Naomi so graphically put it. And after what happened tonight, I'm also scared."

Howie didn't say anything. He just stood and stroked my head and rubbed my back and let me cry. We sat back down and held each other. The night birds called and a sea breeze caressed us. He finally got up and led me to the porch, where he hugged me one more time before urging me into the house.

"I love you, Shel," he said to me through the screen door. "And whatever happens, nothing will ever change that." With those words, he headed back to his van and his empty house.

Chapter Two

I was restless all that night. The little sleep I got was plagued with visions of Naomi and Kara's fight. Naomi's ugly words rang over and over in my head. I grieved, knowing our friendship was probably over and we would never be the Six again.

Diffused by the curtain of Spanish moss hanging from the tree, the sun was just beginning to peek in the windows of my alcove. The summer sky was white along the horizon; another hot, humid day loomed. I was tempted to hide from the day in my johnboat out on the tidal marshes, but I knew doing so wouldn't change things.

I was about to gather my things to take a shower when there was a timid knock at my door. The door opened slowly and Melissa peeked in. I grabbed her and pulled her into a big hug, pushing the door shut with my foot.

"Are you okay?" I asked, my voice muffled in her short, black, strawberry scented hair.

I felt her nod, but her arms tightened around me. I loosened her grip and led her to the bed. Her big brown eyes brimmed with tears. "Are you sure you're okay?"

"Oh, Shelby! Last night at the beach was so scary. But I'm glad Kara and I don't have to hide from y'all anymore. Are you mad at us?"

"You never had to hide from us to start with, silly. And no, I'm not mad at y'all."

"That's so good to hear." Melissa swiped at hair that no longer hung over her shoulder.

"Why do you do that?" I asked, laughing. "Why do you keep trying to push your hair over your shoulder when it's not there anymore?"

Melissa laughed too, pink tinting her cheekbones. "I still can't get used to not having long hair. I like it like this, but I think I'll let it grow out again." She went to my dresser and looked in the mirror. "Dorothy Hamill looks a lot better with this haircut than I do."

I stood behind her. Our reflections couldn't have been more different. Melissa's diminutive frame and dark features contrasted with my stocky frame and pale, almost anemic complexion. I kissed the top of her head.

"How's Kara?"

"She was still asleep when I left the house. She has a black eye and a bit of a fat lip, but I think she's kind of proud of them."

"Think they'll heal before we go to Beaufort next week for our senior pictures?"

"Oh, my gawd!" Melissa's hand flew to her mouth and she spun around to face me. "I completely forgot about that. What if she still has a black eye?"

"I guess she'll have to reschedule," I said, laughing.

"You girls want some breakfast?" Mom called from the base of the stairs.

"We're on our way," I called back.

Melissa and I ate our French toast and scrambled eggs on the back porch, enjoying the morning breeze. Heat waves were already rising off the marsh, but the humidity wasn't oppressive yet. As we ate, the smell of low tide mingled with the aroma of our breakfast and the coffee brewing behind us in the kitchen.

After we ate, Melissa went home to check on Kara. I showered and did my chores before calling Carolyn and Howie and asking them to meet at Melissa's. Howie had to work, but Carolyn and I agreed I would pick her up and we'd go to Melissa's right after lunch.

My '68 blue sedan grunted and groaned and complained about not being driven for a few days, but after Kyle showed me how to prime the carburetor I was able to pick up Carolyn. Her long blond hair was pulled back in a loose braid, showing off her tan shoulders, bare in a multi-colored peasant shirt. Her red shorts barely peeked out from below the shirt and long brown legs finally ended in white sandals. Her beauty astounded me yet again as she climbed into the car, leaning over to kiss me on the cheek.

"Did you get any sleep, Shelby?"

"A little bit. Do I look that bad?" I strained to see my face in the rear view mirror.

"A bit of a raccoon face, but not too bad." Carolyn laughed. "A little make-up would hide those shadows under your eyes, you know."

Carolyn and Melissa both loved to tease Kara and me about make-up. They both wore it and looked wonderful, but the two of us refused to touch the stuff. Kara said it was too much trouble and I felt like a clown when I tried to wear it.

The Ballard home with its pale yellow paint and bright white shutters had always been a safe haven for the Six. Mrs. Ballard and her friend Sue Ellen always had a hug for us, and, when we were younger, lemonade and cookies and now cola and Moon Pies.

Carolyn and I found Melissa and Kara in Melissa's room, lounging on the floor, digging bare toes into the pink shag carpeting. Kara's right eye sported a deep blue and purple bruise and a small cut just above her eyebrow.

"Wow!" I exclaimed when I saw her. "I wonder if Naomi looks as bad."

"Thanks." Kara laughed, then turned serious. "I hope Naomi looks worse. I still can't believe how she acted."

"I tried to call her this morning," Carolyn said. "She wouldn't talk to me. Her mom asked me what happened and I told her there was a misunderstanding that led to a fight and that Naomi would have to explain."

"She wouldn't even talk to you?" I was surprised. Carolyn and Naomi had been practically inseparable since first grade.

We sat in silence a few minutes. I replayed the night before in my head, still stunned and shocked.

Carolyn wiped her eyes with the back of her hand. "Has anyone talked to Howie today?"

"I did," I said, reaching out and patting her shoulder. "He had to work at the Burger Barn today or he'd be here. He seemed okay. We talked a long time last night when he took me home."

"Let's go to the Barn for a malt later and give him a hard time," Kara said.

"Hey, what did your mom say when she saw Kara's eye?" I asked.

Melissa sighed. "She was upset, but we were honest about what happened and why."

"You told your mom y'all are a couple?" Carolyn sounded surprised.

Melissa and Kara smiled and nodded. Their hands were entwined and Kara brought Melissa's to her mouth and kissed it, nodding again, this time to Melissa.

"Yeah, we told her and Sue Ellen the truth," Melissa said.

"How did they take it?" I asked.

The girls grinned at each other again and then Melissa let us in on a secret.

"Y'all have to promise not to tell anyone except Howie," she said. "Mom and Sue Ellen have been a couple since I was three years old." Kara and Melissa laughed at our reactions. "If y'all don't close your mouths, you're gonna catch some flies," Melissa said, reaching over and pushing my jaw up as Kara did the same to Carolyn.

"Wow!" I finally said, at the same time feeling a sense of relief I didn't really understand. "Wow!"

"I don't know what to say, either," Carolyn said. "How long have you known they were more than friends?"

"In a way, I've always known," Melissa said. "But they sat me down and explained their love when I was in fourth grade and wanted to know why I didn't have a father to take me to the Father-Daughter Banquet at the Girl's Club that year."

"I remember that banquet," I said. "Your uncle or someone came down from Greenville to take you, didn't they?"

"It was actually Sue Ellen's brother, but it was easier to call him my uncle than try to explain."

"So when you told them about you and Kara, they weren't real upset?" Carolyn asked.

"They were upset because they know how hard it is to live as a couple and not let people know," Melissa said. "They want our lives to be easier than theirs have been, but at the same time they're happy we have each other."

"Momma Kay didn't seem too shocked, and when I asked her about it, she said she had suspected for a long time that we were closer than just friends."

"Momma Kay?" I asked.

Kara laughed. "I've been calling Mrs. Ballard 'Momma Kay' in private for so many years, I forget y'all don't know."

"Can I ask y'all a personal question?" Carolyn's voice was quiet, unsure. "Y'all don't have to answer if you don't want to."

Kara reached across and patted Carolyn's tan knee reassuringly. "Go ahead, Carolyn. What do you want to know?"

"How long have y'all known you're more than just friends?"

Kara put her arm around Melissa's shoulder and pulled her close. They looked at each other for a long moment before Melissa gave a slight nod.

"Actually, I've known longer than Melissa has, but when she and Eric broke up last winter is when we really got together."

"Kara came over to spend the night that night. I broke up with Eric 'cuz he kept wanting to touch me in places I didn't want him to touch. Kara and I were lying in bed that night and I was trying to explain to her how his touch just didn't feel right, how his hands were so rough."

Melissa ducked her head, peeking shyly up at Kara who pulled her close and kissed her forehead.

"Anyway, Kara was lying behind me in bed, holding me while I cried and tried to understand why I felt so much of nothing with

Eric. I usually wear a nightgown, but that night I had on a pair of baby-doll PJs and the top had ridden up a bit."

"My hand touched the skin on her side and I couldn't help but caress her. It was amazing how her skin warmed up under my hand and how the warmth seemed to spread up my arm."

Kara stopped speaking, turning redder than I'd ever seen her. Melissa's color was high, too.

"Y'all don't have to say any more," Carolyn said, also blushing. "I think Shel and I get the picture."

Secretly I wanted to hear more, but I knew there was no real need.

"That was the day I knew I never wanted another boy to touch me," Melissa said. "I realized later that emotionally I had known for a long time before that. Kara and I connected from the time we met in third grade and that connection just seems to grow stronger."

"Have you told your mom, Kara?" I asked. Mrs. Ashley was the one mom of the Six I didn't know well. She worked two jobs and was seldom home when the rest of us were at Kara's little house on the edge of town.

"Mom just wrinkled her nose and shrugged," Kara said, wrinkling her own nose. "She basically said she wasn't surprised but to try not to let anyone else know. She's afraid she'll lose her job at the primary school if anyone finds out."

"Hopefully Naomi will keep her mouth shut and your mom won't have anything to worry about," Melissa said, cuddling closer to Kara.

We sat in silence a few minutes, each with our own thoughts. I felt safe with these three special friends; I realized I could tell them anything.

"Do y'all remember last spring when Justin Haygood kept asking me out?" I asked.

"Yeah, I remember," Kara said. "He just wouldn't take no for an answer."

"Didn't he try to talk your mom into making you go to the prom with him?" Melissa reached over and smoothed a stray hair back from my forehead.

"Oh, she did try to force me to go." I shivered at the memory. "She actually bought me this horrible green lacy creation she called a formal and she made an appointment for me to get my hair fixed!"

"You're kidding!" Kara shook her head. "I don't remember that part. What happened?"

Melissa sat back to look at her partner. "You don't remember her telling us about Justin showing up at the house in a tux, with a corsage for her?" Kara shook her head again. "Geesh, you've got an awful memory sometimes." Melissa wrinkled her forehead in mock disgust. "Tell her what your mom did, Shel."

"Mom followed Justin down to the dock where I was fishing. When I still refused to go, she tried to tell me my privileges were going to be revoked if I didn't go to the dance. Fortunately, Dad had followed her and he put a stop to that. Neither Mom nor Justin understood why I'd rather fish than go to that stupid dance."

"That begs the question," Carolyn said formally. "Exactly why didn't you want to go to the prom? Justin's a handsome guy, one of the most popular boys in school. Almost any of the other girls would have killed to have him ask them."

"Geez, Carolyn," I said, laughing. "You sound like Dad when he's got someone on the stand. Are you planning on being a lawyer?"

"No." Carolyn shook her head, her braid swaying with the motion. "But truly, why didn't you want to go out with Justin?"

"Yeah, Shel. What gives?" Kara reached over and lightly punched my arm. "Why not date Justin?"

I hesitated a moment too long. Scooting over to sit directly in front of me, Melissa took my face in her small hands and looked me straight in the eye. Without any warning, she threw her head back and roared with laughter. The rest of us could only look at her.

Scooting back over to Kara, she took Kara's face the same way, and I watched as they made the same kind of eye contact. Almost as if they communicated without words, Kara was suddenly laughing as well. Carolyn and I looked at each other and shrugged. Finally Melissa lifted herself from where she had fallen helplessly into Kara's arms and looked at me.

"You're one of us, aren't you, Shelby?"

Carolyn looked over at me, then at them, then back at me. Her brown eyes were big with surprise and realization. "Shelby! I believe Melissa hit the nail on the head," she said.

I nodded, not quite trusting my voice to actually say the words. Before I could think what to say, all three girls were hugging me, giving me the courage I needed.

"Yeah, I'm a lesbian too," I whispered. "Justin accused me of being one that day on the dock. I denied it then, but after I thought about it for a long time, I realized he was right. I told Howie last night and he said he already knew, had always known."

The four of us sat in a close circle, our secrets making us closer than we had been in all the years we were friends. I felt a strength flow into me and I knew I would be okay, that my friends wouldn't leave me because of who I chose to love.

Kara looked at Melissa out of the corner of her eyes and nudged her playfully in the ribs.

"I told you so. You owe me ten dollars," she said, holding her hand out.

Melissa shook her head and started to giggle. Her giggles were notoriously contagious and it wasn't long before we were all laughing, although Carolyn and I weren't sure why. The four of us finally settled down, but if any of us looked up and met anyone else's eyes, we all started again.

"Melissa," Kara said, squeaking to keep from laughing again, "you either pay up or I tickle it out of you."

"Why does Melissa owe you ten dollars?" Carolyn asked, careful not to look up and start the giggling again.

Melissa jumped up and went to her dresser. She pulled a ten dollar bill from her wallet and waved it at Kara before tucking it into the top of her halter. "You can get it later," she teased, turning pink as she realized what she had done.

Kara started to get up, but I tackled her and held her down. "I'm not letting you up until I know why she owes you ten dollars."

"You know you can't win a wrestling match with me, wimp," Kara said, trying to get hold of my arms to get me off of her.

Carolyn sat on Kara's feet and started to tickle the tender soles. Kara finally cried mercy and we let her sit up. "Okay, out with it," Carolyn said, winded.

"Oh, Shelby!" Melissa grabbed me around the neck from behind. "Kara figured out what was going on when you wouldn't date Justin. She didn't say anything to me about it until last night. I wasn't absolutely sure until I looked you in the eye a while ago."

"You still haven't told me why you have to pay her." I turned so that I could see Melissa's face.

"Well, ummm, well," Melissa stammered, looking at Kara.

I spun to face Kara.

"After I told her I thought you are a lesbian, we made a wager about whether or not you are and when you would tell us," Kara confessed. "I said I bet you would tell us by the end of the week and Melissa bet me it wouldn't be until Christmas or later. And I was right."

We all laughed again, and again I realized how blessed I was to have friends who loved me and accepted me.

"Well, I guess I'm the only normal one around," Carolyn said quietly.

I had to look at her to see if she was teasing. She had a half-smile on her face, but a distant look in her eye.

"Carolyn, you've always been the only normal one in the group." I laughed, reaching over and giving her a hug.

With that, we scrambled to put our sandals on and drove to the Burger Barn for a malt and to harass Howie in his blue Burger Barn apron.

Chapter Three

"Shelby, what's going on with you and the rest of the Six? Naomi's mom told me today y'all aren't having anything to do with her."

My fork stopped halfway to my mouth. Mom sipped from her water glass, never taking her eyes off me. Even though a week had passed since the night at the beach, Naomi hadn't made any effort to speak to any of us and if we tried to contact her, we were told she was not available.

"Ummm-mmm, well," I stammered.

Dad and Kyle looked up from their plates in surprise. I wasn't usually one to stammer. Mom's smug look made me wonder if she already knew the whole story.

"Lorraine told me Naomi has been moping around the house complaining y'all don't like her anymore. What happened, Shelby?"

"Naomi and Kara had a disagreement the other night. Naomi's the one who doesn't want anything to do with us."

"There's no need to snap at me, young lady," Mom said. "There is more to this story than you're telling, and I want you to tell me right now."

"Anne Marie, why is it so important you know why Naomi and the others aren't getting along?" Dad reached for the mashed potatoes.

"Because I think your daughter is keeping secrets from us, and you know I don't condone secrets."

Actually, you're just a nosy old biddy, I thought, struggling with what to tell her without giving away my friends' secrets.

"I'm waiting, Shelby."

"Naomi accused me and Kara of being lesbians and it caused a big fight," I blurted out, wondering as I did why I included me in the statement and not Melissa.

Mom looked at me over the top of her glasses, her blue eyes piercing mine. "Is it true, Shelby? Are you a lesbian?"

I gulped. *Do I tell the truth?* I thought. *Or do I keep hiding?*

"Yes. I'm a lesbian," I said quietly.

The silence that followed my announcement was oppressive; the only sounds the clanging of silverware hitting the plates. I waited for the explosion I knew was coming.

"Excuse me?" Mom's voice was much quieter than I expected.

Dad stood up, deliberately pushing his chair gently away from the table. The look on his face broke my heart. Dad and I were close, and I was afraid that closeness was shattered forever. Dad left the room without even looking over his shoulder.

"Kyle, you're excused."

"Aw, Mom, I'm not done eating."

"You are excused," Mom repeated.

Knowing better than to argue with the tone in Mom's voice, Kyle left the room, throwing a look of compassion over his shoulder at me.

Once we were alone, Mom sat and stared at me for what seemed like a long time. I sat frozen in my chair, my fork still in my hand, the peas long since rolled back on the plate.

"Why do you insist on causing this family embarrassment?" Mom finally said. "You wear your hair like a man's; you insist on wearing jeans instead of dressing like the young lady we've raised you to be; and now you say you're a lesbian. Did you see the look on your father's face? Do you think this shock is going to make his heart any healthier? I know you're lying and I want to know why."

I set my fork down and reached for my glass of water. I used the time it took to get a drink of water to try to calm down. It would do no good to get in a screaming match with Mom. I couldn't win; I never did.

"I'm not lying, Mom. I've known for a long time I don't like boys. I don't want to date them and I don't want them touching me. And I do want to date girls. That makes me a lesbian."

Before I could take a breath, Mom was around the table and slapped me so hard I almost fell out of my chair. Shocked, I stood up and backed away. In seventeen years, neither of my parents had ever slapped my face.

"You are not a lesbian!" Venom seeped from Mom's voice. "There are no deviants in this family."

I turned and ran from the dining room, stumbling in the half light of dusk out to the dock, the only place I felt safe. My face stung where Mom slapped me, but my heart stung worse. Her words reverberated in my head. *Was I really a deviant?* I wondered, as I watched heat lightning flash over the ocean in the distance.

Kyle appeared at my side, a soda bottle in each hand. "Shelby, are you okay?" I took one as I shook my head. "Mom can be rough, I know. But, Sis, she only wants what's best for you."

"So she calls me a deviant to show me what's best for me. Do you think I'm a deviant, Kyle?"

"No, Sis, I don't." Kyle's muscular arm went around my shoulders. "I don't understand why you like girls more than guys, but it doesn't change who you are. Heck, I like girls more than guys, too, so maybe we can go girl watching together some time."

We laughed in the gathering darkness, knowing our lives were forever changed. It was good to know Kyle still loved me and accepted me. Now I just worried about Dad. I didn't want to lose the special relationship we had. *Will our relationship survive this? Will the news cause him to have another heart attack?* I wondered.

The following week was horrible. Dad avoided me as much as possible. When we were together, he didn't look at me and had little to say beyond "pass the salt" at the dinner table.

Mom hounded me unmercifully to see the preacher at the church we attended only twice a year. I refused and our relationship became more and more strained. I tried to stay away from the house as much as I could, spending many nights with Melissa, Kara, or Carolyn.

One afternoon, about a week later, Dad found me sitting on the dock, my fishing line in the water but my mind a thousand miles away.

"Let's take the boat out and see if we can hook us some supper." Dad was already untying the boat from its moorings.

Out on the water, the waves and breeze gently rocking us, we fished in silence. Even though we had a few nibbles, neither of us caught anything. Finally Dad looked up at me and spoke.

"Shelby, I'm sorry I've been avoiding you. I had to think about what you told us the other night."

"Okay." I didn't really know what else to say.

"Sweetheart, I don't understand, but if being a lesbian is what makes you happy, then I can be happy for you. I wish...hope...you eventually realize you're wrong, but if you don't, that's okay."

I wanted to hug Dad and started to reach for him when suddenly both of our poles bent with bites. Amid laughter and relief, we reeled in supper.

With school starting in less than a week, I decided I needed to take inventory of my closet and the school supplies left over from my junior year. I realized I needed new jeans, preferably bell bottom jeans — the wider the bell, the better — and more button down shirts. Reluctantly I went looking for Mom.

"Excuse me, Mom?"

"What do you want, Shelby? Can't you see I'm busy?"

"I'm sorry to interrupt your reading, but I need to go shopping for school clothes and I was wondering if I could have the Harold's charge card?"

"If you need clothes, I'll take you shopping. I want to be sure you buy respectable clothing and not the trash your friends wear."

"Mom, I want bell bottoms, a few shirts, and a pair of shoes. Those are respectable clothes, and I can pick them out without you."

"Argue with me and you'll get nothing."

The next day Mom and I drove to downtown Yancey and the only department store in town. Harold's had been around for a hundred years but carried up to date clothing for the teens in town. I knew what I wanted and exactly where in the store to find it, but Mom had other ideas. She immediately tried to steer me toward the racks of dresses.

"I'm not wearing dresses to school, Mom."

"Then just go get back in the car, because that's all I'm buying you."

"In that case, I'll buy her clothes." Dad's voice caught us both off guard. "You go on home, Anne Marie; we'll see you when we're done."

"Larry! What are you doing here?"

"I knew you'd try to force Shelby into clothes she hates and things would get ugly, so I decided to join y'all. Now you can either let her pick out her own clothes, or you can go home."

Sighing in resignation, Mom followed us to the racks of bell bottom jeans. She tried to argue with every selection I made — from disagreeing with the colors to objecting to the fact most of them were hip huggers, but Dad hushed her, usually with just a stern look.

By the time we left Harold's, I had enough jeans and button down shirts to get me through the school year, as well as the Earth Shoes I'd been saving my money for. Dad paid for everything, then handed me another twenty dollars.

"I know you're going to Beaufort tomorrow with the others to get y'all's senior pictures taken," he said. "Use that for lunch and to have some fun. You deserve it."

"Thanks, Dad!" I hugged his neck, then got permission to meet Howie for a malt. I glanced over my shoulder as I hurried down the sidewalk. Mom and Dad stood next to his car, obviously in a heated discussion. I was so glad Dad had rescued me and I wouldn't have to listen to Mom's lectures on the ride home.

The next day Kara, Melissa, Carolyn, Howie, and I drove to Beaufort. The first item on our agenda was a visit to the portrait studio the school had contracted to take our senior pictures.

Howie was first to have his pictures taken. The studio provided him with a tuxedo shirt, bow tie, and jacket. He came out of the dressing room wearing them over his blue jean shorts and the rest of us roared with laughter. We wanted to accompany him into the studio, but the photographer wisely banished us to the waiting room.

Kara's black eye was mostly healed, although there was still a bit of discoloration next to her nose. She protested when the photographer suggested she use a bit of make-up to disguise it, but Melissa and Carolyn insisted, so Kara grudgingly allowed them to apply some foundation and powder to hide the bruise. Once she was done with her session, she fled to the restroom to wash her face.

When it was my turn, I donned the fake fur stole and the faux diamond necklace the photographer insisted we wear. I made a face at the others as I followed the photographer into the studio and sat on the small round stool he indicated.

"Cross your arms on the table in front of you, Miss Livingston," he said, standing directly behind me. "Relax your fingers so they rest naturally across your arm. Now, turn your shoulders this way," he turned the stool so that my body was at a strange angle to the table, "tilt your head a bit to the left, and lower your chin some."

"Excuse me, sir," I said, "but I'm not Gumby. My body doesn't twist like that."

"I know you're uncomfortable, but hold that pose," he said, hurrying to the camera. He picked up a cable release and held his free hand directly above the camera. "Look right here and smile."

I forced a smile through the pain and winced as lights flashed all around me.

"Are we done?" I asked.

The photographer laughed as he approached me. "That was just the first picture, Miss Livingston. We'll take about ten altogether."

I groaned and submitted to the torture.

All of us were relieved when the ordeal at the photographer's was over. Carolyn and Melissa had looked beautiful in the stole and necklace, but both Kara and I felt we looked ridiculous. The others assured us we didn't, but we weren't so sure.

The rest of the day we spent exploring downtown Beaufort. Located on the Intracoastal Waterway, Beaufort had a beautiful waterfront park and restaurants along the waterway. We splurged on shrimp and crawfish, eating our lunch at an outdoor table overlooking the water.

"It feels weird not having all of us here," Melissa said, wiping her hands with her napkin. "I wish Naomi could get over whatever's bothering her."

"You mean actually accept the fact you and I love each other? You have to know that's not going to happen." Kara looked out at the boats moving up the river. "One of those boats will sprout wings and fly first."

"I've tried so many times to talk to her," Carolyn said. "I feel so sad that she'll barely even speak to me. We've been best friends since first grade."

"I'm sorry, Carolyn." Kara patted her on the shoulder. "I feel this is all my fault."

"It's not anyone's fault, except Naomi's." Howie's eyes flashed with anger. "She's the one who chooses not to be our friend any longer. She's the one who's afraid of being around people different from herself. Just leave her alone. I don't even want to talk about her anymore."

Surprised at Howie's vehemence, the rest of us glanced at one another. He was usually an easygoing, forgiving person. Naomi had obviously gone too far by calling him a fag.

We finished our lunch and decided to take a horse drawn carriage ride through town before heading back to Yancey. While Carolyn made the arrangements, I watched as Howie talked with a young man lounging under one of the large moss-laden oak trees.

"Who was that?" I asked him when he rejoined us.

"A friend of mine," was his elusive answer.

Our carriage driver was a wizened black man named Jonah. He enthralled us with the history of the Union occupation of Beaufort during the War Between the States. He showed us houses where slaves quietly rebelled against their owners through subtle disobedience, pointed out homes where the richest people in Beaufort lived, and took us down narrow, tree lined streets along the Point. We hated it when our ride was over and we had to bid him goodbye.

As we walked back to the lot where Carolyn had parked her car, I noticed Howie talking to the same young man as before. Howie raced to catch up with us.

"Hey, my friend asked me to stay here tonight; he'll bring me home tomorrow," he said. "There's a play over at the university we're going to go see."

"Are you sure that's a good idea, Howie?" the ever cautious Carolyn asked. "What about your folks? Aren't you expected home for dinner?"

"Good grief, Carolyn." Howie laughed, grabbing her and spinning her around. "Would you stop worrying and enjoy life for once? I'll call Mom and Dad and tell them I'm staying to go to a play. Mom will think I'm getting a little bit of culture and there won't be any problem."

Carolyn playfully pounded him on the back. "Put me down, you big lug."

"Y'all drive safe and I'll see you tomorrow." Howie waved over his shoulder as he ran back to his friend.

Chapter Four

School started the following Tuesday. Our senior year! The excitement was palpable as we settled into our classes. Since we were graduating in 1976, our nation's Bicentennial year, our senior class felt as though it was more special than any that came before it.

Melissa and I had most of our classes together, a heavy concentration of English, Journalism, and Creative Writing courses. Kara and Howie shared a number of general classes, and Carolyn had a heavy course load of math and science along with her art studies. Naomi would have shared most of Kara and Howie's classes, but she was able to get her schedule changed so that she was in only two of their classes. All of us still had lunch at the same time, but Naomi ate with a different crowd, a crowd none of us had much to do with before.

One day, during the third week of school, the door to my second period English Literature class opened and a vision of beauty walked in. I nudged Melissa.

"Who is that?" I whispered.

"Put your eyes back in your head, Shelby. You're making a spectacle of yourself." Melissa covered a giggle with a faked cough.

Ms. Gilmore, a slender brunette with eyes that danced with excitement and joy, was going to be our student teacher through the New Year, and not only in English Lit, but also in our college prep composition class, our Journalism class, and our Creative Writing classes. I was thrilled when I found out she would also be assisting the newspaper and yearbook staff.

"Come on, you two," Kara said. "I'm starved, and the lunchroom is already crowded."

As Kara stepped into the classroom, Melissa and I looked up from the project we were working on for Journalism. Ms. Gilmore laughed at our looks of consternation.

"The bell rang for lunch five minutes ago, girls. Go eat. This will still be here tomorrow."

The three of us raced to our lockers and then down the stairs to the lunchroom. The line for hot lunches had already dwindled, so we were able to get our food quickly and go out to join Carolyn and Howie.

Usually a cacophony of noise, the lunchroom went silent as we entered. We looked at each other and then at the sea of faces staring at us. We started for the table where Carolyn and Howie were waiting for us, when suddenly a foot came out into the aisle, nearly tripping me.

"Watch out, Justin!"

"You watch out, dyke!"

My eyes got wide and my mouth dropped open. Without responding, I stepped over Justin's leg and continued to our table. It felt as though the three of us were running a gauntlet as catcalls were thrown at us.

"What the hell is going on here?" I whispered as I sat down.

"I think Naomi told Justin and his friends about Melissa and Kara," Howie said. "Almost as soon as I came in, Tony and Justin started asking me where my 'dyke friends' were."

"Well, apparently Justin thinks he was right that day on the dock last spring; he called me 'dyke' just now."

"Hey, dykes, where were y'all?" The deep voice of another football player boomed across the room. "Were y'all out having a threesome somewhere? Can we watch next time?"

"Oh, shit," Kara said.

"Take me home, Kara," Melissa said, obviously close to tears.

"Don't go yet." Carolyn put her hand on Melissa's arm. "If y'all do, you'll just be adding fuel to the fire. Let's try to eat as though nothing happened."

"Hey, Howie, do they let you watch?" a voice called out. More derisive questions and comments were made as we choked down a few bites.

Finally, as lunch drew to a close and other students were making their way out, Melissa and Kara left. I expected to see them in our pre-Calculus class after lunch, but they weren't there. Later I found out they were able to get excused from classes for the rest of the day.

The nasty comments followed me from class to class. I tried my best to ignore them, but since Melissa had gone home, I was the only one of our group in most of my afternoon classes and I felt vulnerable in a way I never had before.

Creative Writing was my last class of the day and Mrs. Williams had left Ms. Gilmore in charge. She wrote a prompt on the board and asked us to free write for fifteen minutes. I couldn't get my pen to move. Ms. Gilmore noticed I wasn't writing and asked me to step into the hallway for a moment.

"Shelby, is there something wrong? You're usually the first to start writing and the last to quit."

"I'm fine, Ms. Gilmore. It's just...it's been a difficult day."

"I've heard some of the things being said about you and Kara and Melissa. It isn't any of my business, but if you ever need anyone to talk to, know I'm here for y'all, okay?"

"Thanks, Ms. Gilmore. I don't know why those guys are being so horrible, but they're, every one of them, male chauvinist pigs."

"Hang in there, dear. They'll find someone else to pick on soon."

I could only hope she was right as I ran from the hatefulness when the last bell rang. Howie was waiting for me out front in his van, Carolyn with him.

"You okay, sugar?" he asked as I climbed in. Exhausted, I just shrugged.

A few minutes later we pulled up behind Kara's pickup truck in front of Melissa's house. It was nice to know the pale yellow house was a safe haven for us, a comfortable place for us to try to understand the turmoil inside us. Sue Ellen met us on the porch with hugs and pats on the back.

"The girls are out back," she said. "Y'all go on out and I'll bring out some cokes."

"Thanks," we said in unison, breaking the tension.

Kara and Melissa were stretched out side by side on a chaise lounge in the screened in Carolina room. At first I thought they were asleep, but then Kara opened her eyes.

"Shhhh," she whispered.

"Why?" Melissa whispered back.

We all laughed as the girls sat up. I sat down on the floor on Melissa's side of the chair and took her hand. "Are you okay, hon?" I asked.

"Not really, but what can we do about it?"

"You be strong and you lean on each other," Sue Ellen said as she set the tray of Cokes on the glass topped table. "Life isn't fair, and things like this happen to people, but with friends and family, y'all can get through anything."

Melissa rose from the chaise lounge and hugged Sue Ellen, standing on her tiptoes to reach the taller woman's neck. Sue Ellen patted her on the back before disentangling herself and going back into the house.

"I love having two moms," Melissa said as she rejoined Kara.

"Sometimes I wish I didn't have one," I mumbled.

"Okay, y'all," Howie said. "We know how everyone found out about Kara and Melissa being lesbians. But why did Justin and the others call Shelby 'dyke', too?"

"That's a good question, Howie." Carolyn held the green glass bottle to her lips as though she was going to blow in it. "Last spring Justin accused her of being gay, but I don't think he said anything about it to anyone else then. Now everyone seemed to know about Shelby, and I know none of us told anyone."

"I'm so angry about how everyone is acting about this whole thing," Kara said, shaking her head. "What is so wrong with two people loving each other?"

We sat in silence, each with our own thoughts and fears. The only sound was the clinking of glass as bottles touched tabletop.

Kara stood up, stretching as she rose. "Look, we can't change how anyone thinks, so we better come up with a strategy about how to handle all of this."

"For one thing, I don't think any of you girls should be alone at all," Howie said, his brow furrowed in thought and worry. "I don't trust any of those football players. I see how they look at the cheerleaders when we're out practicing routines. I don't think any one of 'em would hesitate to try to set y'all 'straight'."

"Howie's right," Carolyn said, brushing her hair back over her shoulder. "Except for Kara's PE classes, we all share at least one class with each other. Let's be sure the three of y'all have someone with you all the time."

"We could all just drop out and become beach bums," I said.

"That might work for you, but Melissa and I have scholarships to protect, so that won't work." Kara slugged me on the arm as she paced past me.

"Ouch! You don't know your strength. I'm going to have a bruise," I said, rubbing my arm.

Everyone laughed, relieving the tension we all felt. We spent the next couple of hours figuring out how Melissa, Kara, and I could always have someone else with us. I wasn't too worried about either Kara or myself, but Melissa was tiny and fragile. We all wanted to be sure she was protected from the bullies the rest of the student body seemed to have become.

Chapter Five

The next three months were hellish. We kept hoping our classmates would find another issue on which to focus and forget about us, but Naomi and a few others made sure to keep us on the front burner. Things finally came to a boiling point the Monday of Thanksgiving week.

Everyone was excited because it was an abbreviated school week. We had school on Monday and half a day Tuesday, then we were off the rest of the week for the holiday. Few students had their minds on schoolwork and the teachers were well aware of that, as theirs weren't really either. The assignments we were given were basically just busywork.

The last period of the day, Ms. Gilmore took our Creative Writing class out to the courtyard to write, not really expecting any Pulitzer Prize winning writing from any of us, even though I had, with Ms. Gilmore's encouragement, already competed for and won several awards in journalism competitions held earlier in the school year. Melissa and I had the class together, Kara had sports, and Howie and Carolyn had already left school for the day, as they didn't have as many classes as the rest of us. Melissa and I found a bench at the far side of the courtyard and took our notebooks out to begin writing. Most of the students in this class took it for an easy credit, but Melissa and I took our writing seriously and were soon totally engrossed.

After about twenty minutes of writing, I heard Melissa groan. She told me she was cramping and was going to the ladies room. We had been careful not to let Melissa go anywhere alone since that horrible day in September, but I was absorbed by the poem screaming to get out of my head. I watched her walk into the building and then bent my head back to my paper.

Before I knew it, the bell was ringing to signal the end of the school day. I was gathering my things when I realized Melissa hadn't returned. I grabbed my bag and hers and bucked the tide of students coming out of the building as I was trying to get inside. I was panicking by the time I reached the door to the downstairs ladies room. I pushed at the door, but it wouldn't open more than a tiny crack. Something was blocking it from the inside.

"Melissa! Melissa!" I yelled through the small opening. "Melissa, are you in there?"

I pushed and pushed on the door as I called out, but I couldn't hear if I was getting a response because of the crowd of students milling in the hallway. "Melissa!"

"What's going on here?"

Mr. Miller's voice startled me. "Mr. Miller, I can't get the door open. Something's blocking it and I think Melissa Ballard is in there."

"Jason, Butch, come help me push this door open." Mr. Miller and the two boys were able to get the door open enough for us to see the feet of someone lying on the floor behind the door. "Push harder, boys. It looks like someone's in trouble in there."

Mr. Miller grabbed at my arm as I bolted into the restroom, almost tripping over Tony Boone's legs. "Shelby! I don't think you should go in there."

"Melissa, where are you, baby?" I pushed open the door of the first stall, then the next one and the next one. I found her in the last one, huddled against the wall as far away from the door as she could get.

"Oh gawd, Melissa! What happened to you?" I knelt in front of her and tried to wipe the blood off her face with a piece of toilet tissue. "Come on, sweetie. Get up, please?"

Melissa wrapped her arms tighter around herself, squeezing her eyes shut, rocking and babbling incoherently. She seemed to be trying to disappear into the corner behind the toilet.

"Come on, Melissa. I won't let anything else happen to you. I promise," I said. I put my hand on her elbow and gently urged her to stand. Finally she opened her eyes and looked up at me. "Come on, baby. Let me help you."

She stood up, wobbling a bit. I put my arm around her waist to steady her and led her out to the sinks. She glanced over at the crowd gathered around Tony and shut her eyes again. I wet a bunch of paper towels and started wiping the blood off Melissa's face to find where she was hurt, then gently washed her face until I found a small gash beside one eye. I knew head wounds bled worse than any other, but I was still scared there might be more damage, so I continued to clean her up.

"What happened in here, Melissa?" I kept asking her, but she only shook her head and muttered under her breath.

An ambulance had been called and shortly the wail of the siren could be heard in front of the school. The now mostly conscious football player was put on a gurney and wheeled out. His head was pretty badly cut and I heard one of the medics tell a teacher he would need a number of stitches.

Another medic came to tend to Melissa so I stepped back to let him care for her.

"No, no, no!" Melissa started screaming and flailing out at him. "Get away! Don't touch me! No!"

"See if you can get her to calm down," he said to me as he put both hands up and backed off.

"It's okay, Melissa," I said quietly. She flung herself into my arms and buried her face in my shirt. "He just wants to be sure you're not hurt. Won't you let him take a look at you?" I felt her shake her head no.

"See if you can get her to sit here on the gurney," the medic said as he lowered the gurney almost to the floor.

"Melissa, baby, sit down here, okay?" I backed her up until her legs hit the stretcher. She stiffened and then allowed me to help her sit down. I squatted in front of her. "Sweetie, the medic just wants to look at that cut and see if you're okay. Will you let him do that?"

Melissa had a death grip on my hands. She shook her head wildly, spit spattering from her mouth. "No, no, no," she groaned.

Two other medics and Mrs. Williams approached us.

"Shelby, you have to let these men take care of Melissa," Mrs. Williams said, her hand on my shoulder.

"Yes, ma'am, I know that. But I don't think she's going to let them."

Mrs. Williams knelt beside me and pried Melissa's hands off mine. "Melissa, listen to me," she said. "These men want to take you to the hospital and make sure you're okay. I'm afraid you don't have a choice. I can see you're scared, but I promise you, they won't hurt you."

I stood up to get out of the way and was mortified when Melissa started screaming and crying and kicking as the medics moved closer to her. It took the three medics and Mrs. Williams to get her strapped to the gurney. I started to follow them as they rolled her down the hallway toward the exit.

"Shelby, I'm afraid you can't go with her." Mr. Henderson, the principal, gently took my elbow. "Come with me to my office and tell me what happened, okay?"

When he opened the door, I saw Howie, Carolyn, and Kara waiting for me and I rushed into the comfort of their collective arms. We stood in a group hug for several minutes while I regained my composure. Finally I stepped back and looked into each of their faces, finally stopping at Kara. The pain I saw there almost started my tears flowing again.

"What happened?" she asked. "Why did Melissa have to go to the hospital? I wanted to follow the ambulance to the hospital but Coach stopped me. She told me to come to the office instead. Is Melissa hurt? What?"

I had no answers for her, so I just shook my head.

"Come on," said Howie as he started out the door. "We'll go up there and find out ourselves."

The rest of us started to follow him but Mr. Henderson stopped us before we got far.

"Kara, the coach was right not to let you follow the ambulance. I don't think it's a good idea for y'all to go to the hospital. I doubt y'all would be able to see Melissa anyway. Now, go sit in my office, and as soon as I know anything, I'll let y'all know," Mr. Henderson said. "Use my phone to let your folks know where y'all are."

Grateful for his kindness, we returned to the quiet sanctuary of his office. One by one we called our parents.

"I'm still at the school, Dad." I was glad he answered the phone instead of Mom. "Something happened to Melissa in the restroom and she had to go to the hospital."

"Are you okay, sweetie?" he asked. The concern in his voice made me start crying again.

"I'm okay, Dad. I'm just worried about Melissa."

"Do you want me to come wait with you?"

"Howie and Carolyn and Kara are here with me. Mr. Henderson said we could wait in his office until he heard something and then he'll let us know. I'm okay, I promise."

"Okay, babe. We'll see you when you get home. I love you."

"I love you too, Dad. Thank you."

We hung up and I turned to the others. "Should we call Mrs. Ballard and tell her what happened?" I asked.

Carolyn shook her head. "I heard Mr. Henderson ask Mrs. Craig to call her. I'm sure she's probably already at the hospital. The bank is only a couple of blocks from there."

I nodded and returned to my chair. Kara reached out and took one hand and Howie took the other. Carolyn held Howie's other hand. We sat in silence and waited for Mr. Henderson to return.

"Tony Boone needed twelve stitches to his head," Mr. Henderson told us. "Except for a small cut beside her eye, Melissa didn't have any serious injuries." He paused a moment, seemingly studying his hands before he continued. "Unfortunately, what happened in the restroom will haunt both of these young people for years to come." He stopped again.

"Mr. Henderson, please tell us!" Kara begged. "Melissa is my best friend. I need to know if she is okay!"

"Kara, Tony had his way with Melissa." Mr. Henderson was so blunt it caught us off guard. It took a few seconds for the reality of what he said to sink in.

Kara buried her head in her hands and shook her head from side to side, a guttural moan escaping from her throat. Carolyn knelt in front of her and tried to hug her, but Kara pushed her away.

"You mean that SOB raped Melissa!" Howie yelled. "I'll kill him!" He was on his feet, his face red.

Mr. Henderson came around the desk and put his hands on Howie's shoulders and then pulled him into a hug. They rocked in unison a moment before Mr. Henderson sat Howie back down. He stepped back and perched on the corner of his desk.

Tears streamed from my eyes. I felt so guilty. I should never have let Melissa go to the ladies room alone. This was all my fault and I was sure my friends were blaming me. I laid my arms on the edge of the desk and rested my forehead on them. I felt I was going to be physically ill. Words would not come to me in my grief and rage.

For several minutes, the only sounds in the office were sobbing and Kara's moans. None of us knew what to say, what to do. Finally, Mr. Henderson spoke again.

"Melissa's mom is with her at the hospital and she asked me to tell y'all you can come up there tomorrow, but please not to come tonight. Melissa is heavily sedated and wouldn't know y'all were there anyway." He took a deep breath and then continued. "All of you need to go home to your families and let them hug you and comfort you. Since tomorrow is only a half day, I'm excusing y'all if you don't want to come to school. Go be with Melissa tomorrow and we'll see you back here a week from today."

We filed out of the office in silence and then down the long, now quiet hallways of the school and out to the student parking lot. Howie's van and Kara's pickup were the only vehicles left. We stood between them, reluctant to leave the company of the only people we really felt safe with.

"Oh, gawd," my tears threatened again, "if I hadn't let Melissa go by herself, this wouldn't have happened!" I buried my face against Howie's chest, afraid to look at him or the others, afraid I would see only accusation and hate in their faces.

Howie lifted my chin and looked deep into my eyes; his eyes reflected love and concern, no hate whatsoever. Kara and Carolyn joined him in hugging me.

"It wasn't your fault, Shel," Kara said. "I know in my heart Melissa won't blame you either."

Kara gave me another hug. It was a relief to know they didn't hold me responsible for what happened to Melissa on my watch. Then something occurred to me.

"If Tony was the one doing the hurting, how did he end up with a huge gash on his head and unconscious by the door?" I asked.

The others looked at me, as dumbfounded as I was. None of us had an answer, of course, and we finally parted ways, Kara and Carolyn in the pickup, Howie and me in the van.

When we got to my house, Howie walked me to the door.

"Are you going to be okay?" he asked as he gave me a hug.

I shrugged. He gave me a gentle peck on the lips, a kiss of friendship and reassurance, and then urged me into the house.

My family was already at the dinner table. I had no desire to join them, but I knew my mother would go on the warpath if I didn't, so I washed up and sat in my usual place. Mom wordlessly passed me the meatloaf and potatoes. I helped myself to as little as I knew I could get away with without getting a lecture. The usual family conversation was strained. Kyle and Dad tried to act as if everything was normal, while Mom and I ate in silence. Finally Mom looked at me, disgust plainly written across her face.

"We heard what happened to Melissa. I don't know why you hang around with people like that. Those kids are why you think you're a homosexual. That girl got what she deserved."

I stood up from the table so fast I knocked my chair over backwards and spilled my glass of tea into my plate. Fists clenched, I had to refrain from pummeling my own mother.

"You don't know what you're talking about," I said, my voice so low in my throat that I didn't even recognize it. "Melissa is a sweet girl, one of my best friends. She didn't deserve to get raped; no one deserves to get raped!" I was shaking with rage. "I am a lesbian. I don't think I'm one; I know I'm one! And my friends have nothing to do with that."

My dad was beside me by then, his arm around my shoulders. He looked at my mom in a way I'd never seen before. "Anne Marie," he said quietly, "leave this table, now."

She looked at him in shock. He never ordered her around. As far as she was concerned, she was head of our household, and my quiet, seemingly docile father let her think so. She seemed to know he would brook no resistance this time and she rose and went into the living room. Shortly we heard the TV on, tuned into *The Brady Bunch*.

Dad turned me to look at him. He was not a tall man, we were just about the same height. He hugged me to him and rocked me for a few minutes. Then holding me at arm's length, he looked me in the eye.

"Shelby," he began, "I'm so sorry about what happened to Melissa, but I am inclined to agree with your mom that you should look for new friends. As long as you run around with Kara and Melissa, you'll also be a target of hatred. I don't want you hurt."

I couldn't believe what I was hearing. There was no way I would desert my friends, especially not now.

"I'm sorry, Dad," I said. "I love Kara and Melissa like they're my own sisters. In a way, they are. And I'm going to stand with them through whatever comes our way."

A deep sadness creased his face but he said, "I understand." Then he added something I needed to hear. "I'm proud of you, Shelby Louise. You're a strong young lady and that will serve you well. If you had said anything else, I would've been disappointed. Always remember that I love you."

We hugged again, tighter this time, then I climbed the stairs to my bedroom and a shower. I was exhausted and wanted nothing more than to wash the hatred and anguish of the day from my body and fall into bed.

The next morning when I woke, I panicked when I realized my alarm clock hadn't gone off in time for me to get ready for school. Then the previous day's events came rushing back and being late for school was nothing in comparison. I wanted to burrow down under the covers and not come out of hibernation for a long while. I did get up, though, and after a quick shower dressed in a pair of bright yellow, hip hugger, bell bottom jeans and multi-color tie-dyed t-shirt. I figured that if I dressed in bright colors, the gray feelings in my head and heart would go away.

Howie and Carolyn showed up at my house about nine and laughed when they saw how I was dressed. We'd been friends for so long, we all thought alike even when apart.

"Good grief, Howie," I said. "If people don't already know you're gay, they will when they see you today."

Howie wore eggplant purple bell bottom jeans with a loose fitting purple shirt covered in huge pink flowers. His outfit was completed with purple platform sneakers. Carolyn wore a flowing red peasant skirt with a matching top and red, fluffy boots. Taken together, we were a rainbow of bright contrasts.

Already at the hospital when we arrived, Kara shook her head in amazement as she watched us come in. She was dressed in her usual uniform of blue jeans and a short-sleeved sweatshirt, white with blue sleeves. She twirled her blue and white baseball cap on a finger on her right hand.

"Have you seen Melissa yet?" I asked after greeting her with a hug.

"I went up, but Mrs. Ballard said Melissa didn't want to see anyone quite yet." Kara sounded so sad, I hugged her again. "We can go up and wait in the waiting room, but I don't know whether or not we'll be able to see her."

We spent most of the day hanging around the fourth floor waiting room, hoping Melissa would change her mind and see us. Sue Ellen or Mrs. Ballard would come out periodically to let us know how she was doing and to check on us. They were apologetic about Melissa refusing to see any of us. Finally, at the end of the day, Mrs. Ballard insisted that Melissa see Kara. Melissa agreed, but didn't want to see the rest of us.

Nevertheless, we all followed Mrs. Ballard down to room 416 and waited at the door as she escorted Kara inside. She conveniently left the door open, so the rest of us crowded around but stayed in the hallway. The lights in the room were dim, but we could make out Melissa's tiny form in the bed, looking smaller than ever.

Kara approached the bed gingerly. We could see her take Melissa's hand and bend down to her. We couldn't hear what was being said, but we all wanted to be in there too. After a few moments, Kara turned and motioned for me to come in. I hesitated. I just knew Melissa blamed me for what happened. Howie gave me a little push to encourage me. I tiptoed into the room and up to the opposite side of the bed.

Melissa had a butterfly bandage across the small cut next to her eye. Bruises I hadn't noticed yesterday were evident on her cheek and forehead. I took Melissa's hand. It was so cold. She turned her head to look at me and smiled, but the smile didn't make it to her eyes.

"Thank you, Shel," she whispered. I had to bend close to hear her. "Thank you for helping me yesterday. I love you, you know."

"I love you, too, Melissa." My tears tracked down my cheeks. "I'm so sorry I let this happen."

Carolyn and Howie joined me and Kara at the bed and Howie put his arm around my waist.

"Shel. It's not your fault," Melissa said. "You didn't know Tony was going to hurt me. Y'all can't babysit me all the time."

We all protested in unison and Melissa finally laughed. The sound of her laughter lifted our spirits and we all climbed onto the bed with her. Mrs. Ballard and Sue Ellen slipped from the room, closing the door behind them. For the next two hours, the five of us laughed and cried together and our bond became even stronger.

The doctors allowed Melissa to go home the next day. She would be seeing a counselor the following week, and probably for a while, to help her come to terms with what had happened to her. She said her best therapy was spending time with Kara and the rest of us, so we spent as much time together as our families and our individual responsibilities would allow.

The Saturday after Thanksgiving, the five of us were on the dock below our boathouse. We were supposedly fishing, but none of us were paying particular attention to our poles. We were enjoying each other's company and the unusually warm weather of late November. I finally got up the courage to ask the question that had haunted me since Monday.

"Melissa, I have to ask you a question about what happened Monday. Do you feel okay enough?"

"Sure, Shel; what's the question?"

I rose from my prone position on the dock and turned to look squarely at her. She was leaning against Kara, who was leaning against one of the support poles.

"How did Tony get knocked unconscious and get that gash on his head?"

Carolyn and Howie sat up and turned to look at her, too.

Melissa's chin dropped to her chest and her shoulders started shaking. Kara's arms tightened around her and I rushed over to her.

"Melissa! I'm sorry! You don't have to tell us! Please don't cry!" I was nearly in tears thinking I'd upset her.

Melissa looked up at us. She was laughing. I sat back on my heels and looked at her, wondering if she was hysterical and whether I should slap her.

"I still can't believe I did that to him!" she crowed.

"What did you do?" the rest of us asked in unison. That got us started laughing, too, and it was a few minutes before she could answer us.

"After he...he did what he did..." She hesitated and we could hear the pain in her voice. "He just left me lying on the floor, like a piece of garbage, and I suddenly got really mad. I jumped up and started after him, and he just laughed at me and slapped me. I fell against the counter and that's when I got this." She tentatively touched a finger to the bandage. "I got up and, just as he opened the door to leave, I ran full force into him. His head hit the edge of the door and the next thing I knew, he was laying there unconscious and bleeding. That's when I went and hid."

We all looked at her in astonishment. Tony Boone had to weigh close to two hundred pounds and Melissa didn't tip the scales at one hundred. Where she found the strength to hit him so hard, none of us could fathom.

"Wow!" Howie said. "Remind me not to make you mad."

Laughter exploded from us then. We lay on the sun-warmed wood of the dock and held our sides until we couldn't breathe for laughing. If one of us looked at another, the laughter would start anew. At one point, I was aware of my mother looking down at us from the yard, but I couldn't stop laughing long enough to even acknowledge her presence.

When we settled down at last, we gathered up the fishing gear and stowed it in the boathouse, then climbed the little hill to my back porch and flopped down in chairs, on the steps, and on the swing. Things were beginning to feel almost normal again, and it felt good.

Mom brought out a tray of bottled cola and cookies, always the gracious hostess, except for the pursed lips and pinched look of disapproval on her face. We all thanked her and she smiled her stiff little smile that didn't show any teeth and retreated back to the kitchen. For some reason, her attitude set us all to giggling again. The evening ended with Kara and Melissa driving off in Kara's pickup, singing *Love Will Keep Us Together* at the top of their lungs, and Carolyn and Howie following in Howie's van. I stood on the porch and waved until I couldn't see them anymore.

Chapter Six

The next few months were rough on all of us. The Monday after Thanksgiving, Tony Boone was arrested and charged with Melissa's rape. People at school finally began to leave us alone, although Naomi continued to try to fuel the fire. She constantly called us names and reminded people we were dykes. Even after Mr. Henderson spoke to her, she kept on. Only after he threatened to suspend her did she stop overtly harassing us. It wasn't long before her new-found friends began to tire of her pointed reminders to them about the deviants among them and started to avoid her. By New Year's, she wandered the halls of school alone and ate alone, ostracized by nearly everyone.

One day in mid-February, Kara and Melissa and Carolyn and I were sitting in a booth at the Burger Barn, waiting for Howie to get off work. Kara and Melissa were teasing each other about something and I was watching Howie, when I realized Carolyn was sniffling. I turned to see if she was okay and caught her wiping a tear from her face with the back of her hand.

"Carolyn, what's wrong?" I asked, handing her a napkin. Melissa and Kara looked up, concern on their faces.

"Nothing. I'm okay."

"Hey. You don't cry for 'nothing'," Melissa said, reaching across the table for her hand. "What's up?"

Carolyn shook her head, but when Kara's hand and mine settled atop hers and Melissa's, the tears started to fall.

"Y'all remember how Naomi used to start our hand stack?" she said between sniffles. "She'd put her hand on top of one of ours and then we would alternate hands. Once we had all our hands together, she'd pull hers out and put it on top."

"I remember," I said, pulling my hand out and putting it on top. "We'd do it and do it until we were all laughing so hard we couldn't do it anymore."

Kara pulled her hand out and put it on top of the stack.

"I miss Naomi," Carolyn said, pulling her hand out and reaching for her napkin. "I know she's not the same Naomi we all used to love, but sometimes I feel like a fifth wheel."

"You're not a fifth wheel," Melissa said, grabbing Carolyn's hand and adding it back to the stack.

"But when you and Kara are together, and Howie and Shel have their heads together, I just feel like...like a fifth wheel,"

Carolyn repeated. "Oh, I feel like I'm whining. I know how blessed I am to have y'all for my friends. I'm sorry."

"Don't be sorry," Melissa and I said in unison. "Jinx, you owe me a Coke," in unison once again. Our laughter rang through the restaurant, catching Howie's attention.

"Hey, y'all can't be having fun without me," he called from the counter. "Five more minutes and then we'll have some fun together."

The reality of Tony's trial loomed over us. It was scheduled for late March. We all dreaded it, but at the same time wanted it over and done with. We hoped justice would prevail and Tony would get what we felt he deserved. He'd been expelled from school, so none of us had seen him since that fateful day.

A couple of weeks before the trial, Melissa showed up at my door, pale and shaken. I led her into the house and up to my room.

"What's wrong, sweetie?" I asked after shutting the door. "You're as white as a ghost."

"I'm sorry to come lay this on you, but Kara's at softball practice and I just had to talk to someone."

"It's okay. What's up?" I sat down beside her on the window seat and put my arm around her petite frame.

Tears filled Melissa's eyes. "Tony and his family have filed charges against me for assault! Can you believe that?"

"You've got to be kidding! You were only defending yourself."

"That's what I thought, too. But since I rammed him into the door after he assaulted me, the courts may decide it wasn't in self-defense. Shel, I could go to jail!"

I didn't know what to say, so I just sat and held her, stroking her thick dark hair. My mind was racing, as was my heart. I couldn't imagine our sweet Melissa sitting behind bars. She wouldn't survive.

As soon as she quieted, I called Howie. I asked him to get Kara to my house as soon as he could and to bring Carolyn with them, too. I also found Dad and told him what happened. Dad had been a lawyer before he had his heart attack and took early retirement, so he knew almost everyone at the courthouse. He went down to see the district attorney and find out what he could.

About an hour later, we were all gathered in my room, venting our outrage that something like this could happen. Kara was sitting in my rocking chair, Melissa on her lap, shaking like she was freezing. Howie was sitting cross-legged in the middle of my bed, manhandling my pillows until I thought he would tear them apart.

Carolyn and I sat on the floor — me leaning against the dresser, Carolyn against the bed. We were more afraid now than we'd ever been from the nastiness we'd faced in school.

Dad knocked on the open door and I motioned him inside. He perched on the foot of my bed and rescued my favorite pillow from Howie's hands. He looked at each of us before speaking.

"Melissa, I don't think you have much to worry about," he said. "The charges will probably be dropped as soon as Tony is found guilty. Even if they aren't, because of the circumstances, you most likely would not get any punishment more punitive than a year's probation."

We all sighed with relief, except for Melissa. She still looked pale and scared to death. Kara hugged her tight and whispered something in her ear. Melissa shook her head.

"Even if all I get is probation, I still won't get my scholarship to USC. It clearly states in the paperwork that it isn't awarded to anyone with so much as a traffic violation." Tears slid down Melissa's face and she angrily swiped at them. "Damn, it feels I've cried enough tears in the last six months to fill a lake!"

We all laughed, shocked to hear a curse word come out of that precious little mouth. All of us tended to use rather coarse language from time to time, but I didn't remember ever hearing anything worse than "heck" or "darn" from Melissa.

"Mr. Livingston, sir," said Melissa after the laughter died down, "I surely do appreciate all you've done for me." She rose from Kara's lap and hugged Dad's neck. Kara and Carolyn also got up and took turns hugging him. Dad blushed at the attention; our family wasn't in the habit of showing a lot of affection. I got up and followed him onto the landing.

"Thank you, Dad," I whispered, afraid I'd cry again if I spoke out loud. Mom had been making life rough for me since I had come out to them, and Dad was my only ally at home now that Kyle had moved to Charleston to go to school. It meant more to me than I could articulate that he was trying to help Melissa.

"I love you, honey," he said. "And don't you worry about Melissa. I'm not a practicing attorney, but I'll see what I can do on her behalf."

I nodded and turned to rejoin my friends. Out of the corner of my eye, I saw Mom watching from their bedroom door.

Two weeks later, Tony's trial began. Since I had to testify, I wasn't allowed in the courtroom during the proceedings. Dad sat with me in the great hall outside and waited for me to be called. Kara,

Howie, and Carolyn had to be in school that day, but promised to join us as soon as they could. Melissa was the first witness to be called by the prosecution, so she was already in the courtroom. I wanted to be in there to give her moral support, but I knew her mom and Sue Ellen were there for her.

Dad and I chatted about trivial matters, neither of us wanting to think about what was happening beyond those big double doors. He held my hand, something he hadn't done since I was eight or nine years old and we went to see *Bambi* at the theater. I was taking everything in, knowing I would want to record the details in my journal later that evening — the architecture, the proceedings, and my feelings. As I looked down the hall, I was shocked by who I saw coming toward us.

"Dad," I nudged him. "Mom and Naomi are coming this way. What are they doing here, and what are they doing together?"

He looked up as they came to stand in front of us. Mom's eyes were filled with thinly veiled disdain as she stared down at us. Naomi stood slightly behind her, her face and eyes full of scorn. I cringed inside, but refused to let either of them see me squirm.

"Anne Marie, what are you doing here?" Dad asked as he rose from the bench.

"Naomi has been asked to testify for the defense," she said, "and I'm here to give her moral support." Suddenly I realized how Naomi had known I was a lesbian. My own mother told her and exposed me to the cruelty and nastiness I faced on a daily basis. My heart broke at the realization.

"What do you mean? What does Naomi have to say for that scumbag?"

I was surprised at the vehemence I heard in Dad's voice.

"I guess you'll just have to wait and find out, won't you?" Mom smirked and led Naomi to a bench further down the hall, where they sat with their heads together.

Shortly after their arrival, I was called to testify. I answered all the prosecutor's questions about what I saw, but I wasn't allowed to tell about the events that had led up to that day.

Dad had come in with me and sat with Mrs. Ballard, Sue Ellen, and Melissa. I joined them to listen to the rest of the testimony. Since court was still in session, I wasn't able to tell Melissa about Mom and Naomi right away.

The medics who responded to the scene and a doctor and nurse who tended to Melissa at the hospital testified next. Then the judge recessed the court for lunch, letting us know the defense would present their case when we returned. We stood as he left the bench. I turned to Melissa and her mother.

"Naomi is going to testify for the defense," I said, unable to hold it in any longer.

"The prosecutor told us that this morning. What in the world could she have to say in Tony's defense?" Melissa asked.

I shrugged and gave her a quick hug. "I don't know; I guess we'll find out together. I also realized my own mom is the one who told Naomi that I'm a lesbian."

Mrs. Ballard and Sue Ellen looked at me in astonishment. Dad took my hand, sorrow evident on his face.

"Your own mother!" Mrs. Ballard exclaimed. "Now that, I just don't believe."

"You don't know Anne Marie," my dad said, his voice quiet. "When she gets on the warpath about something, no one is safe, not even her own children."

Sue Ellen patted him on the shoulder in sympathy as Mrs. Ballard gave me a tight, one-armed hug. Melissa gave me a quick hug and suddenly I felt guilty. She was reliving a horrible event in her life, and I was worrying about something my mom had done months earlier. I stood up and hugged her.

"Let's go eat," I said. "We'll worry about all this later."

Dad chuckled. "That's my girl. Worry about the tummy first, world peace later." Everyone laughed and we left the courtroom in search of food.

After lunch, Howie, Carolyn, and Kara joined us in the courtroom. Knowing they wouldn't be able to concentrate on their studies, Mr. Henderson excused them from afternoon classes. We filled them in on what they missed, including Mom outing me to Naomi and the fact that Naomi would be testifying for the defense.

The judge called the court to order and the defense began the task of convincing the jury of Tony's innocence. They called Tony to the stand first.

Tony's attorney leaned against the railing that enclosed the witness chair, one foot on the bottom rail. "Mr. Boone, will you please describe the events that led to the injuries you sustained on Monday, November 24, 1975?"

"A couple of weeks before that, a friend came to me and told me that Melissa thought I was cute and would like to get to know me better. I said I thought Melissa was a dyke."

"Objection! On two grounds." The prosecutor was on his feet. "Number one — testimony about what the friend said is hearsay. And number two — the term 'dyke' is derogatory."

"What the friend said is central to Mr. Boone's defense," the attorney contended.

"Then let the friend testify," the judge ordered. "Both objections are sustained. Jury, disregard Mr. Boone's testimony so far, especially the use of the derogatory term for lesbian."

The defense attorney turned back to Tony. "Mr. Boone, was the sex with Melissa Ballard consensual?"

"Yes, sir, it was."

Melissa's gasp was audible. The judge frowned in her direction and she buried her face in her hands.

"The two of you planned to meet and have sex?"

"Yes, sir."

"And how did you know when and where to meet her?"

"A mutual friend set it up for us."

"And Miss Ballard was in the restroom of her own volition? She wasn't being forced to meet you?"

"Melissa was by herself when she met me. Is that what you meant?"

"Yes. Thank you, Mr. Boone. No more questions."

"Your witness, Mr. Prosecutor."

"Thank you, Your Honor." The prosecutor rose, but remained standing behind his table. He shoved his hands deep into his pockets. "Mr. Boone, is it normal practice for couples to meet and have consensual sex in the restrooms at your high school?"

"Well, um, well, sometimes, maybe. People make out there all the time."

"Couples make out in the restrooms at your school? Does the school administration know about this practice?"

"Objection!" This time the defense attorney was on his feet.

"I withdraw the last question," the prosecutor said before the judge had a chance to rule on the objection. "I have no more questions for this witness at this time."

The judge excused Tony, who practically slunk from the witness stand back to the defense table.

After several character witnesses testified on Tony's behalf, Naomi was called. We all sat on the edge of our seats to hear what she had to say. After having her state her name and age, the examination began.

"What is your relationship to Melissa Ballard?"

"She and I have been best friends since third grade. We talk on the phone nearly every day."

We looked at each other in utter shock and consternation. Dad wrote a note on the notepad he always carried with him and handed it over the banister to the prosecutor.

"What can you tell us about the events that led up to Tony Boone's arrest?"

"Well, Melissa had confided in me she thought she might be a lesbian and that the thought scared her. She told me she thought if a boy would have sex with her, that she would be able to stay straight. She asked me to set her up with someone."

Melissa's eyes were big, bright with tears. She shook her head in disbelief. Kara put an arm around her shoulders from one side, while Mrs. Ballard did the same from the other side.

"Go on," prodded Tony's attorney.

"I went to Tony 'cuz I knew he thought Melissa was cute. I told him what she wanted. He got real excited and told me to have her meet him outside the restroom that day. So I did."

"What happened next?"

"The next thing I knew, there was an ambulance in front of the school and Tony and Melissa were being taken to the hospital. I didn't know what was going on 'til the next day when everyone at school was saying Tony raped Melissa."

"Did you tell anyone about your conversations with Melissa and Tony?"

"No. I was in shock and I didn't want to out Melissa to anyone. I figured she was yelling rape because she decided she was definitely a lesbian."

"Objection!" The prosecutor was on his feet. "Speculation."

"Sustained," said the judge. Turning to the jury, he added, "The jury will disregard the last statement made by the witness."

"Your witness," said the attorney, nodding to the prosecutor.

"Ms. Jasper," the prosecutor began, glancing at the note Dad had handed him, "isn't it true that you and Ms. Ballard have not spoken since the last week of August?"

"No, we talk almost every day."

"Ms. Jasper, isn't it also true you spread the rumor around school that Ms. Ballard is a lesbian?"

"I wouldn't do something like that."

"Ms. Jasper, you do realize there is an entire high school student body, as well as your principal, I could call as witnesses to the fact that you continually tell people that Ms. Ballard and two other students are lesbians."

Naomi suddenly looked frightened. She didn't answer right away and I suddenly realized she was looking past the prosecutor. I turned to see where she was looking and discovered she was looking to my mom for reassurance and help. Mom was nodding at her, encouraging her. I scowled at my mother until she looked in my direction. She scowled right back.

"Ms. Jasper, you need to answer the question," the judge instructed.

Naomi remained silent.

"Ms. Jasper, you're not answering because you realize you've already committed perjury. Isn't that correct? You do know what perjury is, don't you?" the prosecutor asked.

Naomi nodded and gulped.

"Ms. Jasper, you must answer out loud so the court can hear you. Do you need me to repeat the question?"

"No, sir," Naomi whispered.

"Louder, please, Ms. Jasper."

"No, sir, I have not spoken to Melissa since August," Naomi said, her hands over her face.

"And you didn't really ask Tony to have sex with her to help her decide if she's a lesbian or not, did you?"

"No, sir."

"Ms. Jasper, can you please tell the court why you swore an oath to tell the truth and then lied to everyone here today?"

Naomi suddenly sat up straight in her chair and her eyes shot daggers at us. She looked as angry as she had that night at the beach. I know I flinched, and I'm pretty sure everyone else did as well.

"Sir, Melissa's so-called friends are all deviants. They sin against man and God. They need to be punished! I knew Tony had a crush on Melissa, so I told him to watch her and to catch her alone and to show her what it's like to be with a real man. I knew if she was with a man just once, she'd know she wasn't a lesbo and would leave her evil friends behind. I talked to Mrs. Livingston about it and she agreed I did the right thing, and that Tony was only trying to help Melissa and so it couldn't really be rape." Naomi spat out her speech with such venom the prosecutor actually took a step back.

The prosecutor looked at the judge, at the jury, at the defense table where Tony had his face in his hands, and then turned and looked Melissa square in the eye. He gave her a smile before turning back to the judge.

"I have no more questions for this witness."

"You are excused for now, Ms. Jasper, but don't go too far. I'm pretty sure the police will want to talk to you," the judge admonished. He then looked at the defense attorney and asked, "Any more witnesses for the defense?"

"The defense rests," Tony's attorney said.

"Closing arguments tomorrow morning at nine o'clock sharp. Let's be on time, people. Court dismissed."

We all rose as the judge left the bench and then just stood looking at each other. It was hard to believe all that we'd heard in the final testimony. We knew Naomi had come to hate us, but we had no idea of the extent of her hatred. I couldn't fathom why her prejudice had made her single Melissa out for punishment.

Dad left us and made his way to where Mom and Naomi stood talking. He took Mom by the elbow and quite forcibly escorted her from the courtroom. I could see her protesting the entire way.

"Shelby," Mrs. Ballard was at my side, her hand on my back, "your dad wants you to stay with us tonight. He and your mom have some serious talking to do and he thinks it would be best for you to be somewhere else. He'll bring you some clothes later and then see you here in the morning, okay?"

I nodded numbly. Mom and I had never been close. Kyle had always been her favorite, the star child who could do no wrong, while I had always been the apple of Dad's eye. But the pain I felt from knowing she had turned on me and my friends was immeasurable.

I barely remembered the drive to Melissa's house, although I do know we were quite a caravan — with Howie's van just behind Mrs. Ballard's car, and Kara's pickup bringing up the rear. Later that evening, the five of us were sitting on the Ballard's wide front porch, our shoes off and feet up on the porch railing, drinking lemonade and listening to the crickets.

Spring had arrived in the Lowcountry, and the aroma of blooming flowers mixed with the smell of the ocean on the night breeze. I inhaled deeply, imprinting the scent on my memory.

Sitting there with the people I loved most, I made a decision, a decision I knew none of them would be happy with. As soon as I crossed the stage at graduation, I was leaving this place, probably never to return. I would go to a big city in another state and either go to college there or find a job on a newspaper. I was confident that I had the talent to work for a newspaper. Because of the journalism prizes I won in the fall, and more I won later in the school year, I'd been approached by a newspaper in Columbia about working for them after I graduated. Despite their interest, I wanted to go to a different state altogether, so I doubted I would take them up on their offer. I felt a hand on my arm and looked up.

"You're awfully quiet, Shel," Carolyn said, concern in her face.

"Yeah," Howie agreed. "I don't think you've been this quiet since you had laryngitis back in ninth grade."

We all laughed, but it was obvious our hearts weren't in the laughter. I looked out at the night sky, at all the stars that could be seen from our perch on the porch.

"You know," I said, "there's a lot of world out there I'd like to see one of these days. I think I'll start the day after graduation."

"I know," Carolyn said. "I think we all want to see what's beyond our city limits. But we have to make a pact to always stay in touch, no matter what happens or where any of us goes."

We all agreed, each solemnly placing a hand atop another and promising to always remain friends and to stay in touch. Suddenly the screen door banged open and Sue Ellen ran out on the porch wearing a grass skirt and lei over her jeans and t-shirt.

"Y'all are way too melancholy!" she yelled. "Let's dance!"

Mrs. Ballard was leaning out the window and, on cue, cranked up the stereo. *Do the Hustle* blared from the speakers and the five of us jumped up and joined Sue Ellen on the sidewalk, line dancing to the beat. We were laughing and hollering and were soon joined by other people on the street. Our impromptu party lasted until close to eleven that night, when the police came by and politely insisted we turn down the music. Howie, Kara, and Carolyn gave us all hugs before departing for their respective homes. Melissa and I went to her room and climbed into her big four poster bed. We talked into the early morning hours about the long day we had just survived and how we both dreaded the next day. Just before we fell asleep, I hugged Melissa. She snuggled up to me and we fell asleep with our arms around each other, sisters comforting one another.

Chapter Seven

The tension in the courtroom the next morning was palpable. Howie, Carolyn, and Kara skipped school — with Mr. Henderson's permission — to be there with us. The defense attorney, Tony, and Tony's parents were huddled around their table talking. Every once in a while Tony would nod his head. After a few minutes, he stood up and hugged his mom, who was crying. The defense attorney went and talked to the prosecutor and the two of them disappeared through a door at the rear of the courtroom. The Boones walked to their seats behind the banister that separated the spectators from the court, giving Mrs. Ballard and Melissa a strangely sorrowful look as they passed.

Nine o'clock came and went. The judge, the attorneys, and the jury didn't come in. We were getting worried that something had happened. As time passed, the chatter in the room began to get a little louder. Finally, close to ten o'clock, the attorneys returned to their seats. The prosecutor turned to say something to Melissa, but before he could, court was called to order and the judge entered the room. He called for the jury. The courtroom was quiet as they filed in.

"The defense and the prosecution will please rise," the judge said unexpectedly. The attorneys and Tony got to their feet.

"I understand y'all have reached a plea arrangement," he said.

"We have, Your Honor," Tony's lawyer and the prosecutor said in unison.

"Well, let's hear it." He nodded at the defense.

"Our client would like to change his plea from innocent to guilty, sir. The defendant would also like to request all counter charges against Melissa Ballard be dropped."

The gasps in the courtroom were audible. I looked over at Melissa. We all reached over and clasped hands in her lap.

"Does the prosecution have any objections?" asked the judge.

"None, sir," said the prosecutor, giving us a thumbs up behind his back.

"Fine. Ladies and gentleman of the jury, thank you for your service. You are dismissed. Sentencing will be next Tuesday, at nine o'clock sharp. No one be late. Court adjourned." The judge left the bench in a flurry of black robes.

I looked at my dear friends. There wasn't a dry eye among us. Melissa and Kara had their arms around each other and were jumping up and down; Howie and Carolyn were hugging; Sue Ellen and Mrs. Ballard were hugging; and Dad was beside me, his arm around my shoulders. I looked up into his eyes and knew I was loved, but the uncertainty about what had happened between him and Mom weighed on my heart.

"We won! We won!" Melissa repeated over and over, the relief and excitement evident in her voice. "Let's go celebrate."

"Tonight, after you get out of school," Mrs. Ballard said.

"School. I can't concentrate on school right now." Melissa was practically giddy.

"Yes, if you want that scholarship, school. It's still early in the day and you can get to your afternoon classes. All five of you, off to school," Mrs. Ballard ordered, laughing. "Come over to the house afterwards and we'll have a good ol' cookout. And bring your folks."

We left the courthouse hoping things would regain some semblance of normalcy, at least until graduation. When we got to school, we traipsed into the office and told Mr. Henderson about the change in Tony's plea, and got our passes to class. Some of the students continued to give us the cold shoulder, but we felt too good to let it bother us.

The cookout that night at the Ballard home once again turned into a party, but this time with my dad, Howie's parents and little sister, Emma, Carolyn's mom and dad and two brothers, and Kara's mom. My mother didn't put in an appearance, but I didn't expect her to.

Afterwards I climbed into the car, leaned back, and stretched. Dad smiled at me as he turned the key in the ignition.

"Tired?" he asked.

"Yeah, I am. This has been a hard week. Heck, it's been a hard year."

"I know, sweetheart."

Dad was silent and I looked over at him. The glow from the dashboard lights illuminated his many wrinkles, made deeper by the frown on his face and by the weight he had lost since his heart attack.

"I'm sorry things have been so tough. Your senior year should have been your best."

I put my hand on his slumped shoulder. "Thank you, Daddy."

He rubbed his cheek on my hand, his five o'clock shadow lightly scratching me.

"I'm sorry your mother has been so ugly to you and your friends, Shel," he said quietly. "She just can't wrap her mind around the fact you'll never marry and give her grandbabies."

"I wish she could just accept me as I am," I said, the tremor in my voice catching me off guard. "I love her; I just don't know how to get her to love me."

"She does love you, Shelby Louise." Dad handed me the large white handkerchief he always carried. "But there's going to be a lot of changes around the house and Anne Marie doesn't like them, so don't expect her to warm up to you. If I were you, I'd avoid her as much as possible."

I was scared, but I asked anyway, "What's happening, Dad?"

He drove along in silence for a few minutes. I could see his jaw working as he considered what he wanted to say.

"I moved your mother into the guestroom last night," he finally said. "I told her never to darken my doorway again. I'd like to move her out of the house, but she has no skills with which to support herself and I can't do that to her."

I sat up straighter in my seat and turned so I could see him better. His face was silhouetted against the bright moon over the marsh, but I could see a tear trailing down his creased face. I handed him back his handkerchief.

"Daddy, I'm so sorry. I feel like so much of this is my fault."

"Don't think like that, Shelby. None of this is your fault. You've been honest and truthful with us all along. Anne Marie could learn a lesson in morality from you. You've matured into a strong and responsible young woman over the last few months; I'm proud of you."

"Thank you, Daddy," I whispered as we pulled into our gravel driveway. The light was on in the guestroom and we watched as a figure pulled back the curtains and looked down at us as Daddy parked the car.

Daddy and I hugged at the foot of the stairs before I climbed to my bedroom and he retired to his study. I clung to him, knowing in my heart he would be my only true parent for a long time to come, if not for the rest of my life. I grieved for my mother, for the love we never could seem to find for each other. I cried that night until my pillowcase was wringing wet, more tears than I'd cried the rest of the year put together.

April and May flew by. Before we knew it, finals were upon us and then the big day itself. We got our class standings the week before graduation and were pleased we all did so well. Carolyn made

Salutatorian. She'd hoped for Valedictorian, but a lower than expected grade on her calculus final dropped her from the running. Melissa, despite the problems she'd faced through the school year, still graduated eighth in our class. Kara was behind her in the top twenty, and Howie and I followed in the top twenty-five. With a total of two hundred twenty-eight students graduating, we all felt pretty good about our accomplishments.

Kara and Melissa received their hoped for scholarships to the University of South Carolina. Carolyn applied to the Savannah College of Art and Design. Howie made it clear he had no desire to go to college. My plans were already made. I was going to Atlanta to stay with Dad's sister, my Aunt Mae, until I decided what I wanted to do and where. I was leaving two days after graduation.

The day before graduation, the five of us sat in a circle on the dock below the boathouse. We talked about all the years we had known each other and about all that had transpired over the year. Naomi was charged with perjury and also as an accessory to the rape. She was given a substantial fine for the perjury charge. She pled guilty to being an accessory and, at the insistence of Melissa and Mrs. Ballard, was sentenced to probation and community service working at the Rape Crisis Line. Tony was sentenced to ten to fifteen years in prison for raping Melissa. She cried at the sentencing, not in relief that he would be off the streets but because she felt his sentence was too harsh, but we all rested better knowing he would never bother her again.

"I can't believe you're leaving so soon." Carolyn had tried for weeks to talk me into waiting until the end of the summer to go to Atlanta.

"I can't wait," I explained once again. "I can't stay in this house one more night than is absolutely necessary. Mom and I tiptoe around hoping we don't run into each other; it's like living with a ghost. I want to go someplace I can spread my wings."

"Me, too," Howie said. "I'm ready to find out what it's like to really live and not have to hide anymore. I'm going to San Fran as soon as I can can."

We all laughed at his attempt at rhyme, but the laughter covered sadness. We realized that once graduation was over and Howie and I were gone, there was no reclaiming what we once had. We knew things were changing and would be changed forever.

"Just don't forget our pact to always stay in touch." Carolyn started to cry and her tears were as contagious as our laughter usually was. Before we knew it we were all sniffling and snuffling.

I put my hand on hers; Howie followed with his. Kara and Melissa followed suit and we sat in silence, looking at our stack of hands. No one wanted to be the first to move.

"Well, look at the crew of graduates." We all jumped at the sound of Mom's voice. I looked up, surprised to see her standing there with a tray of sandwiches and a pitcher of lemonade. I jumped up to help her. Our hands touched for an instant when I took the tray from her and something in her eyes flashed. She returned to the house, stopping once and looking back over her shoulder, a wistful look on her face.

Carolyn stood up and put her arm around my shoulder. I realized I'd been standing, staring up at the house rather than serving my friends our unexpected refreshments.

"Stay the summer, Shel," she pleaded. "Maybe you and your mother can reconcile."

I looked at her, knowing she meant well, but also knowing even if I stayed, mending fences with my mom now would only open the floodgate for more abuse later. Mom had proven over the years that her forgiveness always had strings attached.

"I'm sorry, Carolyn," I said, handing her the tray. "I can't. My plans are already made and I'm catching the bus out of Beaufort for Atlanta in three days."

"Hey," Howie said. "I have a great idea. Instead of taking the bus, why don't I drive you to Atlanta? I plan on seeing some of the good ol' U S of A on my way to San Francisco and I can start in Atlanta. Whatcha say?"

I looked at him in amazement. I didn't know why we hadn't thought of that sooner. I would be able to spend one more day with one of my favorite people. I hugged him tight and he spun me around, almost hitting Kara and Melissa in the process.

Graduation day dawned bright and warm. The weather promised to turn muggy by the end of the day, but the humidity didn't dampen the excitement in the air. Graduation, like football, was a major part of Yancey's hometown tradition. Everyone came, even people who didn't have relatives graduating. The football stadium was turned into a great outdoor auditorium, with a stage set up on the fifty yard line for the dignitaries and highest ranking students. Rows of chairs were lined up facing the stage to accommodate the graduates. Black and gold streamers and balloons festooned the stage and the end of each row.

The graduates gathered at the field house before marching onto the field. We milled around, hugging and wishing each other luck. Regardless of class standing or popularity, everyone got along on this day. Soon the teachers began lining us up in alphabetical order, with the exception of Valedictorian and Salutatorian, who led the procession onto the field to the strains of our high school band playing *Pomp and Circumstance*. We were met with cheers from the crowd gathered in the stands.

I searched for my dad and there he was — Kyle on one side of him and Mrs. Ballard and Sue Ellen on the other. I waved enthusiastically at them and they all waved back. Mom was nowhere in sight.

The ceremony went off without a hitch. Lora Krantz was the Valedictorian and gave a mushy speech about lifelong friendships and futures seen through rose-colored glass. I rolled my eyes throughout, thinking she must live in a fantasy world.

Then Carolyn, her beautiful blond hair pulled back in a French roll, her mortarboard perched squarely on her head, rose to give the Salutatorian speech. I sat up straighter and leaned forward, not wanting to miss one word she said. She stood for a moment, looking out at the gathering of classmates seated in front of her. She held her arms out as though to gather us all to her and then spoke, simply and elegantly.

"Honored guests and fellow classmates of the great year 1976, I am honored to be your Salutatorian and I am more honored to be a member of this class. You are all very special people; you all have so much to offer. I wish you much luck, much love, much laughter. Go forth from here today and let the world beware — we have arrived!"

She stepped back as the class rose in unison and cheered her. Her face turned red at the realization that over two hundred people were on their feet, chanting her name and clapping. The ovation lasted close to three minutes and would probably have lasted longer if Mr. Henderson hadn't stepped to the podium and motioned for us to sit down. Carolyn turned to leave the stage and return to her seat, but Mr. Henderson reached out and stopped her.

"Before you sit down, Miss Shipley, there is someone here who would like to speak to you." Mr. Henderson nodded at a woman standing beside the stage. The woman climbed the five steps and joined Mr. Henderson and Carolyn at the podium.

"Good afternoon, Carolyn," the woman said as she shook Carolyn's hand. "My name is Thelma Johnstone and I'm from the Savannah College of Art and Design. After reviewing the artwork you sent in along with your application, SCAD is pleased to present you with a full scholarship for your freshman year with options to renew the scholarship each subsequent year you attend our school."

Carolyn's face flushed as her mouth fell open and tears flowed down her face. The student body was once again on its feet. Mr. Henderson hugged her and led her down the steps, where Howie met her and escorted her to her seat.

"It's now my great privilege to present the graduates with their hard earned diplomas," Mr. Henderson said as everyone but the first row of students sat down.

"Sarah Lou Adams; Billy Frank Ainsworth; Howard Lesley Akins..." As Mr. Henderson said each graduate's name, a cheer rose from the students and the crowd in the stands. As Howie's name was called, I stood and waved my arms in the air. I didn't care if I did look like a fool; he was my best friend and I was proud of him.

"Kara Renee Ashley; Melissa Sue Ballard..." Howie and Carolyn and I were on our feet as their names were called. Kara waited at the far side of the stage for Melissa, even though the teacher there kept urging her down the stairs. Melissa joined her and they left the stage hand in hand, a bold move considering all that happened. I cheered even louder as I cried tears of pride.

Suddenly it was my turn to approach the stage. As I followed Lewis Langley to the stage, I heard Naomi's name called. There was a smattering of applause, but little of the cheering the rest of the students enjoyed. I wanted to be embarrassed for her, but found instead a strange apathy towards her.

Standing at the base of the steps, I realized I was nervous. In just a few minutes I would have my high school diploma in my hand and the beginning of my new life would be just hours away.

Mr. Henderson called my name and I walked across the stage. As he shook my hand, he winked at me. I had to bite my lip to keep from laughing out loud. We had formed a close relationship since that horrible day in November when I poured my heart out to him in his office. I reached the end of the stage, and, as tradition would have me do, I faced the field and moved my tassel from the right of my mortarboard to the left. As I did so, a camera flashed. Once the spots in front of my eyes cleared, I looked to see who snapped the picture. Mom smiled at me as I left the stage. I wordlessly hugged her and returned to my seat.

Carolyn's name was the last of the Six to be called. The rest of us, including Naomi, stood and cheered as she crossed the stage to receive her diploma. As Carolyn moved her tassel, I saw her nod almost imperceptibly toward Naomi, but Naomi ducked her head and sat down without acknowledging her. Carolyn's smile faded, but just for a moment, as her father met her at the base of the steps with an armful of roses and escorted her to her seat.

After the ceremony, Mrs. Ballard and Sue Ellen hosted a come-and-go party at their house for the entire class and their families, not just the members of our small group. Several other families hosted similar parties, so the evening was spent going from home to home celebrating our new freedom. Carolyn's family insisted she remain with them, but Howie, Kara, Melissa and I went to every party. We hugged the necks of people we barely knew and some we wished we didn't know. We encountered Naomi at a couple of the parties, but we ignored her. At one of the parties, I caught her watching us, a sad, wistful look on her face. I almost felt sorry for her, but then the same apathy I felt at the graduation ceremony took over and I didn't approach her.

It was late when Howie took me home. One last time, we sat on the swing in our usual way.

"I had fun tonight," I said, leaning back against Howie as he set the swing in motion.

"Me, too. It was cool seeing everyone actually being nice to each other," he said. "People even seemed to accept Melissa and Kara as a couple."

"I think part of that was because of the way Kara took Melissa's hand at the graduation ceremony."

"I was so proud of her for doing that." Howie chuckled quietly. "That took a lot of guts."

"A lot more than I think I would have had," I said. "It was hard saying good-bye to Mrs. Ballard and Sue Ellen and to Carolyn's folks."

"I know." Howie sniffled and I wondered if he was as close to crying as I was. "I love Mrs. Ballard and Sue Ellen almost as much as I love my own parents. It was nice knowing we always had a place to go if we needed it."

I wiped my eyes with the back of my hand and didn't say anything. I didn't trust myself not to start bawling.

"You okay?" Howie asked, wrapping his long arms around me and resting his cheek against mine. I nodded. "Are you sure you want to go to Atlanta? Leave Melissa and Kara and Carolyn behind for who knows what?"

I nodded again, but still didn't speak. My tears were flowing in earnest.

"Oh, hon."

Howie stood me up and hugged me to him. I laid my head on his shoulder and allowed myself to grieve the friends and family I was leaving behind. When I finally cried myself out, left only with the hiccups, I turned around and sat down, but Howie stood me up and led me to the back porch.

"It's getting late, Shel. We're supposed to meet the girls for breakfast at Robbie's pretty early tomorrow. Are you going to be okay?"

"Yes, I'll be fine. I love you, Howie. Thank you for taking such good care of me."

"Goes both ways. I'll see you in the morning, bright and early, okay?"

I reached up and kissed him on the cheek before going inside. I stood and watched through the screen door as he drove out of the driveway.

Upstairs, I looked around my bedroom. Even though Aunt Mae had promised me her garage apartment, I would miss the coziness of my bedroom. I loved my room with its window seat looking over the oak tree. I could see the marsh grass swaying in the breeze, the marsh itself catching the moonlight. I sat in the window and reminisced. I was ready to move on, but leaving this place was proving harder than I'd anticipated. I was about to go to bed when there was a quiet knock on my door. I crossed the room and opened the door, expecting to see Dad but was surprised to find Mom.

"May I come in?" Her voice was cautious. I stepped back so she could walk past me. She glanced around, her gaze stopping on the suitcases and boxes I planned on taking with me to Aunt Mae's. "You really are leaving, huh? You sure are taking a lot of stuff."

"Yes, Mom, I am. Since I decided to ride with Howie instead of taking the bus, I packed a lot more of my books and other things." I wondered if I was in for one of her tirades about how selfish I was to leave right now. Dad's health was worse, but the one time I offered to stay, he refused to hear of it. He knew I needed to leave Yancey.

"Shelby," she began, then stopped. She looked at me and started again. "Shelby, I know this has been a tough year for you. And I know I haven't made it any easier. You've grown into a beautiful young woman. I hope someday you'll forgive me, but I just can't accept that you're a lesbian. I'll pray every day you will realize how wrong it is and change."

I wanted to shake her. Her little speech started off with such promise and ended on a note of pain. It was okay if she couldn't accept the fact I was a lesbian, but her little comment about the prayer grated on my nerves. I decided to take the high road.

"Thank you, Mom. Now, if you'll excuse me, I've got to get some sleep. I'm really tired, and tomorrow's going to be a long day."

I stood at the open door of my bedroom, indicating it was time she left. She got the message. On her way out, she stopped in front of me, reached out, and touched my arm. I closed the door behind her and went to bed. Sleep finally came, but it wasn't a restful sleep. I tossed and turned until the jangling of the alarm clock signaled the beginning of the first day of my new life.

Chapter Eight

Shortly after eight, Howie drove up to the back door. His van was already packed to the gills with as many of his belongings as he could cram into it. I wondered if there was room for my things, but he somehow managed to find a place for them. Dad stood on the porch and watched, one eyebrow cocked.

"Will that rattle trap get y'all to Atlanta?" he asked.

"Why, yes, sir, it certainly will," Howie drawled. "And from there it will get me to the City by the Bay and the Golden Gate Bridge."

Dad shook his head in amazement and doubt, but grinned at the two of us all the same. Suddenly I realized I might never see him again. My heart caught in my throat as I climbed the steps to stand beside him. I laid my head on his shoulder. His arms came around me and we hugged each other.

"My darling daughter," he said into my ear, "I'll miss your bright smile and the sunshine you bring into an old man's life."

"You aren't an old man, Dad," I whispered back, knowing his poor health made him feel like one. "I love you so much. Thank you for always being there for me."

"You will always be my baby," he said, a sad note in his voice. "You call me when y'all get to Atlanta. Give my sister a hug for me. I love you, always will. Don't ever forget that."

I stood back and looked at him again. His eyes were bright with tears. He hugged me again, then turned me around to head down the stairs to the van. He waved at Howie who was waiting patiently. Howie waved back as I climbed into the navigator's seat. I leaned out the window and waved until we were out of the driveway. My tears fell freely as Howie drove in silence to Robbie's Coffee Shop.

I dried my face as we drove into the parking lot. Howie parked the van and rubbed my shoulder. "You okay?" he asked. I nodded.

Inside, Carolyn, Melissa, and Kara had snagged our regular meeting place — the round booth in the corner — and had already ordered sweet tea all around. We joined them and ordered a robust breakfast of eggs, grits, hash browns, sausage, biscuits, and gravy. The five of us talked and laughed and giggled as though it were any other day, not the last day we would be together in the foreseeable future. We finished breakfast and the waitress cleared away our dirty dishes. We sat in silence for a few minutes, knowing Howie and I needed to hit the road but reluctant to leave. Finally, Howie spoke.

"We've got to go, sweetie," he said to me. "It's going to be hot today and the A/C in the van isn't working."

"I know," I said, looking at the faces of the three young women with us; faces that reflected the way I felt. I hated leaving them behind. We'd been friends for so long we could finish each other's sentences and sometimes knew what the others were thinking before they did.

We slid out of the booth and walked up to pay our bill. Robbie herself was at the cash register. She came from behind the counter and hugged Howie and me. She, along with most of the rest of the population of Yancey, knew we were leaving town.

"You kids be careful, and be sure y'all come back to see us once you've made your fortunes and are famous, ya hear?" she said. We laughed and promised we would. "Y'all's breakfast is on me today. I'm goin' to miss y'all taking up space back there in the corner. Now hit the road, and don't forget me, okay?"

We thanked her and went out to the van. Standing beside it, we looked at each other, reluctant to take that final parting step. We knew we had to go, but it was so hard to say goodbye. Carolyn finally took charge. She grabbed Howie in a tight hug and then urged him around the van to the driver's seat. Kara and Melissa followed and hugged him before he climbed in.

I stood with my hand on the door handle, waiting for them to come back around to me. When they did, Carolyn stood looking at me. The feelings I felt for her when I had a crush on her came rushing back. I grabbed her and hugged her tight. I knew I would miss her the most and worry about her the most. Kara and Melissa had each other, after all. No words were spoken, but I could tell by the way she hugged me that she knew how I felt. She stepped back and her hand caressed my cheek. I leaned my face against her hand and kissed her palm. She smiled and put her palm to her mouth. I could feel the tears threatening to overflow.

"Shel." Melissa was standing at my elbow. I turned to her. "I'll never be able to thank you enough for being my friend and helping me get through this year. You'll always have a special place in my heart. Please, let's always stay in touch."

Not trusting my voice, I nodded. I knew if I tried to speak I would start crying and not be able to stop. I scooped her up in my arms, raising her feet off the ground. She was so tiny and seemed so fragile.

"Take care of her," I said to Kara, my voice husky with emotion. "Take care of yourself."

Kara hugged me then. It was a great bear hug that threatened to crack my ribs. I returned the hug with as much strength as I had. I was going to miss this intimacy between friends. I knew it was rare, and I might never experience it with anyone else ever again.

Howie got out of the van and came back around to where the four of us stood. We linked arms, forming a circle, and bent our heads together. We stood that way for a few minutes before falling into a great group hug, our tears mingling.

It was time to go. Howie and I climbed into the van. As he started the engine, I found I was secretly hoping it would quit and not start again, but it stubbornly kept running. He moved slowly out of the parking lot.

"Bye, bye, bye!" The three girls raced behind the van, waving as they ran. I leaned out the window, waving back until I couldn't see them any longer, and then I put my head on the dashboard and cried, Howie's hand resting on my back in comfort.

"Are you going to be okay?" he finally asked, his own voice husky with emotion.

"Yes, and so are you," I said, sitting up. I looked at him and grinned through my tears. He grinned back, and the rest of the drive to Atlanta was spent singing at the top of our lungs and laughing uproariously about everything and nothing.

Eight and a half years later, one quiet Saturday afternoon in January, 1985, my telephone rang, its jangling startling me out of a reverie of memories. I hoped Janice, my partner, would answer it, but it kept ringing. I struggled out of my stupor and into the kitchen. A note was propped on the table. I picked it up at the same time I answered the phone.

"Hey, Shel."

"Howie? Is that you?" I laid the note down, unread. "You sound awful. Do you have the flu or something?"

"Or something," he said, trying to laugh but coughing instead. "I've been in and out of the hospital with pneumonia for a month. I just can't kick it."

"Oh, honey. Who's taking care of you?"

"That's kind of why I'm calling, Shel. All of my friends are sick and most of us are too sick to help each other anymore. I can't go home. Mom and Dad...well, you know how they feel about me. Can I come stay with you until I'm better?"

Howie's speech ended in a paroxysm of coughs. I winced at how bad he sounded.

"Of course you can, Howie. You know my door is always open for you. Come to Atlanta and I'll be your Nurse Nancy until you're back on your feet."

"Oh, God, Shel, don't make me laugh," he choked out. Then, more seriously, "Some of my friends aren't getting better, Shelby. My friend Jonathan died last week."

"I'm so sorry, Howie. But we're going to get you better so fast your head will spin. Now when do you want to come out?"

After we decided on a date for his arrival, we hung up and I read the note lying on the table.

You were a million miles away, not awake and not asleep. I got tired of being ignored so I went to Peachtree Café for coffee with Millie. Be back later. Janice.

I cringed. Janice had been complaining a lot lately of being ignored. It was a complaint I had heard from other partners, as well, and I had a feeling this might be the beginning of the end for Janice and me. We had been together six years, but something was missing and we both knew it.

When Janice got home a couple of hours later, I had fixed dinner and opened a nice bottle of wine. I apologized for not paying her enough attention, and we had a pleasant dinner together. We were lucky, or maybe unlucky, to live in an apartment complex with several other gay and lesbian couples. She caught me up on the neighborhood gossip.

"Jake, over in 10D, is sick again," Janice said. "He can't seem to shake this flu he caught a few months ago. A lot of the guys seem to be getting sick."

"I know. I talked to my friend Howie while you were out," I said. "He's had pneumonia for a month and there's no one to take care of him out there in San Francisco. He asked if he could come stay with us until he's better."

Janice looked up from her dessert, the spoonful of ice cream halfway to her mouth.

"And you told him yes, didn't you?" she said, lowering the spoon to the bowl.

"Of course I did," I said. "His folks disowned him and he doesn't have anyplace else to go."

"And how do you plan on taking care of him with your schedule at the newspaper? You're gone all hours of the day and sometimes night; you never know when they're going to call you."

Janice pushed back from the table and carried her dishes to the sink. "You don't expect me to take care of some stranger, do you?"

I joined her at the sink, put my hands on her shoulders and turned her to look at me.

"Janice, Howie is my best friend. You know that. You've known that since before we got together. You don't really expect me to tell him he can't come, do you?"

"I guess I expected you to talk it over with me first. This is my apartment too, you know. It's supposed to be our life, but you made a really big decision without even asking me what I think." Janice wriggled away from me and stomped into the living room where she plopped down on the sofa. "You just told a sick man he can come stay with us when you really don't know how sick he is. And you can barely take care of yourself when you're sick — or of me when I'm sick, for that matter. How do you expect to take care of him?"

"You're right, Janice. I should have talked to you about it first," I said, moving her feet and sitting down beside her. "But I've already said yes and I can't go back on my word. Once he's here and feeling a bit better, I'll help him find his own apartment, but for now, I'm going to fix up the spare bedroom for him. Please say you'll welcome him. You don't have to help me take care of him; just be nice, please?"

A week later, I pulled my car into the parking garage of the Delta terminal at Hartsfield International Airport. I was almost giddy with excitement; I couldn't wait to see my oldest and dearest friend again. I found the gate where his flight was about to deplane and studied the people around me, also waiting for friends and family. As always, I found myself imagining their stories. Before I got too lost in my imagination, the doors opened and the passengers began streaming into the terminal.

I watched as the man in the overcoat and bowler coolly greeted another man in an overcoat and bowler, both burdened with briefcases. A young mother with a twins stroller raced forward when an older couple came through the doors, tears rolling down her face as she kissed them and handed them each a tiny baby. The girl who stood by the window biting her nails watched anxiously until a tall, handsome sailor sauntered out. Then her face lit up and she practically flew across the waiting room into his arms. But in this crowd of people, I didn't see Howie. I was becoming concerned that he might have missed his connection in Dallas when a flight attendant approached me.

"Are you Shelby Livingston?" she asked quietly.

"Yes, I am."

"Your friend, Howard Akins, needs assistance exiting the plane. He asked me to come get you. If you'll follow me, please?"

Before I could ask any questions, she turned toward the gangway leading back to the airplane. I followed her, wondering why Howie needed help. My jaw dropped open when the flight attendant stopped and retrieved a wheelchair from behind the service desk.

"Is that for Howie?" I asked.

"Yes, ma'am." She gave me a sympathetic look. "Mr. Akins is quite weak; this will make it easier for him."

My heart pounded in my throat as we approached the door to the airplane. *Just how sick is Howie?* I wondered. The flight attendant led me through the first class section into coach, where an emaciated figure sat hunched all alone about halfway back. When the flight attendant bent over him and lightly touched his shoulder, his head came up and dull eyes focused on me.

"Hey, Shel. I'm here," Howie said with a tired smile.

I was shocked at the gauntness of his face, the pallor of his skin. I tried unsuccessfully to hide my dismay at his appearance.

"I guess I should have warned you I lost some weight, huh?" he said as the flight attendant helped him into the wheelchair. I moved out of the aisle so she could push the chair past me. "Shel, you push me out of here, okay?"

The flight attendant stepped back and I took the handles of the chair. My shock grew as the extent of Howie's weight loss became even more apparent as I wheeled the chair off the airplane. I felt tears building behind my eyes and struggled to control them.

Forty-five minutes later I had Howie settled in the passenger seat of my car and his two pieces of luggage stowed in the trunk. He leaned his head back and took a deep breath. I glanced over at him as soon as I had merged onto the highway. He was looking at me.

"How long have you been sick, Howie?" I asked.

He shifted in the seat so he was facing me as much as he could within the confines of the seatbelt. "Almost four months," he answered. "It started out with a cold that turned into bronchitis, then into pneumonia. I couldn't shake it; I kept getting sicker and sicker. Jonathan and Bruce and Greg were all sick, too."

He stopped talking to cough, pulled a large red bandana from his back pocket and held it over his face, which was almost as red as the bandana.

"Are you okay?" I asked. "Do you need me to stop and get you some water?"

He shook his head as the coughing began to subside. He wiped his mouth and gave me an apologetic look. "I'm sorry, Shel. I wasn't completely honest with you about how sick I am."

"Obviously," I muttered. I glanced at him, hoping he hadn't heard me and was stunned to see tears rolling down his face. "I'm sorry, Howie. I shouldn't have said that," I said, reaching out for his hand.

He grasped my hand with his skeletal fingers, holding on as though for dear life. "It's okay, Shelby. I don't blame you. I should have been more honest. Maybe you better pull off at the next exit so we can talk. You might not want to take me home once you hear the whole story."

I wasn't sure I wanted to hear the whole story. "I'm taking you home, Howie, regardless of what the problem is. We're going to get you well again," I said around the lump in my throat.

"Please, Shel, pull over so we can talk."

The next exit was a few miles away and we drove along in silence. Once we were off the highway, I pulled into the parking lot of a McDonald's and parked as far from the restaurant as I could. We unbuckled our seatbelts and faced each other.

"Okay, Howie. I'm listening."

"Have you heard of the 'gay man's cancer'?"

"Yes, I have. There's been talk at the paper of someone doing a piece on it. I heard the CDC has come up with a different name for it, but I can't remember what it is."

"AIDS," Howie said. "The new name is AIDS. It stands for AutoImmune Deficiency Syndrome. And that's what the doctor says Jonathan died of. And it's what Bruce and Greg and I have."

"Well, there's got to be a cure," I said. "We'll find the best doctors in Atlanta and find out what you need to do to get well."

"Shelby, there aren't many doctors that treat AIDS. There isn't a lot known about it, except that it's considered highly contagious and the doctors aren't sure how it's passed from one person to another." Howie coughed into his bandana. "Shel, I don't want to take a chance that I'll make you sick. I'll understand if you say I can't stay with you and Janice, I just don't know where else to go."

I sat in silence for a moment, thoughts flying through my head so fast I couldn't catch any of them. *What will Janice say? How can I take care of him when he's so sick? I can't turn him away now. How could he manipulate me this way? Oh, please, don't let him die!*

"You're coming home with me, Howie, and don't worry about anything except getting well." I leaned over and hugged him then rubbed my hand up and down his knobby backbone, sad and taken aback that I could feel each vertebrae.

Janice was less than happy when, later that evening in the privacy of our bedroom, I explained the severity of Howie's illness.

"And you're going to let him stay here, even though you don't know whether he'll give us what he has?" she asked. She paced the room, wearing a path around the bed. "I don't like it one bit, Shelby."

"Janice, please come sit down and let's talk about this," I said, patting the bed beside me.

"Why talk about it now?" she said. "You didn't bother to talk to me about it to start with." She shook her head, rubbing her forehead. "Your friend is more important to you than I am."

I couldn't argue with her; she was right. Howie was a lot more important to me than Janice, or anybody else on Earth right then, except maybe Melissa, Kara, and Carolyn, whom I hadn't seen or spoken to for several years. I closed my eyes and wished they were here with me instead of Janice.

"You're not even going to try to convince me otherwise, are you?" Janice stopped pacing and stood directly in front of me. I shook my head. "I'm packing a bag and I'm going to stay with Millie until you've found someplace else for Howie to live. Let me know when you're ready for me to come back."

Ten minutes later, Janice slammed the front door behind her. I tapped on Howie's bedroom door and peeked inside. He was sitting up in bed writing in a notebook.

"Whatcha doing?" I asked.

"I've taken a book out of your page and started keeping a journal."

I laughed. "A book out of my page, huh? When did you start that?"

"Right after I got to San Francisco," he said. "I have about thirty notebooks full. It's fun to pull out the ones I wrote when I first got there. I had so much to learn about the place and about living on my own. I was so naïve in so many ways."

Talking so much set off his coughing again. I handed him a glass of water once his coughing subsided.

"Can I read your journals someday?"

"Maybe someday," he said. "Did I hear Janice leave? Is everything okay?"

Tears welled in my eyes as I shook my head. "Yes, you did hear Janice leave. And, no, I don't think everything's okay."

"Did she leave because I'm here, or because I'm so sick?"

"That was only a part of it. We've been growing apart for a long time. I think she's been looking for an excuse to go."

Howie reached over and pulled me into a hug. As I snuggled into him, I realized again just how thin he was. When we were in high school, his frame was well muscled, firm in all the right places and soft where it counted. Now he was all bones.

"What do you think about calling Melissa and Kara and Carolyn and inviting them to come down to see us?" I asked. I felt the shake of his head.

"I don't want to see anyone from home until I'm doing better," he said. "Once I'm feeling better, let's have a party."

"Now that sounds like a plan."

Of course he didn't get better. He got worse and worse. Few doctors knew how to treat the disease, only the symptoms, and then their treatments rarely did much for Howie. I rented a hospital bed for him, but finding a nurse who was willing to help was difficult. There were a few devoted angels who helped as much as they could. I took a leave of absence from the newspaper and devoted all my time to taking care of Howie. Janice came back only long enough to pack the rest of her belongings and move out.

During the few months Howie was with me, we talked at length about the events of our senior year. One night I heard him crying and went to him.

"I think I should talk to Naomi," he said. "I want her to know I forgive her. I want to know whether she really hated us as much as she seemed to, and whether she still does. Can we please try to call her?"

"Howie, I don't think that's a good idea. Naomi knew exactly what she was doing. I doubt she would talk to us if we called."

I crawled into bed with him, gently pushing his IV tube over so I wouldn't pull on it. I dried his tears, embarrassed about the latex gloves I wore as I did so. The nurses and his doctor insisted I wear the gloves whenever I helped Howie. They wanted me to wear a mask, too, but I drew the line there.

Howie died a week later. As he left me, I held him in my arms, whispering to him how much I loved him. My tears didn't come when he died; I had cried them all while I was taking care of him.

I took his body back to Yancey. There I planned and paid for his funeral and interment since his family refused to have any more to do with him in death than they had in life. I also contacted our friends and let them know what had happened. Carolyn traveled up from Savannah, where she and her husband made their home in the affluent Jekyll Island community. Melissa and Kara, still together and now living and working in Columbia, came also. Melissa's mom attended the funeral, but Sue Ellen was out of town on business. Dad was the only other person in attendance. Howie had been popular in school, but in death he was shunned.

Later that year, a spread I did about poverty in the inner cities of America caught the eye of the editor of a major newspaper, and I was offered an opportunity to travel and cover some of the major events of the time. I jumped at the chance and soon made a name for myself and was able to branch out into freelance work, picking and choosing the stories I covered. I won several awards, which made it possible for me to start asking top dollar for the work I did. I could have lived comfortably anywhere I chose, but instead I squirreled away my money for a rainy day, and pursued a nomadic lifestyle.

Traveling extensively, I didn't make the effort I should have to stay in touch with my friends. When Dad passed away, it took Kyle several days to find me to give me the sad news. Mom stayed on in the house after Dad died. We were never close, and when I was home to bury Howie and later to attend Dad's funeral, it was more like staying in a boarding house than my own home. I could have stayed in a hotel, but out of misplaced loyalty chose not to.

When Carolyn took her life, I almost missed her funeral because I was in Europe. I saw Kara and Melissa at Carolyn's funeral and we once again renewed our pact to stay in touch, but I almost immediately broke it. After a month or so of emails, I got "too busy" to respond, and after a while, they quit trying.

Carolyn's funeral in September of 2000 was the last time I returned to Yancey for a long time.

In the years that followed, there were a few times when I tried to settle down. I would have a relationship that would last three or four months, and then a lucrative assignment would come my way and I would be off again. No one was willing to wait for me, and after a while I swore off ever having another relationship. I continued to bury myself in my work.

On January 3, 2006, I was standing outside the entrance to the Sago Mine in West Virginia, waiting with other members of the media for news of the trapped miners, when my cell phone rang. After checking the caller ID, I answered the phone.

"Hey, Colleen," I said to the editor-in-chief of the newspaper for which I was working. "We're still waiting for word about the miners."

"Shelby, I can barely hear you for all the background noise there. Go find someplace quiet and call me back. It's important."

"I can hear you just fine. If I leave now, I might miss an update on what's going on with the rescue."

"Shelby, I don't want to tell you this with you in the middle of a bunch of people. Now go find someplace quiet and call me back."

Colleen hung up the phone before I could protest. *What is in her craw?* I wondered as I gathered my camera equipment and left the crowd of reporters.

"Shelby, your mother died last week," Colleen told me when I called her back. "Her lawyer contacted me and asked me to have you call him."

"Mom's dead?" I waited to feel something, anything.

"Yes, Shelby. I'm so sorry."

"Why didn't the lawyer call me himself?"

"I don't know. You'll have to ask him when you call him back. Here's his number; are you ready?"

I jotted down the lawyer's name and phone number.

"If you need to go home to take care of things, I understand. John and Stacey are there; they can cover the story for us."

"Yeah, but you wouldn't have any good pictures. I'll call the lawyer, but I'm staying here until the miners come out of that mine."

"That's your call, Shelby. I know better than to try to argue with you."

We both laughed and then the click of her phone ended the call. I leaned back in the seat of the car and closed my eyes for a moment. I could see Mom standing in the kitchen of the house back in Yancey, her red gingham apron tied primly around her waist. She was stirring cake batter and singing softly to herself. Then she turned towards me and I could see the disdain and disappointment in her face. I shook my head and opened my eyes. There were no tears of grief. I called the lawyer.

"Ms. Livingston, thank you for calling back so promptly," Mr. Maddox said. "I'm terribly sorry for your loss."

"Thank you, sir. May I ask why you called my editor rather than calling me, and why it took a week to do so?" *And why didn't Kyle call me?* I suddenly thought, but didn't voice.

"Your mother didn't give me a contact number for you other than the one for your editor," Mr. Maddox explained. "She also asked that you and your brother not be notified of her death until after she'd been cremated."

"Kyle wasn't with her when she died?"

"No, ma'am. Your mother died alone. Her choice." Mr. Maddox cleared his throat. "The reason I asked you to call me, Ms. Livingston, is concerning your mother's will. In it, she leaves you the house and all its contents."

I was stunned into silence. I knew my mouth was hanging open, but I was powerless to shut it.

"Ms. Livingston? Are you still there?"

I nodded, then realized he couldn't hear a nod. "Yes, sir, I'm still here. Did you say Mom left me the house? And all its contents?"

"Yes, ma'am; that is according to the dictates of the will. I need an address to send you some paperwork to sign and then the house is yours, free and clear."

I gave the lawyer the information he needed and hung up. I needed time to process the news that Mom had died and that I had inherited the house, but people were gathering near the mine entrance and I could feel the excitement and tension in the air. I sprang out of the car and hurried to cover whatever news they were bringing us. I didn't realize until later that I hadn't asked him what had happened to Mom's ashes.

I knew I needed to return to Yancey to take care of the house, and either give it to Kyle — who should probably have received it in the first place, since he had a family — or put it on the market. But I didn't. Instead of facing what I knew I would eventually have to do, I hired someone to take care of the house and continued to travel.

As time went by, I gradually came to realize that I was tiring of the nomadic existence and decided to try to find a job that would allow me to stay in the same place for the rest of my life. In April I read in a trade publication that *Charleston Magazine* was accepting applications for a regional reporter and photographer. I contacted them and asked for an opportunity to bid on the position. They invited me to come for an interview and I accepted. We set a date and I began looking forward to possibly moving back to the Lowcountry.

About the same time, I received an invitation to my high school graduating class' thirty-year reunion. It was hard to believe so much time had passed since I'd left Yancey. I had received invitations to previous reunions and just tossed them in the garbage. The thirty-year reunion was being held the weekend before my interview with *Charleston Magazine*, so I decided to attend to see how much people had changed, if they had at all.

Part Two

Chapter Nine
June, 2006

I sat up, stretching. I couldn't believe I'd fallen asleep on the window seat; I was too old to sleep in awkward positions. I stood, gingerly stretching each limb, hoping the corresponding joints would pop easily into place. Looking out the window, I noticed the sun was up, well above the limbs of the oak tree. A glance at the clock showed me that it was nearly nine. I started to panic. Was today the day I had to be in Charleston? I quickly checked my Day Planner and was relieved to realize not only was it Saturday, but my interview was still three days away.

Showered and dressed in a pair of Bermuda shorts and a white t-shirt, I sat on the back porch with my coffee, listening to the birds and smelling the breeze coming off the tidal marsh. I was struck by how much I loved this place and sincerely hoped I would get the position in Charleston. It would be an easy commute from Yancey.

I heard a vehicle pull into the driveway and walked around the side of the house to see who was coming to visit. A bright red SUV pulled in, my brother Kyle at the wheel. His wife, Paula, rode shotgun, and their boys, Rod and Tom, sat sullen in the backseat. I hadn't seen any of them since Carolyn's funeral, when Rod was barely ten and Tom was nine. They were big strapping teens now, obviously not happy about being dragged to visit an aunt they barely knew.

"Kyle! What a wonderful surprise." Once he was out of the SUV, I threw myself into his arms. "Paula, I'm so glad to see y'all."

I hugged Paula while the boys hung back, their hands stubbornly shoved in the pockets of their blue jean shorts. Rod looked like Dad must have at his age. He had a thick shock of dark brown hair that refused to be tamed and the same blue eyes Kyle and I inherited from Dad. Tom was the spitting image of his mother. He and Paula shared sun-streaked blond hair and green eyes with an unusual brown halo around the iris. Tom and Paula were tall and thin, while Rod had inherited Dad and Kyle's squat, thick stature. Not wanting to embarrass them with a hug, I shook their hands.

"The caretaker I hired left some chicken necks in the freezer. Why don't you boys grab them and go down to the dock to see if you can catch us a mess of crabs for lunch?" I said. "Kyle, are the nets still hanging in the boathouse?"

"Yep," he said. "The cast net is there, too, if y'all want to see if any shrimp happen to be running yet."

The boys' faces lit up. I could see the relief in their eyes that they wouldn't have to sit with us grownups and pretend to be interested in our conversation. Rod ran into the house to get the chicken while Tom started down the hill to the boathouse.

Paula laughed. "Well, you made their day. They tried everything under the sun to get out of coming with us."

"Y'all come get some coffee and let's sit out here," I said.

We went inside and I filled a cup for each of then and refilled mine. I found some pastries in the cabinet and was thankful the caretaker had stocked my pantry when I let her know I would be in town. I heated the pastries in the microwave and joined my brother and sister-in-law on the back porch.

"How was the drive down from Charleston?" I asked.

"Not bad," Kyle said. "I don't know if I told you we're in the process of refurbishing a house on Tradd Street. We spent our first night there last night and it only took about ninety minutes to get here."

Tradd Street was right in the middle of the Battery, the oldest and most historic section of Charleston. "Wow! I can't wait to see it. Are y'all doing all the work yourselves?"

"A good part of it, but since the historic society is such a stickler for detail, we've had to hire contractors for some of it," Kyle said. "Everything that's done has to maintain the historic integrity of the house, and some of that is beyond me."

"We found a great guy that specializes in restoring these old houses and he's worked wonders," Paula said. "When are you coming up for your interview? Maybe you can come by and see the house then."

"My interview is Tuesday morning at nine," I said. "I'm ready, too. I have my portfolio together and have already chosen what I'm going to wear. I really hope I get this position."

"Tired of traveling?" Kyle laughed. "I remember when you decided to leave Yancey. Dad said all you talked about was seeing the world and setting foot on every continent at least once. Did you reach your goal?"

I answered his last question first. "I haven't been to Antarctica, but not from lack of trying. The closest I came was Patagonia in Argentina. But, yes, I'm tired of traveling. I'll be forty-eight soon and I think I'm finally ready to settle in one place. I can't think of a better place to do that than here."

"I think that's why Dad insisted Mom leave you the house," Kyle said. "He always hoped you'd come home."

I sat up straight and turned to look Kyle in the face. "What do you mean, Dad insisted Mom leave me the house?"

"You didn't know?" Kyle was incredulous. "One of the stipulations in Dad's will was that if Mom wanted to stay here after his death, she had to leave you the house. Actually, Dad left you the house, but you weren't to get it until after Mom died or you turned fifty, whichever came first."

Now it was my turn to be overwhelmed. I couldn't believe Dad had done that for me. Tears threatened to spill over.

"If you start crying, we're leaving," Kyle said with a teasing laugh.

Just then Rod and Tom came flying up the hill, carrying a bucket full of blue crab and shrimp. Kyle fired up the grill and set up a pot to start the crab and shrimp cooking. Paula and I went inside and found the fixings for a salad and some frozen corn-on-the-cob in the freezer, which we immediately put on to boil. The boys washed up and set the picnic table. In a short time we had a feast waiting.

After we cleaned up, the boys stretched out on the hammocks strung on the porch. Kyle, Paula, and I visited until the sun started to sink below the marsh. Once they left, I went down to the dock and watched the sun set. I forgot how beautiful the sunsets were here. I found myself hoping once again that *Charleston Magazine* would take a chance on an old reporter.

Sunday morning I woke to the sound of rain on the roof. I sat in my window seat and enjoyed the cool breeze that accompanied the shower, reflecting on my life up to that point. I'd been blessed with a brother and father who loved me dearly, a mother who taught me to have a backbone of steel, and a career I could be proud of. Things hadn't always been easy. In fact, there were times I felt it would be easier to crawl into a cave and be a hermit rather than try to continue, but that backbone Mom helped create kept me going. Failure wasn't in my vocabulary.

I also had dear friends who would have supported me and encouraged me if I'd given them the chance and kept in touch. Here, where we'd spent so much wonderful time together, I missed my friends.

Howie had been such an important part of my life from well before either of us could walk or talk. Some of my earliest memories involved him. And Naomi, too, when I really thought about it. Even though Howie had been gone for over twenty years, my soul still grieved and my heart still ached for him.

And Carolyn. I would never forget the crush I had on her in high school. Her hand on my face just before we left Robbie's that day stayed in my memory and brought a smile to my face at times when it was hard to smile. I don't know if Carolyn ever realized I had a crush on her, but I always knew she loved me the way a friend is supposed to love another friend. What a loss we all suffered when the demons of depression claimed her life. I missed her smile, her wisdom, the calming effect she had on me when I stormed down a warpath. I often wondered if things had been different and I hadn't left Yancey, would Carolyn still be alive? Realistically I knew my proximity probably wouldn't have made any difference, but I still couldn't help but wonder.

Kara and Melissa lived in Columbia, not that far from Yancey. I hadn't seen them since Carolyn's funeral, and I couldn't blame anyone but myself that we were no longer in touch. *Maybe I'll drive up to see them after I know how my interview turns out.*

The rain made me feel lazy, but I forced myself into the shower and then downstairs to fix myself some breakfast. I didn't have any plans for the day, so I decided to start sorting through some of the books and paperwork still in Dad's study. Most of the paperwork found its way into the shredder, but the books I couldn't bear to part with. I decided to do some remodeling if I ended up staying in Yancey. I would turn the seldom used formal dining room into a library. Over the years, I'd collected books and artifacts from all over the world, and I wanted a place to display them. I also still had all of Howie's journals, none of which I'd had the heart to read. Right now my collection resided in a secured storage unit in Atlanta.

After lunch, I kicked back in Dad's old reclining chair with the copy of *Treasure Island* Dad used to read to Kyle and me on days like today. I hadn't read it since I left Yancey. As I read, I could almost hear Dad's voice as he made each character come alive. Tears filled my eyes. I missed him, and yes, I also missed Mom. For the first time since I'd received the news of her death six months earlier, I cried for her. I cried for the relationship we should have had and didn't. There in the house where I was raised, I finally was able to begin to grieve for my mom.

After crying myself out, I fell asleep in Dad's chair. When I woke, the house was beginning to darken in the dusk. At first I couldn't figure out what woke me, but then the old telephone rang again. Having become accustomed to the Melissa Etheridge ringtone on my cell phone, this ring was quite a foreign sound. In fact, until that moment, I didn't even realize the phone in the house was still working. I jumped up and stumbled into the hallway where the telephone sat in its little alcove carved in the wall.

"Hello?"

"Shelby, this is Valerie Gilmore. How are you?"

"Ms. Gilmore, I mean Valerie... It was good to see you at the reunion. I'm sorry I haven't called you." I didn't want to admit I'd forgotten.

"That's okay, Shelby." She laughed. "I know you're probably playing catch up with a number of people. I was calling to see if you'd like to meet for lunch sometime this week."

"I'd love to." I went on to explain I had to be in Charleston on Tuesday and why.

"How about if we get together at Robbie's on Thursday then?" Valerie said.

I was surprised. Robbie had seemed old when I was in high school and I couldn't imagine she would still be running our old haunt. "Is Robbie's still open?"

"Robbie retired, but her daughter-in-law and granddaughter still run the place. They've kept the name out of respect," Valerie said. "Robbie still shows up once or twice a week and handles the register. I think it helps her feel she still has a place there."

We talked a few more minutes before ringing off. I went to the kitchen and made myself a sandwich and a salad and took my light dinner out to the porch. The rain had stopped, but water still dripped off the eaves. Steam rose from the marsh, eerie in the moonlight that peeked from behind the clouds. The night birds were singing, crickets rasped out their greetings, and the breeze ruffled the marsh grass. I felt more at home with each passing day.

Chapter Ten

I woke up well before my alarm clock announced it was Tuesday morning. I was more nervous about the interview with *Charleston Magazine* than any interview since the one for my first job thirty years earlier. I was confident of my portfolio and of my ability to fill the position, but I was nervous because the outcome of this interview would determine my future more than any other. I already knew I no longer wanted to travel extensively. If the job in Charleston didn't pan out, I was determined to find something similar somewhere else, preferably close to Yancey.

I showered and then dressed carefully. I'd laid out my best dark blue linen suit the night before, making sure the slacks were creased to within an inch of their lives and that there wasn't a piece of lint to be found on the slacks or the blazer. I chose a simple white button down shirt and a blue and gold scarf to wear under the collar. Simple gold stud earrings and the gold chain Howie gave me for my twentieth birthday completed my outfit. I combed my short auburn hair down rather than opting for my usual spiked hairstyle. I learned many years earlier, after a rather disastrous experience, that a conservative appearance was best until the job was landed.

I glanced at the clock and was surprised to see it was barely 6:30. I was completely dressed and ready to go, and I still had a half hour before I had to leave. The interview was at nine. It would take approximately an hour and a half to get to Charleston and I decided a half hour cushion would be good in case of bad traffic or inaccurate directions to the magazine's office.

It made sense to stop at Robbie's for breakfast rather than fix my own. I knew if the little diner's food was half as good as it had been when Robbie herself ran the place, I could count on eggs and grits cooked to perfection and a decent cup of coffee. I wasn't disappointed. The service was good and the food was as wonderful as I remembered. I proceeded to Charleston with a full stomach, ready to face the challenge of the interview.

I found the offices of *Charleston Magazine* with no problem and checked in with the receptionist at 8:45, then sat in a comfortable overstuffed leather chair in the lobby with my portfolio balanced on my knee. Several past issues of the magazine were stacked on the table at my elbow. Having obtained samples when I originally applied for the position, I was familiar with the magazine but I flipped through them anyway, re-familiarizing myself with the layout and the scope of the reporting. I liked what I saw and it redoubled my determination to get the position.

At nine o'clock sharp, I was escorted into a dark paneled conference room. I took a seat at the end of a long mahogany table while the editor-in-chief and the CEO of the magazine took seats to either side of me. I opened my portfolio for the editor-in-chief, Mr. Thompson.

"Ms. Livingston," the CEO said, "thank you for coming in today. Would you tell Mr. Thompson and me about some of your work?"

"Thank you for inviting me," I said. "I've done mostly freelance photography and photo-journalism for the past twenty-plus years. My work has been published in major news magazines and newspapers."

"Why are you giving up your freelance work?" Mr. Thompson handed my portfolio to Mr. Lubick.

"I've been on the road for a long time," I said. "I don't remember what it's like to be in one place for more than a week or so, and I'm ready to settle down. I'd like to stay in my hometown, Yancey, and work here at *Charleston Magazine*."

Mr. Lubick looked up from one of the layouts I had done in Afghanistan the year before. "You don't think you'll get restless and want to move on again?"

"Mr. Lubick, as you can see from that layout, I've seen some really awful things in my life. I'm tired of feeling sad all the time. I'm tired of never knowing where I'm going to lay my head the next night. I honestly don't anticipate becoming restless."

"Why do you believe you'll be an asset to *Charleston Magazine*?" Mr. Thompson asked.

"I was raised in the Lowcountry and I love the people here. I'm looking forward to doing stories about their lives and their lifestyles. I'm thorough in my reporting, whether in photos or in words."

Mr. Thompson told me more about the position and its responsibilities. At the end of an hour, they promised I would have an answer from them by the end of business on Wednesday. I left more nervous than when I arrived.

I spent the rest of the day with my sister-in-law, admiring the work she and Kyle had done and were doing on their new home on Tradd Street. We drove out to John's Island and feasted on shrimp and crab and buttery corn-on-the-cob at the best seafood restaurant in the Lowcountry, at least as far as I was concerned. I was glad I had thought to bring a change of clothes with me. Eating there was not something to be done in a linen suit.

When I returned home to my house on the marsh late Tuesday afternoon, I went down to the dock and sat down. I took off my sandals and hung my feet over the edge, remembering sitting that way so many evenings — a fishing pole at my side and surrounded by my friends. The ghosts of those long ago evenings joined me and I told them about my day and about my hopes to be able to stay in the Lowcountry permanently. They didn't answer, but I knew they were sending me encouragement and love.

I sat there until the sun set and then walked up to the house. I'd left the back porch light and a small lamp in the kitchen on in case I returned after dark. Summer moths and June bugs buzzed around the porch light. I went into the house and jumped when I realized someone was sitting at the kitchen table. I snapped on the overhead light.

"Naomi!" I wished I'd remembered to lock the back door when I left that morning. "What are you doing here?"

She looked up at me, her green eyes dull. I remembered when they had flashed with excitement and sparkled when she laughed. I suddenly realized Naomi looked much older than I felt.

"I knew you wouldn't see me if I didn't just show up," she said, standing up as she spoke. "When you weren't home, I had my son drop me off. I really need to talk to you."

Tears rolled down her cheeks but I stood still, not moving to comfort her. The pain she caused thirty years earlier still made me leery of her. Like my mother, Naomi had proven to be unpredictable, and I was not anxious to put myself in a position to be hurt again, especially with my future already hanging in the balance. She took a step toward me.

"Sit down, Naomi," I said. "What do you want to talk about?"

"Shelby, I'm so sorry," Naomi said. "For thirty years I wanted to tell you that — you and Howie and Carolyn and Kara and Melissa. I waited too long, though."

"Yes, you did. You should have told all of us that, and meant it, a long time ago. Howie went to his grave thinking you hated him. When he was sick, we talked a lot about regrets and one of his biggest ones was the fact the two of you never reconciled."

"It's one of my biggest regrets, too," Naomi whispered.

I was having a hard time working up any sympathy for her. I'd watched Howie cry too many times while he was ill. He cried about losing Naomi's friendship, about the mistakes he made throughout his life, about the grim situation in which he found himself. He wanted to try to contact Naomi, but I wouldn't let him. Howie was too sick and I was afraid she would reject him and make him worse than he already was.

"Shelby, please believe me." Naomi looked up at me. I still stood by the back door. "Please, come sit down. Please."

"I'd rather stand," I said, aware of how cold my voice was.

"I was so stupid," Naomi said. Her voice, already gravelly from smoking, was now hoarse with emotion. "I didn't realize how much harm I'd caused until after the trial. I saw the five of y'all together and I hurt so bad I wasn't a part of the group anymore and I realized how much I lost."

"How much you lost!" I screamed at her. "Are you really sitting here in my kitchen, probably in the same chair you sat in when you and Mom cooked up your horrible scheme, hoping to gain my sympathy by telling me how much you lost?"

I was so angry, I was shaking. The hurt and the pain I had bottled up for thirty years came boiling out.

"You almost destroyed Melissa! You broke Howie's heart when you said you had to put up with a fag. Carolyn tried for months to talk to you and you turned her away every time. How do you think that made her feel? How do you think I felt when I found out my mom outed me to you? And what about how I felt when you told the whole school I was gay and Kara and Melissa were gay? And you're telling me how much you lost!"

Naomi dropped her head into her hands. Her shoulders shook as she sobbed. She finally looked up at me, pale behind her freckles. She reached a hand out to me, trembling. I looked at it and then turned my back on her. My hand was on the screen door, I was ready to bolt, but I turned and looked back at her. "Why?" I whispered. "Why?"

She shook her head and shrugged. She slumped lower in her chair, seemingly trying to sink into the floor. "I don't know," she whispered. "I honestly don't know. I saw Kara and Melissa that night at the beach and something in me broke wide open. I felt more anger than I knew what to do with."

I crossed the kitchen and sat down across from her, pushing my chair far away from the table. I crossed my arms over my chest. I didn't want to touch Naomi or for her to touch me. We looked at each other for what felt like an eternity before she spoke again.

"Shelby, there was so much going on in my life back then that y'all didn't know about, and I didn't want y'all to know about. I didn't know how to deal with those things and I know that's no excuse for what I did, but it's the only real explanation I have," she said. "I had so much anger in me that didn't have anywhere to go and I took it out on the five people I loved most instead of letting y'all help me. I was in a lot of pain, so I guess I did my best to make sure y'all were too."

I didn't know what Naomi was talking about, so I just let her talk.

"When you and Howie left town the day after graduation, I was so hurt y'all didn't say bye to me. I stood across the street from Robbie's and watched y'all in the parking lot. I wanted to join y'all so bad, but I knew I didn't dare. It took me years to realize you couldn't say goodbye. You couldn't, and it was my fault. Then I heard Howie died and I was devastated. I waited too long to try to make things right. That's when I decided to get some counseling, for Earl's sake as much as my own. I wanted to raise him to be tolerant and loving and accepting and to not have any regrets. Since his daddy left me as soon as he found out I was pregnant, I was his only parent."

She stopped and looked at me. She was on a roll and I didn't really know what to say anyway. I cocked my head at her to let her know I was listening.

"By then Daddy was gone and Mom had moved back to Nashville, so I finally felt safe. Daddy was always so mean, so I was pretty surprised when he left the land and horses to me. Anyway, the counselor helped me understand why I was so angry and see how what I did to y'all was an extension of that anger. He tried to get me to contact y'all, but I was so ashamed, I couldn't do it.

"Then Carolyn killed herself. I was at her funeral, but I stayed in the back, away from y'all. I was afraid y'all would blame me for her death; I know I blamed myself. After that I knew I couldn't contact any of the rest of you. And you, you were getting so famous. Every time I opened a newsmagazine, there was an article by you or a photograph you took. I knew you wouldn't want anything to do with a lowlife like me."

She stopped again. This time I allowed her to make eye contact with me. I could see the exhaustion in her eyes. Suddenly I realized how thin she was. Naomi's face was gaunt; her cheekbones sharp and her eyes sunken. I looked at her hands. Her right hand was nicotine stained; both hands were rough and callused. They looked like they belonged to a skeleton with skin.

"Shelby, I don't know what to do or what to say to tell you how sorry I am that I turned on y'all. Daddy and Uncle Tyrone started molesting me when I turned thirteen. They would take turns holding me down while the other one... Well, you get the idea.

Mom knew about it but did nothing, and I didn't think I could tell anyone else. Daddy was so well respected; I knew no one would believe me. By that night at the beach, I hated all of them and that hate spilled over onto all of you. I knew things weren't good 'tween your mom and you, but to me, y'all had a wonderful relationship compared to what I had. And Melissa's mom was so great and Carolyn's folks always doted on her. They wouldn't have let something awful happen to their girls the way my mom did."

I was shocked. I knew Naomi wasn't happy when we were in high school and hated going home. There were many nights she would beg to stay overnight with one of us girls, but we never questioned why. It was my turn to feel guilty. Shouldn't we have seen the signs?

"My counselor tried to explain to me how I transferred my anger for my folks to y'all. He tried to tell me that it isn't such an unusual thing to do, but I still have so much pain inside me for what I did. Even if you never forgive me, and I won't blame you if you don't, I had to at least try. I hope Melissa and Kara will let me talk to them. My son Earl has offered to drive me to Columbia next week."

"Naomi," I started, then stopped. I gulped, the tears close to the surface. I started again. "Naomi, I wish you'd told us what was happening to you. We would have done something. Dad would have done something."

"I know," she said. "But I was too ashamed. I thought y'all would think less of me if you knew. I was so scared."

I finally reached across the table to her. She latched onto my hand like it was a life preserver. The thinness of her hand shocked me again.

"Shelby, do you think you'll ever be able to forgive me?"

"I don't know, Naomi. When I think about what happened to Melissa, the pain is still severe. I want to, though. Now that I have some sense of why you did it, I want to. I don't know how long it will take."

The look on Naomi's face reflected both relief and panic.

"Shelby, I don't have a long time left. I have lung cancer that's not treatable. I've had all the chemo and radiation treatments this old body can tolerate. I'm on medical maintenance now. I honestly don't know how much longer I'll be alive."

"Oh my God!" I reacted the only way I knew how. I rose and went around the table and gathered Naomi into my arms. As my tears fell, I realized how much I'd missed her. We hung onto each other for dear life, both of us crying — crying in sorrow for the friends we had already lost, crying for the time we had lost, crying for our uncertain futures. When we finally cried ourselves out, we sat down, this time side by side.

"Naomi, I'll take you to Columbia. I haven't seen Melissa and Kara since Carolyn's funeral and we've kind of lost touch. We'll go see them together. Maybe when they see you and I have reconciled, they'll be able to forgive you, too."

Naomi looked at me, her eyes still bright with tears, relief written clearly across her face.

"Does this mean you'll forgive me?" The hope in her voice was edged with caution.

"Naomi, it means I'm going to try my best to forgive you. I want to say yes so badly, but it isn't that easy." I suddenly realized a huge weight was gone from my heart.

"I understand," Naomi said. "I wish you could say yes, but I understand."

I was utterly exhausted. I'd had a long day even before my encounter with Naomi. I glanced at the clock and was shocked to see it was well past midnight.

"Naomi, it's far too late for your son to come pick you up. Why don't you stay here tonight?"

She nodded. I could see she was also exhausted. We staggered up the stairs together and I made up the bed in my mother's room. We hugged and then I stumbled to my own bed. I barely got my shorts and t-shirt off before I was asleep.

Chapter Eleven

I woke to the feel of bright sunshine pouring through my window, the enticing smell of coffee brewing and eggs and bacon cooking wafting up the stairs. I pried my eyes open and was shocked to find it was almost ten o'clock. Until I returned to Yancey, I probably had not slept past six in the morning more than half a dozen times in over twenty years, and now I had slept late three times in less than a week.

I dragged myself to the shower and then put on clean shorts and t-shirt. Downstairs, I found Naomi wrapped in one of Mom's old robes, water droplets glistening on her frizzy hair. She was standing at the stove, cooking breakfast and swaying to a tune only she could hear.

I laughed as I watched her, memories flooding back. Naomi always seemed to have music playing in her head. She whistled or hummed a tune she was sure we would all know, but since she was tone deaf, the tune was usually unrecognizable.

"Who do you hear in your head this morning?" I asked as she turned to me.

"The Beach Boys," she said, and then proceeded to sing horribly off key.

I laughed again. She sounded so much happier this morning, and looked a little better, too.

"Enough, enough," I said, covering my hands over my ears. "You've never been able to carry a tune in a bucket. Puh-leese stop."

She laughed and turned back to dishing up eggs and bacon and toast. I helped myself to some freshly brewed coffee and leaned back on the counter to watch her. "You look like you feel better this morning."

Naomi set the two plates of food on the table and motioned for me to sit down. I joined her and was surprised when she took my hand and said grace over the food. As teens, none of us went to church or put a lot of stock in prayer. Over the years, especially after Howie's and Carolyn's deaths, I put God in a box in the storeroom of my heart and hadn't planned on letting Him out.

"I do feel better," she said after the prayer. "I slept better last night than I have in thirty years. Thank you for letting me stay."

"I was glad to have you," I said, sincerely. "Especially since you can cook," I teased.

We both laughed and dug into our food. After we ate, we cleaned up in companionable silence and then she went upstairs to get dressed. I dug out my old address book and looked up Mrs. Ballard's telephone number. I laid my cell phone on the table in front of me, trying to find the courage to call her. I didn't even know whether she would be home or at work.

"What are you doing?" Naomi asked as she came back into the kitchen. She held one hand behind her back.

"Trying to find the courage to call Mrs. Ballard and get Melissa and Kara's contact information," I said. "What have you got there?"

Naomi put a silver picture frame down on the table in front of me. I looked at it in surprise. I looked out of the photograph, a confused smile on my face. I was standing on the edge of the stage at graduation, one hand raised to my mortarboard, my fingers on my tassel. It was the graduation photograph Mom took of me the day before I left for Atlanta. I picked it up and ran my fingers down the edge of the ornate frame.

"She was so proud of you, Shelby," Naomi said quietly. "We used to get together for lunch once in a while, and all she could talk about was how well you were doing."

"I wish she'd told me," I whispered, not trusting my voice.

Naomi covered my hand with her thin one. She didn't say anything for a long time.

"Hon, she was as scared to talk to you as I was," she finally said. "You were so cold to her that last night before you left. I know..." She held up her hand to forestall me as I started to protest. "I know she wasn't exactly accepting or warm to you, but she was really intimidated by you."

"Intimidated?"

"Yes," Naomi said. "She could see you inherited your dad's intelligence and she never felt she could live up to either of y'all's expectations. And then when you came out, she was so jealous of your courage. When she told me you were gay, it wasn't to cause trouble but to brag about you. I was the one who used the information to cause trouble."

"Brag about me?" I stammered. "But she was so hateful about it."

"Shelby, neither your mom nor I understood. And when people don't understand something, they're instinctively afraid of it. And when a person is afraid of something, they fight it. In a nutshell, that's why both your mom and I were so horrid."

I looked at Naomi in astonishment. Her level of understanding was so much deeper than mine, even after thirty years in the reporting business. She laughed at the look on my face and gave my hand a quick squeeze.

"Don't go thinking I've all of a sudden got smart or something. I just regurgitated what my counselor took twelve years to pound into my head."

I pulled Naomi to her feet and gave her a hard hug. My heart sunk when I realized how thin she was. I hugged her tighter, wishing we had been able to get to this point before she got sick. I knew in my soul she wouldn't be around much longer.

"Naomi, after all that Mom did to get you in trouble when we were in high school, why did you continue to stay in touch with her, to have lunch with her?"

"Oh, Shel, she honestly felt she was trying to help. She was as confused and hurt as I was; she just never actually admitted it. She did apologize to me for making things so bad for me. Your mom and I were both awfully lonely. Your dad had very little to do with her after you left, and I had no friends. We kind of gravitated to each other. She's who told me y'all would be at Robbie's that day. She wanted me to try to make amends. I just didn't have the courage."

"Mom apologized to you?" I was incredulous. I could never remember Mom apologizing to anyone for anything.

"Yes, she did. I guess that's another reason I stayed her friend. Are you going to call Mrs. Ballard?" Naomi asked as we sat down. "She should be home."

"Home?" I asked. "Shouldn't she be at work on a Wednesday?"

"Oh, she retired. About a year ago, I think. Sue Ellen still works over on Hilton Head Island, but Mrs. Ballard retired."

I laughed. "Do you know everyone's business?"

"You forget what it's like to live in a small town," Naomi said, laughing as well. "Are you going to use your cell phone to call her? If you are, I'm going to use the other phone to call Earl. He must be wondering if you drowned me in the marsh."

"Yeah, I'll use my cell," I said. "Go ahead and give him a call. Tell him I'll bring you home."

Naomi left the kitchen while I picked up my phone and tentatively dialed the Ballard's phone number. Mrs. Ballard picked up on the third ring.

"Hello?"

"Um. Hi, Mrs. Ballard," I said. "This is Shelby."

"Oh my word!" Mrs. Ballard practically screamed. "Shelby Livingston, I heard you were in town. You get your scrawny ass over here and hug my neck."

I started laughing. The clock turned back to my high school days as soon as I heard her voice. She didn't sound as if she'd changed at all.

"Mrs. Ballard," I finally croaked out. "I'll do just that as soon as I run a few errands."

"Just don't be wasting a lot of time," she said.

We hung up and I sat there chuckling, thinking how much I'd missed her, and Sue Ellen, and their earthy humor and abundant love for all of Melissa's friends. Naomi came back into the kitchen and sat down across from me, one red eyebrow cocked.

"I assume she yelled at you for not calling or coming over sooner."

"Yup," I said. I looked at Naomi and noticed a sheen over her eyes. "Are you okay?"

"I need to get on home, Shelby. I don't have my pain meds with me and I really need to go."

I immediately felt guilty for not realizing she might not be feeling well. I jumped up and grabbed my wallet and car keys and then turned to help Naomi out the door. She was unsteady on her feet and I worried she would stumble and fall. I got her situated in the passenger seat of my car and then took the road north to her horse farm.

Earl met us at the door and helped his mom into the house. I followed them inside the house, but not into Naomi's bedroom. After a few minutes, Earl rejoined me in the kitchen.

"Is she going to be okay?" I asked, almost immediately doing a mental head slap. Of course she wasn't going to be okay, but it was too late to rephrase my question. Earl grinned at the look of chagrin on my face.

"I know what you mean, Ms. Livingston. It's okay," he reassured me. "I gave Mom her pain medicine and helped her to bed. She asked me to apologize. She also wants to know if you'll come back or call later and let her know how it went, whatever that means."

"Is y'all's phone number still 555-8726?" He nodded so I continued, "Tell her I'll call this evening."

"Thanks, Ms. Livingston. I'll tell her."

I left then, but had to pull off the road almost as soon as I got out of the driveway. I put my head on the steering wheel and sobbed. So much time had been wasted in hate and misunderstanding. I regretted now that I kept Howie from contacting Naomi. He would have understood and helped us all to forgive. I knew it in my heart and hoped against hope that Kara and Melissa would also understand.

I dried my tears and drove into town. I turned off Main Street onto the oak lined Mink Road. The neighborhood had barely changed except that the trees were larger, forming a tunnel of lacy green. I pulled into the Ballard's driveway, noting the house was still painted a happy yellow. Pots of colorful flowers lined the porch railing and an American flag flew proudly.

Before I was even out of the car, Mrs. Ballard was out the door and down the steps. She practically dragged me from the driver's seat into a huge hug. I returned her hug, tears threatening again, this time happy tears.

"Come in this house and tell me what's going on in your life, where you've been, where you're going, and why you don't write me and Sue Ellen and Melissa and Kara." The words poured out of her mouth so fast it left us both breathless.

I laughed and took her hand as we went up the steps. I stopped on the porch, struck again by how little things had changed. The same yellow, metal lawn chairs were placed in little groups, inviting intimate conversation. The porch swing still hung from the end of the porch, swaying in the slight breeze. White shutters graced the windows, looking newly painted. Mrs. Ballard squeezed my hand.

"Would you like to sit out here?" she asked quietly.

I nodded and sat down in the nearest chair. It rocked back in that comforting way it always did and then the tears did begin to fall. Mrs. Ballard sat down in the chair beside me. She placed her hand on my shoulder and just let me cry.

"I'm sorry," I finally was able to say. "I'm not sure where that came from."

"Oh, Shelby," she soothed, "you've been away from home for a long time; lots of things happened before you left and since you left that you've had to come to grips with. Of course you're going to be emotional. It's okay."

I smiled at her and she patted me on the shoulder. I stood up and hugged her again.

"You just sit here and I'll go get us something cold to drink," she said. "Then you can start talking and filling me in on your life."

I watched her go through the door, amazed at how little she'd changed. Petite like her daughter, Mrs. Ballard was a pretty tough little woman. She lived her life the way she wanted and didn't care how much criticism she faced for it. She carried her shoulders straight and proud, her chin up and her eyes forward. Even though she was only five feet tall, people often mistook her for quite a bit taller. Her hair, once a deep black, was now streaked with gray, the only real indication that she'd aged.

Mrs. Ballard returned with a tray of lemonade and chilled glasses, along with a plate full of cookies, standard fare for a Southern lady to serve to a guest. I accepted my glass of lemonade and plate of cookies graciously and gratefully. I realized how much I missed a good glass of homemade lemonade.

For an hour we talked about me — where I'd been, things and people I'd seen and met, what my hopes were for finally settling down. Mrs. Ballard was happy I was through traveling and sincerely hoped *Charleston Magazine* hired me so I could stay in Yancey.

All the time we were talking, I was trying to get up my courage to ask about Melissa and Kara. I was afraid they wouldn't want me to be in touch with them. Finally, I just asked.

"Mrs. Ballard, I want to go see Melissa and Kara. Do you think they'll want to see me after all this time?"

"Oh for Pete's sake! Don't tell me you're still so insecure that you don't think your best friends would want to see you. You were always afraid of your own shadow and I don't think that part of you has changed."

Insecure? Me? I thought, but didn't challenge her.

"Of course the girls will want to see you. In fact, why don't we call them right now?"

"Will they be home?"

"It's June, Shelby." Mrs. Ballard shook her head. "How is it you can be such a great reporter and not have the common sense God gave a goose? They're teachers, silly. They don't work in the summer."

Mrs. Ballard was laughing as she went in to get her telephone. I sat there feeling like a little kid again. It had been a long time since I'd last been told I had no common sense. I knew that was a shortcoming of mine, but being told sure did bring it home.

I was nervous about talking to "the girls". It had been a long time, but I knew it was crucial that I not delay any longer. I sat quietly, trying to formulate what I would say to them. I had to somehow make them believe that Naomi was sincere, talk them into agreeing to see her and talk to her. I went into my mental tunnel, meditating and breathing deeply to calm myself. The ringing of my cell phone brought me back to reality. I dug it out of my pocket.

"Hello?"

"Ms. Livingston? This is Mr. Thompson."

I nearly stopped breathing when I heard the voice of the editor-in-chief at *Charleston Magazine.*

"Yes, sir. How are you today?" I asked, trying to sound like this wasn't one of the most important conversations I would ever have.

"I'm quite well, thank you," he said, "and I think you'll like why I'm calling. We would like to offer you the position of lead in-house reporter here at *Charleston Magazine.*"

I refrained from whooping with joy and relief and thanked him instead. He went on to make a generous salary offer and welcome me onboard. I thanked him again and assured him I looked forward to seeing him when I began work on the first of August.

After we hung up, I did whoop and dance around the Ballard's porch, and whoop some more. When I calmed down, I realized not only was Mrs. Ballard watching, but also Sue Ellen. I scooped Sue Ellen up in a bear hug and then proceeded to dance her around the porch. The two ladies had no idea what was going on, but joined in my impromptu celebration anyway. We finally collapsed in laughter.

"What was that all about?" Mrs. Ballard asked once she caught her breath.

"I got the job at *Charleston Magazine*! I start on August first." I whooped again.

"Congratulations! One of our babies is coming home," Sue Ellen said. She jumped up and hugged me again.

"When did you get home?" I asked her. "I didn't see you drive up."

"I ride the shuttle bus the transit system set up for people who work on the Island," she said. "It lets me off on Main Street and I walked down the alley. I wanted to surprise you and I guess it worked."

"It did," I said.

"Surprised me, too," Mrs. Ballard said, beaming at Sue Ellen. "I called her at work and told her you were coming to visit, but she didn't say a thing about getting off early. I like surprises like that."

Mindful of small town proprieties, Sue Ellen patted her on the leg. I could tell she wanted to kiss her, but since we were on the porch, she didn't. I watched them make eye contact and was reminded of the sparks I saw flash between Melissa and Kara whenever they looked at each other.

"Are we going to call the girls?" I asked, bringing their attention back to me.

"Oh, yes. I knew I picked up the phone for some reason," Mrs. Ballard said. "Your good news almost made me forget what I was doing."

She pushed a speed dial button on her cordless handset and put the receiver to her ear, winking at me as she did. I could hear the phone ringing on the other end and was afraid there would be no answer. Mrs. Ballard cocked an eyebrow at me as the phone was finally answered.

"Hi, baby. How are you?" she greeted. "Are you enjoying your time off?" She paused for a few minutes, listening and smiling. "Hey, I've got a wonderful surprise for you," she said, smiling at me. "Here, listen to this." She handed me the phone.

For a second I was stunned into silence. I hadn't expected her to hand me the phone. She mouthed, "Say something," at me.

"Hello?" I finally said.

"Hello," said the voice of an angel. "Who is this?"

"Melissa?"

"Yes, this is Melissa, but who... Oh my Gawd!" she screamed. "Shelby! Shelby! Is that you? Is that really you? Kara, come quick! Shelby's on the phone!"

I held the receiver several inches from my ear as Mrs. Ballard and Sue Ellen laughed out loud. Melissa continued to scream and scream, her joy coming through loud and clear over the phone line. Finally I heard Kara take the telephone from her.

"Shelby, is that really you?" she asked, trying to make herself heard over Melissa.

"Yup. I'm sitting on Mrs. Ballard's front porch as we speak," I said, laughing. "Tell Melissa if she doesn't shut up, I won't come up to Columbia to see y'all next week."

"You're coming up here!" Kara exclaimed, setting Melissa off again. "Where are you on your way to this time?"

"Just to see y'all, if you'll have me." I was still a little bit afraid they wouldn't want to see me.

"Oh, Shelby, that would be so awesome! Our house is really tiny, but we'll give you the bed and we'll sleep in the living room."

"No, y'all won't do anything of the kind. I can stay in a motel and be as happy as a lark." I laughed, relieved and gratified they still wanted to see me and were willing to sacrifice their comfort for mine. "I have something really important I need to talk to y'all about, and I want to do it face to face."

"That sounds serious," Kara said. "Can you give me a hint?"

"I'd rather not," I said. "I'd rather wait until I can sit down with y'all."

"Well, okay, if that's the way you want to be." She laughed. "Let me give you our address and phone number."

Mrs. Ballard handed me an ink pen and a notepad and I jotted down the information and directions on how to find them. I told them I would firm up our plans on Sunday and give them an idea of what time I expected to be there the following Monday. After chatting a few more minutes, we hung up. Our conversation was invigorating and I felt like whooping again. Instead I sat quietly, thanking the Universe that my friends still loved me.

"Something important, huh?" Mrs. Ballard interrupted my reverie. "Care to share?"

"Not yet, Mrs. Ballard," I said, hoping she would understand. "After I've talked to them, I'll either let them fill you in or I will when I come back. Right now, I have to get going. I have a lot to do to get ready to move to Yancey and start working in Charleston."

We said our good-byes and I promised faithfully to come back to visit often, a promise I intended to keep. I climbed into my car and drove home, still giddy from the excitement of the day.

Later that day, after making the necessary telephone calls to have my belongings shipped from Atlanta, and calling Kyle and friends I made over the years to tell them about my new job, I called Naomi. Earl answered the phone.

"Hey, Earl," I said. "Is it possible to talk to Naomi?"

He asked me to wait a moment while he took the handset to her.

"Hello?" Naomi sounded tired.

"How are you feeling?" I asked.

"A little better than this morning. I was just waking up from a nap, so excuse me if I'm still yawning."

"I've been so busy today, a nap actually sounds good." I laughed. "I went to see Mrs. Ballard," I continued. "Sue Ellen was there, too, and we had a great visit."

"Did you mention me?" she asked.

"No, hon, I didn't. I want to talk to Kara and Melissa first. After we see how they do, then we'll go back and talk to Melissa's folks. Okay?"

"That's fine," she said, sounding a bit disappointed. "I just figured if anyone had the heart to forgive me it would be Mrs. Ballard. She always tried so hard to understand us and support us."

"I know, Naomi. Do you think you're up for a trip to Columbia?"

"They want us to come visit?" Naomi's voice perked up some.

I explained they were only expecting me, but I wanted her to come, too. I would pay for her hotel room and we would use the time to get reacquainted, regardless of whether Kara and Melissa chose to see her. After some encouragement, Naomi agreed to accompany me to Columbia the following week.

"I got more good news today," I said.

"Did you get the job in Charleston?"

"I sure did. I was so excited, I'm afraid I made a fool of myself."

"Well, if I remember Mrs. Ballard and Sue Ellen like I think I do, they just joined right in."

I laughed, memories of silliness flooding back. We started the "remember when" game and talked for over an hour. When I heard tiredness creeping into her voice, I made up an excuse to get off the phone, promising to call her the next day.

I sat back in Dad's chair and closed my eyes. When I came back to Yancey for the high school reunion and my interview I had no inkling of the turn of events that would occur. I had been home less than a week and the course of my life had taken yet another unexpected path. I opened my eyes and looked around. It was taking some time to get used to the idea that this was my house, in my name, free and clear, thanks to my father and, yes, to my mother, as well. I quietly thanked them for taking care of me, both in life and in death.

Chapter Twelve

Thursday provided another opportunity to travel down memory lane. At one in the afternoon, I parked my car in the parking lot of Robbie's Diner. The lunch crowd was just beginning to thin out. Valerie hadn't yet arrived, so I sat on one of the benches in the small garden out front.

The garden was new to me. The area in front of the diner had been a nondescript lawn when I was a teenager, but someone, probably Robbie's daughter-in-law, had put a lot of time and effort into turning it into an inviting place to wait for friends or just enjoy the day. A simple fountain bubbled in the center. Benches were arranged around the perimeter of the garden, each facing inward so its occupants could enjoy the fountain and the flowers.

I was deep in a daydream when I felt a hand on my shoulder. I looked up to see Valerie smiling down at me. I was struck again at how wonderful she looked. Her thick brown hair was secured on one side with a silver barrette that matched the necklace and bracelet she wore. Her blue tank top accentuated the blue in her eyes, which sparkled with mischief.

"Where were you?" she asked with a laugh. "I stood in front of you for a good two minutes and you didn't even notice me."

"Sorry." I shrugged, laughing along with her. "This has been a week for the books and I was just taking some time to digest it all."

"Speaking of digestion," she said, "I'm starved. Let's go in and eat."

We entered the diner and I was thrilled to see Robbie sitting at the register. I went around the counter to hug her.

"So, you got famous, made your fortune, and came home," she teased.

"Yes, ma'am." I laughed. "And in just that order, too."

"Git on with ya." She lightly punched my shoulder. "Miz Gilmore, it's good to see you today. I hear you're in the running for principal up there at the high school."

I looked at Valerie in surprise. That was the first I'd heard about her possible promotion.

"It's a possibility, Miss Robbie," Valerie said. "I'll find out in another couple of weeks."

"Well, good luck," Robbie said. "Y'all go find you a table and have a good lunch, hear?"

We found a booth by the front window and it didn't take us long to decide on a basket of fried chicken along with mashed potatoes and green beans. A large glass of cold sweet tea made the lunch a true Southern meal, the likes of which I hadn't enjoyed in many years.

Valerie and I reminisced about many things over our food. She reminded me of how I used to argue with her whenever she edited an article I wrote for the high school newspaper.

"Do you still give your editors that much grief?" she asked, a grin on her face.

"Oh, yeah," I said, thinking of all the times I'd had to fight for the integrity of an article. I also thought of the many times editors had helped me improve my writing. "You honed my skills through your tough editing, and I learned how to argue effectively in the process."

Valerie laughed. The sound of her laughter made a part of me melt. Her face lit up and her eyes sparkled. I wanted to reach out and touch her. I was still attracted to her; my crush from high school had never waned. I had a sudden realization that one of the reasons my other relationships had not lasted might have been because none of those women measured up to Valerie Gilmore.

Valerie caught me staring at her and smiled. Reaching across the table, she rested her hand on mine. Its warmth made my hand feel as though it was on fire. I looked down at our two hands and it looked and felt so right. I smiled back.

"Valerie..." I started, hesitating before going on. "Do you remember that day everyone got so hateful, when you took me aside and asked me what was going on?"

"I do," she said. "You told me everyone was full of themselves and you didn't know what was going on."

"I lied."

"I know."

"You do?"

"Yes, and I knew what was going on, too."

"I guess after what happened to Melissa, it was hard not to know."

"That's true, Shelby, but I knew before then. I knew the day it all started."

I shook my head. The memories of that day, of that year, were still hard for me. The wounds just didn't seem to heal, even after the time I'd spent with Naomi earlier in the week.

"It's still hard, isn't it?" Valerie's expression was full of sympathy and concern.

"Yes."

I told her about Naomi coming to my house and the long talk we'd had and how sick Naomi was. I tried to convey how much I wanted to forgive Naomi, but how difficult it was to let go of the pain that had festered for thirty years.

Valerie let me talk without interruption, never taking her hand from mine, nodding from time to time to encourage me to continue. Until then, I hadn't realized how badly I needed to tell someone, anyone, what was in my head and heart. I finally ran out of steam and took a long drink of my tea.

"Do you feel better now?"

I laughed. "I absolutely do."

"Why don't we go for a walk and talk some more?" she said.

"It's amazing how much Yancey has changed in thirty years," I said as we walked along Main Street. "When Howie and I left, most of these stores were boarded up. Harold's Department Store and Robbie's Café were about the only businesses left downtown."

"I know," Valerie said. "It's been refreshing watching Yancey come back to life. Some civic minded leaders were elected about twenty years ago and they took it upon themselves to revive this area. Their efforts certainly have paid off."

I looked at the bright red awning shading the door of a bookstore we were passing and nodded. "I love all the trees and benches they put along here. It's really inviting."

Two young girls greeted Valerie as they came out of the candy store. "Hey, Ms. Gilmore. How's your summer going?"

"Well, hi, Marybeth, Laura. My summer is getting better and better," Valerie said. "Are you girls having a good time off?"

"Yes, ma'am," they answered in unison, giggling. I was reminded of how my friends and I used to giggle and I couldn't help but smile. "We're on our way to the pool now to meet up with Rob and Stan and some of the others."

"Y'all have fun," Valerie said. "See you in August."

The girls groaned and then ran off down the street.

We made our way down Main Street toward the park across from the First Baptist Church. Young mothers watched their children playing on the seesaws and swings at the playground while couples sprawled on blankets spread on the grass of the meadow.

"There's some benches back here," Valerie said, pointing down a path toward a copse of trees. "We can sit in the shade and talk."

"So, you knew back in '75 that I was gay?" I asked, continuing the conversation we started at Robbie's.

"Yes, Shelby, I did," she said, smiling at me.

"What did you think when you found out for sure?"

"I worried about you." Valerie was frank. "I know what a hard time young gay people face today, and back then it was harder. I saw what you and Kara and Melissa, especially Melissa, suffered at the hands of your classmates, and I knew it would be just a taste of what it would be like once you were a part of the real world."

"It was hard," I said. "One of the first things I did when I got to Atlanta was go to a barbershop and get my hair cut really short. I loved it, but I found I faced a lot of discrimination just because of how I looked, without even telling people I was a lesbian."

"Hon," she said with a laugh, "you looked the part before you ever left Yancey. With that shorter haircut, which I assume wasn't even as short as the one you have now, you must have really looked quite butch."

I laughed too. I remembered when I looked in the mirror after the barber finished, and how pleased I was to look like I felt inside. But then I found it disheartening to be turned away from places where I applied for jobs simply because of the way I looked.

"I was lucky. I found a newspaper editor who only cared about the quality of my writing and the fact that I was a good photographer, rather than what I looked like," I said, forever grateful to my first boss in Atlanta. "Mr. Edmonds was almost as tough an editor as you, and I learned a lot about how to get the story, even when the person I was interviewing didn't want to give it to me."

"He must have been a good teacher, then," Valerie said. "I've probably read everything you've had published, and I'm amazed at how you were able to include details other reporters didn't."

We continued talking for a while. Time seemed to stand still. Suddenly Valerie looked at her watch and jumped up.

"Good grief. It's a quarter 'til six. We've been sitting here almost three hours. I need to get home and feed the girls."

"The girls?" I asked as I rose and stood beside her.

"I have two cats and a dog, all gentle ladies unless they aren't fed on time, at which point they turn into monsters." She laughed. "Bella, my little mutt, will destroy anything I leave within reach, and the other two will conveniently forget where their litter box is located. They have me on a strict schedule."

I laughed as we rushed back up Main Street to Robbie's, where we'd left our cars. When we reached the parking lot, we were both out of breath. We leaned on her car for a moment before she unlocked the door and slid into the driver's seat.

"Why don't you follow me home and meet my crew?" she said, looking up at me with clear blue eyes.

I hesitated only a moment before agreeing. I hurried over to my car, climbed in, and pulled in behind her as she drove down Main Street. Valerie lived in a subdivision of town I wasn't familiar with. The nicely sized houses had generous yards and were not too far from the new high school campus. She pulled into the driveway of a pretty white house with hunter green shutters and lots of flowers spilling out of boxes on each windowsill. As I climbed out of the car, I could hear a small dog yapping. Valerie hurried to the front door, key at the ready.

"I'm coming, Bella!" she yelled as she opened the door. A flurry of brown fur flew past her into the yard, did a U-turn, and returned to her. Valerie picked the bundle up and endured a frenzied face licking before setting the dog down again. "I know. I know. You think you're starving to death, don't you? Where are Kelsey and Victoria? Did you eat them for dinner since I'm late?"

I chuckled at how she talked to the little dog. That dog had to be the ugliest thing I'd seen in a long time. She had an abbreviated little snout and great big soulful eyes. She was mostly brown, but had wirehairs that were silver. She stood about twelve inches high, but could jump several times that height, which she demonstrated the entire time we were walking into the house. Clearly glad to see Valerie, the dog completely ignored my presence.

"Sit down, if you dare," Valerie said. "But be aware you will probably leave covered in animal hair. Kelsey? Victoria? Where are you hiding? Dinner time."

I sat down on the beige sofa that took up most of one wall in the small living room and looked around. Valerie had exquisite taste. The house was nicely decorated, a neutral colored throw rug on the floor and deep easy chairs opposite the sofa. The little dog at her heels, Valerie disappeared down the hallway, calling the cats. A few minutes later she returned, an enormous Persian in her arms and a dainty cat that reminded me of a Siamese draped across one shoulder.

"Shelby, I'd like to introduce you to my little family," she said. "The mutt you've already met is Bella, my little rescue from the dog shelter. Then this big girl is Victoria. She's a silver Persian. And my sweet Kelsey is an Abyssinian."

"They're all so pretty," I said, knowing I was lying about Bella. She was anything but pretty.

"Well, thank you," Valerie practically gushed, then laughed. "Excuse me while I go feed these munchkins. Would you like something to drink? I have sweet tea."

"Tea sounds good," I said, following her into the kitchen.

Valerie poured me a glass of tea and then went about feeding her pets. I watched as she prepared them each a bowl of Kibble and canned food, talking to them and to me the entire time. She talked to her animals as though she expected them to answer, which sometimes one would — with a meow or a bark. Bella would occasionally fly through the doggy door leading to the back yard and return with a toy or just to bark at Valerie. She finally settled down when Valerie put her food dish on the floor.

Once they were all eating, she grabbed herself a glass of tea, refreshed mine, and we went back to the living room. I sat on the sofa again and was surprised when she sat down beside me, close enough to touch. We talked about where some of my classmates were, about some of my assignments, and about my new job at *Charleston Magazine*. Time froze again.

"Do you realize it's almost eleven o'clock?" she asked suddenly.

"You're kidding." I looked around and realized that at some point she must have turned the lamps on around the room, as it was quite dark outside.

"Not kidding." She chuckled. "Time flies when you're having fun."

"I've had such a great day, Valerie. I'm so glad we got together."

I stood up, stretching as I rose, closing my eyes as I stretched. When I opened my eyes, Valerie was standing quite close to me. She rested her hand on my arm and looked me in the eye. I wanted desperately to kiss her, but I didn't. My gaydar had never been very keen, and on more than one occasion I'd embarrassed myself, and others, with my assumptions.

"I'm glad we did too, Shelby," Valerie said, a breathlessness in her voice I hadn't heard before.

She lowered her eyes for a moment, but continued to caress my arm with her hand, sending electric currents through my body. She raised her eyes back to mine and I couldn't stop myself. I gathered her into a hug and kissed the side of her neck. She groaned in pleasure and turned her face to mine. Valerie put a hand on each side of my face and brought my lips to hers. I melted into the soft fullness of her mouth. Our lips parted and her tongue found mine. I hadn't been kissed in a long time and never quite like that. When we stopped kissing, I stepped back just enough to look her in the eye.

"Wow!" she said. "I've wanted to kiss you since 1975. It was worth the wait."

I was surprised by the revelation. "You wanted to kiss me?"

"Oh, yes. I knew you were a lesbian the first time I laid eyes on you. You and Kara both, but little Melissa surprised me," she said. "You were so intelligent and so sure of yourself, and so protective of your friends. I had quite a crush on you. Can you believe it? A teacher with a crush on a student."

We both laughed, and then we kissed again, this time falling back onto the sofa. I felt a fire building in me and I had a feeling the same was happening with her. When we finally came up for air, I sat back and took a hard look at her. She was beautiful. Her hair was disheveled and the barrette that had held it back was now hanging at a precarious angle, but that didn't detract from her looks. Her complexion was clear and she wore little make-up, if any. Her tiny ears were adorned with tiny diamond studs.

I realized Valerie was studying me just as intently. I was glad I'd made the time over the years to stay in shape. I knew I had laugh lines around my eyes and other wrinkles from spending too much time in the sun without a hat. My hair was still a deep auburn. I was like my dad in that I had few gray hairs. I took care of myself and I was confident that it showed.

"How old are you now, Shelby? Forty-seven, forty-eight?"

"I'll be forty-eight later this month," I said. "How about you?"

"I turned fifty-four in April," she said. She smiled and pulled me back for another long kiss. Holding me tight, she whispered, "You don't have to go home tonight, you know."

I made myself sit up. I had rushed into too many relationships, only to be hurt or to hurt someone else. I wanted desperately to spend the night in Valerie's arms, to touch her, to taste her, but at the same time, something in me told me to take it slow.

"Valerie," I said, turning to her, "I'd love to stay the night, but I'm not going to. I fell in love with you thirty years ago and now I want to give that love a chance to grow before we become intimate. I want to see you, often. I want to take you out on a real date, several dates. And I want to get to know you and for you to get to know me. I want us to be sure we have something special before we spend the night together."

Valerie sat up and put her arms around me. We hugged and I was acutely aware of the feel of the body pressed against me. I struggled with my decision but knew it was the right one. Our lips barely brushing, I kissed her tenderly.

"And if I don't go now, I won't," I said, standing up again.

Valerie accompanied me to the door, where we kissed one last time and where once again I had to hold firmly to my resolve to wait. She walked me to my car, her hand discreetly on the small of my back. I climbed into the car and rolled down the window. She bent and put her head inside and kissed me gently on the cheek.

"I'll call you tomorrow," I promised, and then backed my car out of her driveway.

Chapter Thirteen

The next few days passed rapidly. On Friday I drove Naomi to Beaufort for her doctor's appointment. Dr. Stephens gave her clearance for the trip to Columbia. He gave her referrals to an oncologist in Columbia in case she needed immediate treatment while we were there. He made sure I knew how to give Naomi her pain medications and gave me specific instructions for how to deal with some of the side effects she might experience from them. I had taken care of Howie and wasn't squeamish about starting an IV in Naomi's port, if necessary, but I sure hoped I wouldn't have to.

Valerie and I spent all day Saturday together. I picked her up early and we drove the hour south to Savannah, where we played tourist all day, strolling the many squares and admiring the historic homes. On a romantic, horse-drawn buggy tour, we stole kisses when we thought we weren't being observed. We ate dinner at one of the most prestigious restaurants in Savannah, pleased and excited when the owner came out and spoke to each and every patron in the restaurant.

That evening we went to Savannah's premier gay bar. The show featured well known drag queens and drag kings, and it was all it was advertised to be and then some. Before and after the show, we danced, and I found Valerie to be an accomplished and sensuous dancer.

We arrived back at her house in Yancey well after midnight. I walked her to the door and as soon as we were inside, she turned and gave me a passionate kiss. I wrapped my arms around her and returned the kiss, but as she tried to lead me to the sofa, I demurred. I knew I wouldn't be able to maintain my resolve if I sat down beside her.

"I really have to go, Valerie," I moaned, my voice full of the desire that was coursing through me.

"You are one stubborn woman, Shelby Livingston," she murmured in my ear, her hands rubbing my back.

"You're making it very difficult to remain stubborn," I said just before capturing her lips in another passionate kiss. After a long, sensual moment, I gently pushed her away from me. "I have to go, now."

She laughed as I scurried backwards out the door. "Coward." I heard her call after me as I stumbled to my car. I wondered if I was making the right decision. *Why, exactly, am I waiting?* I wondered. But I knew the answer. It was because I wanted to be sure this time. I didn't want to rush into something only to find out later that one of us hadn't made the right decision, as I had in the past. I wanted to pursue a relationship only if I was absolutely positive it would be a forever thing.

Sunday dawned bright and clear. The only thing on my agenda was to do laundry and pack for Columbia. I decided to spend the day on the dock, fishing and reading, and wait until evening to do my chores.

Even though the dock was just steps away from the back door of the house, I packed a picnic lunch and some sweet tea to take with me. I grabbed the novel I was reading, my favorite hat, and some sun block, and set off down the hill. From the boathouse I retrieved a lawn chair and a fishing rod.

I baited my hook, cast out, and put the pole in one of the rod holders Dad had fashioned from PVC pipe around the edge of the dock. My feet propped up on one of the dock supports, I leaned back in my chair and made myself comfortable. The day passed quickly and quietly. I had a few nibbles on the fishing line, but only one good bite. I was slow to react, so whatever had been interested got away. I finished the novel, ate my sandwiches, and enjoyed the cool breeze blowing through my hair and the marsh grass. I was more content than I had been in years, and I knew I'd made the right decision to accept the job in Charleston and return home.

Late in the afternoon I returned the fishing rod and lawn chair to the boathouse and climbed the hill to the house. I felt rested and relaxed as I approached the back porch. I knew I had a lot to do to get ready for the trip to Columbia, but I wanted to hear Valerie's voice first. I dug my cell phone out of my pocket and dialed her number.

"Hi, hon," she said.

She called me "hon"! I thought. That felt so good. "Hi, yourself," I said, reveling in the sound of her voice.

"Are you ready for your trip?" she asked.

"No," I admitted. "I took the day off and went fishing."

"Did you catch anything?"

"Nothing but a little bit of a sunburn," I said, peeking at my shoulders. Even with sun block, my very pale skin turned pink if I was exposed for too long. "I did finish reading a good book, though."

We discussed different authors and their merits for twenty minutes or so before I forced myself to ring off. I would have nothing to wear in Columbia if I didn't get busy.

Two hours later, my laundry was done and my bag was packed and in the car. I fixed myself a quick salad and went out on the porch to enjoy yet another beautiful sunset over the marsh, realizing yet again how perfect my home was and how blessed I was to have it.

Monday morning I drove out to the horse farm, where I helped Earl load Naomi's baggage into the car. She had twice as much as I did, but most of it was medication and other paraphernalia she needed to deal with her illness. The special pillows she needed to help her get comfortable enough to sleep took up most of the backseat. The trip to Columbia was uneventful. We laughed and talked the first hour, but then Naomi tired and I urged her to take a nap. I drove in silence the last forty-five minutes, thinking about what we would face once we arrived. I knew Naomi had the courage — she had already proven her courage by fighting cancer and by taking a chance on approaching me. She had made herself more vulnerable than I could ever imagine. I wasn't sure I had her courage. We would soon find out.

I checked us into the hotel about lunchtime. Naomi was still tired, so I went to the hotel restaurant and bought us a carryout lunch. Naomi barely picked at hers.

"Are you okay, Naomi?" I asked, concerned that the trip had already taken too much of a toll on her.

"I'm scared," she whispered, tears glistening on her cheeks.

I knelt by her chair and hugged her gently. I could feel her shaking. "I can't promise everything will be okay," I told her, "but I'm going to do my best to talk Melissa and Kara into hearing what you have to say."

Naomi turned to look at me and put her hand on my shoulder. "Thank you so much. I know you aren't yet able to fully forgive me," she put her finger on my lips when I started to protest, "but I know you're trying and that's all I ask of you, or of them. I don't want to die with what I did to y'all on my conscience."

I hugged her again, gently, because I knew she was in a lot of pain. I helped her to one of the beds, tucked her special pillows behind her and under her legs, and kissed her on the cheek.

"Rest, sweetie," I said. "I'm going to let Melissa and Kara know I'm here and see when I can get together with them. I'll let you know before I leave, okay?" Her nod was barely perceptible as she drifted off into a medicated sleep. I stepped out onto the patio and called Melissa.

"Hi!" Melissa answered. "Are you here?"

"Yes, Melissa," I said with a laugh. "I'm here. I'm in room 115 at the hotel on Third Street."

"I can't wait to see you," she said. "Kara is out right now, but she should be back any minute. Do you want to come here or do you want us to meet you somewhere?"

"There's a restaurant right next door. Why don't we meet there for an early dinner?"

"Ohhhh, I love that place," she said. "It's two now. How about we meet you there about four-thirty?"

"Sounds like a plan," I said, amused at how excited she sounded. I hoped it wouldn't ruin her day when I talked to them about Naomi.

"By the way," she said, "I'll be the one with the red rose behind my right ear."

I laughed as we hung up and stepped back inside. Naomi was still asleep so I dug the latest book I was reading out of my bag and went out to sit by the pool and read.

About three-thirty, I went back to the room. Naomi was sitting up in bed, surfing the channels available on the hotel TV.

"You look much better," I said. "I'm meeting Kara and Melissa next door at four-thirty. I think you have everything you need there on the bedside table, but if you see anything I've forgotten, let me know, okay?" She responded with a smile and a nod, and I went to take a quick shower.

I dressed in my favorite Hawaiian shirt, bright green with yellow hibiscus flowers. When I saw it on the rack at the store, the shirt reminded me of Howie and I knew it was for me. I finished off my outfit with a pair of khakis and my ever-present Earth Shoes. Naomi laughed when I emerged from the bathroom.

"They won't be able to miss you, will they?" She giggled. "That looks like a shirt Howie would've worn."

I joined in her laughter. "That's what I thought when I saw it; that's one of the reasons I bought it. Are you sure you'll be okay while I'm gone?"

"I'll be fine, Shelby," she said. "You've made sure I have everything I need, and I have your cell phone number if I need anything else."

"Okay." I checked the clock and saw I still had a few minutes before I needed to walk over to the restaurant, so I went out on the patio and called Valerie.

She answered the phone on the first ring. "Hi."

"Were you sitting on the phone?" I asked, laughing.

"I just happened to have it in my hand when it rang," she said. "How was the trip?"

"It tired Naomi and she's been in bed since we arrived. Other than that, it was fine I'm about to go meet Kara and Melissa for dinner. I'm kind of nervous."

"Oh, hon, I wish I could be there to hug you. Unless she's changed drastically, Melissa is a total sweetie and I just know she'll accept Naomi's apology. I'm more worried about Kara. She was very protective of Melissa, even back in high school."

"I know, I'm most worried about Kara, too." I checked my watch. "I've got to go, Valerie," I said, reluctant to hang up. Hearing Valerie's voice made me long to be with her. "I'll call you later if you want me to."

"Of course I want you to, silly," she said, then her voice became softer. "I miss you, Shelby. I miss your kisses and the feel of your arms around me. Come home soon, okay?"

I swallowed hard. How was it that she could verbalize the very thoughts I was having?

"I miss you, too, Valerie. I'll talk to you later."

We hung up and I held the cell phone to my chest for a moment. It always surprised me — the intensity of the feelings I was beginning to have for her. The crush I had on her in high school was definitely evolving into something a lot stronger, something close to what I imagined love must feel like. I had sometimes thought I was in love with other women, but I'd never felt a true loss when they left, never felt heart wrenching grief when we broke up. I didn't remember feeling anything like what I already felt about Valerie.

"Shel!" Naomi's voice pulled me back to the moment. "You better get going if you're going to be next door by four-thirty."

I gave her a quick hug and double-checked to be sure she had water, her meds, the phone, and the slip of paper with my cell phone number within reach. I hoped things went well with the girls tonight so Naomi could rest easily for whatever time she had left.

At the front door of the restaurant, before I could get inside, a tiny dynamo burst through the door and into my arms. I hugged her then held her at arm's length to get a good look at her. Melissa wore her long black hair pulled back over her right ear and fastened with a barrette, and she had, indeed, attached a huge red rose. Her tiny frame had not an ounce of fat on it and her form fitting red tank dress flattered her beautiful figure.

Kara followed her out the door. She wore her hair spiked, similar to mine, but a bit longer on top. Unlike mine, Kara's hair was completely silver. Other than that, she had changed very little since high school. She was in excellent shape, setting a good example for the athletes she coached. She wore brown slacks with a short-sleeved button down man's shirt over a white tank top. The two were a striking couple.

I gathered Melissa into my arms and kissed the top of her head. She wrapped her arms around me and the way her shoulders shook, I could tell she was crying. I stroked her hair and fought back my own tears. I met Kara's eyes over Melissa's head and saw she too had tears in her eyes. Melissa stepped back and punched me on the arm, hard.

"Ouch!" I cried, rubbing my arm. "What was that for? I thought you'd be glad to see me."

"I am glad to see you," she said. "That was for not staying in touch like you promised. We've missed you so much."

"I'm sorry, Melissa," I said, my voice catching. "I'm sorrier than you'll ever know that I didn't stay in touch with y'all, and with Carolyn."

She nestled back into my arms, this time reaching for Kara as well. The three of us stood in front of the restaurant, hugging and rocking and crying. Other people walked around us, shooting us questioning looks, but we didn't care. Finally we went inside to be seated.

"Melissa, do you still love teaching as much as you did the last time I saw you?" I asked once we had ordered our food.

"Oh my gosh, yes," she said. "Watching kids learn and flourish, that other teachers have written off as 'unteachable', is such an awesome high. The other two teachers and I work so hard to get these children back into a regular classroom, and then we cry when they leave us."

"Tell her about little Eddie," Kara said.

"Oh, Shel, he's the cutest kid I've ever taught. He has these big brown eyes a person could just drown in. I don't think he'd ever been hugged at home. Once he got over his fear of us, he couldn't get enough hugs."

I laughed as she wrapped her arms around herself and rocked as though she was still hugging the little boy.

"He was in second grade when he came to us and he could barely read or do even the simplest math. I had him tested and discovered he was hard of hearing and near-sighted. Once he had hearing aids and glasses, oh my goodness, Eddie took off. When he left us at the end of the year, he was reading on a fifth grade level and doing middle school math."

"Wow! That's awesome, Melissa," I said as the waitress set our meals in front of us. "You absolutely light up when you talk about teaching. What about you, Kara? Do you still enjoy it, too?"

"I love teaching Health classes and as long as my girls keep winning State in volleyball, I'm going to enjoy coaching them," Kara said as she sank her knife and fork into her perfectly cooked steak. "The team has won four years running and with the kids I have coming up, I wouldn't be a bit surprised if we keep the streak going for a few more years. Softball team isn't too shabby, either."

"If it hadn't been for you, Yancey would never have had a chance of making it to regionals in softball," I said.

"Remember when you tried out for the team?" Melissa asked me, a glint in her eye.

Kara snorted as she tried to keep from laughing with a mouth full of tea. We laughed as she covered her face with her napkin.

"I was embarrassed to admit I knew you," she said once she got herself under control. "You couldn't hit, catch, or run. Heck, Shel, you couldn't even field a grounder. Why in the world did you even want to try out?"

I shook my head, tears in my eyes I was laughing so hard at the memory. "It didn't look so hard when I watched you do it," I said. "But, dang, that ball's hard. I didn't want to catch it; it hurt every time I did."

The three of us continued to laugh and reminisce as we ate our dinner.

"Shelby, what made you decide to finally settle down?" Melissa asked me as our dessert was being served.

"I'm so tired of travelling, of never knowing where I'm going to be next," I said. "When the lawyer told me Mom had left me the house and then I found out *Charleston Magazine* needed a reporter, it just seemed the time was right. And," I paused a moment, catching my breath, "I've fallen in love."

"What?" Kara and Melissa cried in unison.

"You're kidding, right? Our Shelby in love? Enough in love to want to stay in one place?" Kara said.

"Who is she, Shel? Anyone we know?" Melissa chimed in.

"Oh, y'all knew her once upon a time," I said, teasing them by taking a big bite of apple pie and making them wait.

Melissa flicked her napkin at me, snapping me on the nose with the corner of it. "Swallow," she demanded as I chewed slowly and deliberately. "Tell us who she is."

As I acted as if I was going to take another bite, Kara reached across the table and grabbed my dessert plate, sliding it to the middle of the table.

"You get this back only after we have the information we want," she said.

"Oh, all right. Y'all have convinced me you really have to know." I dabbed at the corners of my mouth with my napkin. "Remember the student teacher we had in Journalism and Creative Writing our senior year?"

"The one that caused you to salivate so much you almost drowned in your own slobber?" Kara asked.

"Kara, that was gross." Melissa smacked her partner on the shoulder. "Ms. Gilmore. She's a teacher at Yancey High now, right? You had a crush on her then and now you've renewed it?"

I nodded, smiling as I thought of Valerie then and now. Now was much better I decided.

"Yes, Ms. Valerie Gilmore. She's the most wonderful person I've ever met." I caught their eyes on me and quickly added, "After y'all, of course."

"Of course," Melissa said. "Now, how did you meet up with Ms. Gilmore again, and is she in love with you or is it all one-sided like it was in high school?"

"I ran into her at the reunion," I said. "We had lunch last week and I ended up at her house."

"For the night? Ooo la la," Kara said, fanning herself.

"No, Kara, not for the night. We're taking it slow, not jumping into anything until we're both absolutely sure this is what we want," I said. "Valerie is special, unlike anyone else I've ever dated, and I'm almost sure I want to spend the rest of my life with her."

"Almost sure?" Melissa asked. "Does she feel the same way?"

"Almost sure," I answered, nodding, a little sad that I wasn't one hundred percent sure yet. "And I do think she feels the same way. But it's only been a week since we started seeing each other, so I don't think either one of us is absolutely sure."

"Regardless of how things turn out with Ms. Gilmore, I'm glad you're finally settling down and I'm even happier that it's back in Yancey," Melissa said. She slid my dessert plate back to me.

It was almost the end of the meal and I realized I hadn't yet said anything about Naomi. I knew I had to tell them the primary reason I had come to Columbia to see them. "Girls," nervousness made my voice quiver, "I have something extremely important I need to talk to y'all about."

"You mentioned something about that on the phone the other day," Kara said. "What's up?"

Kara and Melissa looked concerned and I hesitated to broach the subject, but knew it wouldn't be fair to Naomi not to.

"I've seen Naomi," I said. Kara sat bolt upright, tension obvious in the set of her shoulders. Melissa put a calming hand on Kara's arm. "She came to see me last Tuesday to ask for my forgiveness."

"I hope you told her to go to hell!" Kara spat.

"Kara," Melissa said quietly, "let Shel finish what she has to say."

"Thank you, Melissa," I said. "Kara, believe me, I wanted to. I wasn't very open to what she had to say at first, but something made me listen and I'm glad I did."

I told them about that night in my kitchen, about Naomi's pain and why it was so deep, and about her illness. "She would very much like to have the chance to see you both, to tell you herself that she's sorry for the pain she caused us all. She doesn't really expect to be forgiven; she's just hoping for the opportunity to talk to you, to apologize." When I finished, we sat for a time in silence.

Tears flowed down Melissa's face, while Kara's expression was alternately sad and stormy. Melissa rested her face in her hands, her elbows on the table. I knew Kara's hand was on her knee even though I couldn't see it under the table. When Melissa finally looked up, I could tell she'd made a decision. She looked up at Kara and asked her quietly, "When can we go to Yancey to see Naomi, honey?"

"Are you sure you want to do that?" Kara asked, her voice tight. When Melissa nodded, Kara said, "In that case, we'll go tomorrow."

"Y'all don't have to," I said before they could make any specific plans, and they both looked at me, questioning. "Naomi is next door at the hotel."

"Well, let's go," Melissa said, jumping up from her seat.

"Melissa," I stood up beside her and put my hand on her arm. "Naomi is extremely tired from the trip. She was already in bed when I came over here. She was watching TV, but I expect tonight is not a good time for y'all to see her."

As Melissa sat down, I realized Kara was scowling at me.

"You brought Naomi with you?" she asked. "You were that sure we'd agree to see her? Or did she convince you to bring her?"

I was caught off guard by the vehemence in her voice. Melissa seemed to be as well. A scowl on her own face, she turned to Kara.

"What's wrong with you, Kara?" she asked. "Shelby's trying to help Naomi make things right; she did what she felt was best under the circumstances."

"Kara, I offered to bring Naomi up here. I was already planning on coming to see y'all when Naomi showed up at my house. I have a feeling the time Naomi has left is limited and I'm just trying to help an old friend who's in a lot of pain and wants to try to make amends."

Kara shook her head. "I'm sorry, Shelby. Even after all this time, I'm not sure of Naomi's true motives. I don't know if she can be trusted."

"I completely understand, Kara, but wait until you talk to her to decide. Please. I think she's sincere."

"Okay. I'm willing to hear her out. When do y'all want to get together?"

"Either breakfast or lunch tomorrow. I probably should be getting back to the hotel in case she needs anything."

The girls escorted me to the door of the hotel. We walked in silence, each with our own thoughts.

"Y'all be careful driving home," I said as we reached the lobby. "I'll call you later and let you know what time we can meet." We hugged each other and I went back to our room.

Naomi slept sitting up in the bed, snoring quietly. I tiptoed over, took the remote control from her hand, and turned off the TV. The sudden silence woke her. She blinked, yawned and stretched, then grimaced in pain. I got her a glass of water and her pain pills. After she swallowed the pills, she looked at me.

"Well, are you going to tell me how it went?" she asked. "Or was it so bad, you don't want to?"

"They want to see you tomorrow," I told her with no preamble. Her face lit up. "I think Melissa is open to forgiving you; Kara's going to be a harder sell."

Naomi started to cry. I sat down on the edge of her bed and handed her a box of tissues. She leaned forward and put her head on my shoulder and I put my arms around her and held her until she was cried out.

"Thank you, Shel," Naomi finally said. "I know it wasn't easy for you to ask them to see me."

"I had no idea how they'd react, so I admit I was nervous, but it went better than I expected." I patted her arm. "When would you like to meet with them, for breakfast or lunch?"

"I usually feel better in the mornings, so why don't we meet them for breakfast?"

I called the girls and we agreed to meet at nine o'clock at a small diner a few miles from the hotel. Once the plans were confirmed, I made sure Naomi was as comfortable as possible, then I took my cell phone and went out to sit by the pool.

The night was humid, but not unpleasantly so. Some of the hotel guests still splashed in the pool, although the sun had set long ago. I called Valerie, wishing she were there by my side.

"Hello, darlin'," she said. Just her voice made me smile; so did her greeting. "How did dinner go?"

"Hey, Val." Her name on my lips made me miss her all the more. "I miss you."

"Oh, Shelby, I miss you so much. I didn't have any sense of how important you've become to me until this afternoon when I realized I wouldn't be able to see you tonight." Her voice quivered. I had never seen Valerie cry and I hoped she wasn't going to now, since I wasn't there to comfort her.

"You're important to me, too," I told her, a catch in my throat. "I so want to hold you right now."

"Stop or you're going to make me cry," she said. "Tell me what happened with Kara and Melissa."

I filled her in on what the girls were doing, how successful they both were in the teaching field. She was pleased to know I'd told them about us. Then I told her about their reactions to Naomi's request to see them — that Kara wasn't sure she wanted to see her, but would for Melissa.

"Melissa was ready to drive to Yancey right away, so I told them that Naomi was right here in the hotel but would probably want to wait to see them until tomorrow when she would be more rested. We're having breakfast with them in the morning. Naomi is awfully nervous about the meeting, but she's grateful they're at least willing to see her."

Our conversation turned to other things and before I knew it, more than an hour had passed. The pool area was quiet; everyone else had gone to their rooms. I hated to hang up but I knew the next day was going to be stressful and I needed my rest.

"Sweetheart," I said, savoring the endearment on my tongue, "I have to go. I have to get some sleep."

"I know," Valerie said. "I meet with the superintendent of schools tomorrow for one final interview before the board chooses the new principal, so I need to try to get a good night's rest, too."

"Do you want this position?" I asked, aware we hadn't talked about it since Robbie mentioned it on Thursday.

"Yes, I do," she said enthusiastically. "I love the students at Yancey High and I feel I can do more for them as principal than as head of the English department."

"Then I hope you get the job," I told her. "What time is your meeting?"

"It's at eleven, but I won't know anything for another week or so," she said. "What time are you and Naomi meeting Melissa and Kara?"

"At nine. Why don't you call me when you're done?"

"Okay. Shelby?"

"Yes?"

She hesitated a moment before saying only, "Sleep well. Good night."

We hung up and I once again held the cell phone to my chest, wishing it was Valerie's hand. I ached for her touch, her kiss.

I finally got up and went back to the room. Naomi slept soundly, her medication doing its job. I washed up, changed into my favorite sleep shirt, and climbed into the other bed. Sleep was slow to come. My mind replayed the events of the evening and the phone call with Valerie. I closed my eyes and imagined her standing in front of me. I wanted to reach out and touch her. Sleep finally came, and with it, sweet dreams.

Chapter Fourteen

I woke up just before eight the next morning to the sound of the shower running. A few minutes later, Naomi came out of the bathroom dressed in blue slacks and a blue plaid shirt with tiny red flowers embroidered all over it. Her hair was wrapped in a towel. She sat down on the edge of the bed and looked at me intently.

"I don't know what you were dreaming about last night, but it must have been good," she said, unwrapping her hair and shaking it out. Water droplets flew and I shielded my face.

"Good grief, Naomi. You're as bad as any dog I've ever seen when you do that."

She laughed and shook her head again, this time turning it toward me to be sure I got even more water in my face. Her hair was so frizzy it held water like a Brillo pad. She started gingerly pulling a comb through it. I laughed along with her as I climbed out of bed.

"Wait," she called as I headed for the bathroom. "Tell me what was making you smile in your sleep last night. Or is it a who?"

"It's a who, and I'm not quite ready to share," I said, closing the door as she pitched her towel at me.

Twenty minutes later I was showered and dressed. Opting for comfort over style, I chose Bermuda shorts and a t-shirt.

"Are you ready?" I asked Naomi.

"As ready as I'll ever be." I could tell she was worried about the meeting. I grabbed her purse from the dresser and handed it to her. "I hope they haven't changed their minds," she said.

"You know they always keep their word," I reminded her. I helped her into the car, mentally crossing my fingers that all would go well for her today.

Melissa was waiting at the door of the diner when we arrived, but Kara was nowhere in sight. My heart sank. I had so hoped they would both be there. I glanced at Naomi and saw the sorrow in her face.

I parked the car and went around to help Naomi out, giving a little shrug and squeezing her elbow to let her know I was there for her. She gave me a pained smile and we went to meet Melissa.

"Hi, Shel," Melissa said, giving me a quick hug. She looked at Naomi for a long moment and then visibly gathered her courage. "Hi, Naomi. It's been a long time."

"Yes, it has," Naomi said quietly.

I could see Naomi was already getting tired. "Let's go inside," I said.

"Kara's already inside," Melissa said. "She went in to be sure we were able to get a table right away. This little diner is quite popular."

Naomi and I looked at each other. Relief mirrored on our faces, we followed Melissa inside. Kara had been able to snag a booth close to the door and she waved us over. She stood up and gave me a hug, then turned to Naomi and offered her hand. My heart rose to my throat as I watched the two shake hands. I hoped it was a good sign.

We ordered breakfast — lightly scrambled eggs and dry toast for Naomi, and a full Southern feast of fried eggs, bacon, grits, and biscuits for the rest of us. We sipped strong coffee while we waited, silence settling over us like a scratchy wool blanket. Naomi kept her eyes down, obviously afraid and edgy. Finally I couldn't stand the tension any longer.

"I'm glad y'all decided to meet us today," I said. "I know it's not easy, but I know once y'all hear Naomi out, things will make a little more sense."

Melissa and Kara looked at each other, then at me as they nodded in unison.

"We talked a long time last night about what you told us at dinner," Kara said. "We want to hear everything firsthand from Naomi."

I glanced at Naomi; there were tears on her cheeks. I thought Kara was cruel to ask Naomi to repeat what I'd already told them, but it wasn't my opinion that mattered. I touched Naomi's thin hand. She looked up at me, her eyes full of pain. I couldn't tell whether the pain was physical or emotional. She gripped my hand tightly.

"Are you okay?" I whispered.

She nodded, took another sip of her coffee, and finally looked at Kara and Melissa. She took a couple of deep breaths and began speaking. She told about how her dad and uncle had molested her and how her mother had turned a blind eye to the abuse. She told them about how her anger and jealousy had festered because the rest of us seemed to have ideal homes. She tried to explain how that anger made her over-react when she found Melissa and Kara together on the beach, and how an inexplicable insanity took hold of her after that. She acknowledged that none of the things that had hurt her gave her the excuse to out us to the school or to set Melissa up to be raped. She talked through our food being served, food none of us touched. After a while, she stopped. We sat in silence. She looked first at Melissa and then at Kara.

"I'm truly sorry for being that person," she said. "I've lived with the shame for thirty years. My deepest regret is I haven't asked y'all to forgive me before now, and that it's too late to apologize to Howie and Carolyn. I couldn't go to my grave without at least trying to tell y'all how sorry I am for the pain I caused each of you and to beg you for forgiveness. But, I'll understand if you aren't able to forgive me. What I did was unpardonable."

Tears dripped from Naomi's chin as she finished. I had held her hand the entire time she talked. She looked down at our hands entwined and smiled at me through her tears.

"The first time I remember you holding my hand was when we were barely four years old and I was in trouble with my mom," she said. "She was fussing at me about something, and you walked over and took my hand and stood at my side. Mom stopped whatever she was saying, looked at the two of us standing there, and just turned and walked away. I knew then there was strength in numbers. I wish I'd never forgotten that."

I squeezed her hand and looked over at Kara and Melissa. Their hands were also linked on the tabletop. They were looking down, but I could see they were also looking at each other. Finally, Melissa looked up. Her face was wet with tears and I realized all of us were crying.

"Naomi," she started, then hiccupped. We all laughed, Melissa's legendary hiccups relieving some of our tension. She tried again, "Naomi, it took a lot of courage not only to tell us what happened to you, but to have lived through it. I can't imagine what that was like."

She paused as another fit of hiccups made it impossible to speak. The waitress brought her a fresh glass of water and took away our untouched plates without a word. Melissa sipped the water while the rest of us tried to repress giggles every time a hiccup escaped her.

"Y'all are just mean," she said as she continued to hiccup.

She elbowed Kara in the ribs to try to get her to stop laughing, which just set Kara off harder. Before long, the four of us were laughing as hard as we ever had as teenagers sitting in the round booth at Robbie's. Four faces were buried in four sets of hands because we knew if we looked at each other, none of us would be able to stop laughing. We laughed for five solid minutes before any of us dared look up.

"Back to what I was saying," Melissa said, trying not to start laughing again. Sober now, she continued, "Naomi, I forgave you a long time ago, just as I forgave Tony. But I never understood, even though I forgave you, how either of you could have done what you did. I'll probably never know why Tony raped me, why he made that horrible choice. But at least now I have some understanding of the demons you faced every day."

She paused for another drink of water and to catch her breath. Kara slipped her arm around Melissa's shoulders in a show of encouragement and solidarity, not seeming to care who saw her. After a minute or two, Melissa went on. "I just wish you'd been able to tell us what you were going through back then. We would have done whatever we could to help."

"I know," Naomi whispered. She met Melissa's gaze. "I was so scared and so confused; I didn't know what to do or where to turn, so I didn't seek any help. And because of my pain, I hurt the people I loved the most."

"Let's go back to the house," Kara said. "I think we'll all be more comfortable there."

"That sounds like a good idea," I said as I pulled my wallet from my back pocket to pay for our food.

"Put your money away," the waitress — who suddenly materialized at my elbow — said. "Y'all didn't eat a bite of your food and I'm not chargin' ya for somethin' ya didn't eat. Besides that, from what I can see, y'all got a lot more talkin' to do."

Flabbergasted, we all thanked her and made sure to leave a generous tip. Naomi and I followed Kara and Melissa's black SUV back to their little house on the outskirts of Columbia. Situated in an older, well-established neighborhood, it was tan brick with a large front porch and a lovely lawn.

"This is beautiful," Naomi said as we joined them on the porch.

"It's tiny on the inside, but we love it," Melissa said. "We bought it the second year we were here and burned the mortgage last year. It's all ours."

The pride she had for the home she and Kara had made for themselves was obvious in her voice. Kara opened the heavy wood door with the half-moon stained glass window and stood back for us to go inside. The house was cool after the humidity outside. Hardwood floors graced the living room and extended into the dining room beyond. A deep burgundy sofa and matching chair took up most of the room on one side, while a large desk with a state of the art computer occupied the other side. There was no TV in sight.

We heard barking from the back of the house. "Do you mind if I let the dogs inside?" Kara asked.

"Dogs?" I said.

"They're big, but they're harmless," she reassured us.

Naomi and I both smiled and nodded. Kara disappeared through the dining room and returned holding two dogs by the collars — a Golden Retriever, and a dog whose breed was indistinguishable. Both strained to get to Melissa, so Kara let them go and the petite frame immediately disappeared under an avalanche of dogs. We could hear her muffled voice from under them.

"Get off, you big lugs. Get off."

I looked at Kara, wondering if we should go to Melissa's rescue. She grinned and shook her head. Eventually Melissa emerged, hair disheveled, laughing.

"Sit," she said firmly, and both dogs' butts hit the floor, their tails sweeping back and forth. The mutt was almost as tall as Melissa, even sitting down, but it obeyed her every command as she directed them to lie down and to stay. Two pairs of big brown eyes followed her every move as she joined us on the sofa.

As Kara left the room, Melissa introduced her dogs. "The Retriever is Jane and the mix is Dick." Kara returned with a tiny cat and Melissa held out her hands. The kitten leapt from Kara's hands to Melissa's. "And this precious bundle is Charisma," Melissa added, nuzzling the cat's thick multi-colored hair. "These are our babies."

"The dogs are bigger than the house," Naomi said. "May I pet them?"

"Of course." Melissa gestured her forward. "I'd almost forgotten how much of an animal lover you are."

Naomi scooted down the sofa so she could reach the dogs where they lay on the floor. As soon as she touched them, they turned their big brown eyes to her, apparently sensing her love for them. Two thick tails thumped the floor and Jane leaned into Naomi's hand as Naomi scratched behind her ears.

Naomi slid to the floor and buried her face against the dog's neck. Her shoulders were shaking. Before I could get to her, Kara knelt beside her and gathered her into a hug. Melissa moved over and put her hand on Naomi's shoulder. The three sat that way for some time. I sat silently, letting them be together for the first time in thirty years. Naomi finally raised her head and looked at each of us in turn.

"Thank you," she said. "Thank you."

"Well, I'm starved," Melissa said and stood up. "Who else wants a sandwich or something?"

Kara helped Naomi to her feet, but almost as soon as Naomi was up, she slumped backward. Kara lowered her to the sofa and looked at me, panic clear on her face. I hurriedly got Naomi's pain medicine from her purse and handed her two of the pills while Melissa rushed to bring her a glass of water. Naomi gratefully swallowed the pills, all the while trying to apologize for feeling bad.

"Hush," Melissa said. "Why don't you lie down on our bed for a little while? It's okay. We'll all still be here when you wake up."

Naomi nodded. Kara scooped her up and carried her through the doorway to the bedroom. Naomi laughed all the while, protesting she could walk. Melissa and I followed, laughing at the sight of squat, strong Kara, carrying long, lanky, Naomi. The laughter was bittersweet. We realized Kara would not have been able to carry Naomi if Naomi hadn't been so ill.

We sat on the bed with Naomi until her medicine took effect and she nodded off to sleep, then we tiptoed out of the room. Kara pulled the door not quite closed behind us and the three of us went to the kitchen where Melissa made sandwiches and poured glasses of sweet tea.

"Kara, I'd like to know something," I said, looking across the table at her. "Melissa told Naomi she was able to forgive her a long time ago. What about you? Can you forgive her?"

"I'm going to work on it," she said. "I just can't forget what happened."

"Kara, for years I've tried to tell you that forgiving doesn't mean forgetting," Melissa said. "It means letting go of the anger, but learning from it at the same time. If we forget, the same thing might happen again. Geez."

I could tell this was a recurring argument so I didn't say anything. Kara sighed in exasperation. "I know that, darlin'," she said, a hint of frustration along with laughter in her voice. Turning to me, she said, "Have you been able to forgive Naomi?"

"I'm trying," I said, ashamed I couldn't give her a definitive yes. "It's hard. Howie wanted to call her while he was sick to see if she really hated him, but I wouldn't let him. I was afraid of what she would say to him. After she called him a fag, he suffered emotionally a lot more than any of us knew. I know Howie forgave her. He said as much shortly before he died. I know I need to, for her sake and mine."

"That's why I forgave her," Melissa said, adamant we understand. "As much for my sake, for my mental health, as for any other reason. I wasn't going to be able to move on from the rape if I couldn't find it in my heart to forgive the people responsible. The ability to forgive didn't happen instantly, but over a long period of time. But I'm at peace now. No nightmares in twenty years or more, no more fear of being alone. I can go into a ladies room now and not look in every stall to be sure no one's lurking there. I would have been poisoning my own life if I hadn't been able to forgive both Naomi and Tony."

Kara stood up and hugged Melissa. They leaned apart and looked at each other, and the sparks I remembered so well flew between them. They kissed and then hugged again.

We went back into the living room and spent the next several hours reliving the good times we had before that milestone summer night and our senior year in high school, back when we were part of that wonderful group known around Yancey as "the Six". Howie had always been our de facto leader, but Melissa was the one who usually thought up the shenanigans that occasionally landed us in trouble with our parents and sometimes our neighbors. We were laughing about the time we toilet papered the huge oak trees around the police station when Naomi came out of the bedroom. I jumped up to help her to the sofa.

"Did we wake you up?" Melissa asked. "Are you hungry? You should be; you haven't eaten anything all day." Without waiting for an answer, Melissa was up and going into the kitchen.

Naomi shook her head and chuckled. "Well, she hasn't changed much, has she." It was a comment, not a question.

Kara shook her head. "Not much, and I like it that way. She has more energy now than she did when we were kids."

"I heard that," Melissa called from the kitchen. "You want tea, Naomi?"

"Yes, thank you," Naomi called back, laughing.

A few minutes later, Melissa came out carrying a tray. She let us each take a glass of tea and then sat next to Naomi on the sofa, offering her the ham and cheese sandwich. She set the tray down and patted Naomi's knee.

"Naomi, I never finished telling you how courageous I think you are," she said. "I don't know if I would have been able to go through all you have and stay sane. I have one more question for you, though. Do you mind?"

Naomi shook her head. "Ask as many questions as you want."

"When you outed me and Kara and Shel to the school, why didn't you out Howie, too?"

Kara nodded. "I wondered about that, too."

Naomi was quiet a moment. She looked around at each of us. "My counselor asked me the same question. I didn't really know the answer then, but I think I do now. Howie was so popular. He didn't have one enemy; everyone liked him. I guess I thought if I outed him, it would backfire on me and they'd turn on me instead of on y'all. Gawd, I was such a coward."

"For not outing Howie, too?" Kara said. I looked over at her and could tell her anger was near the surface. Melissa put her hand on Kara's arm.

"No. For outing any of you," Naomi said, tears once again rolling down her face.

I handed Naomi the box of tissue and gently hugged her.

"But you're not a coward anymore," I said. "You're one of the most courageous people I've ever known."

Melissa nodded, but before she could say anything my cell phone rang. Melissa made a face at me as I dug it out of my pocket. The caller ID told me it was Valerie. I excused myself and went to the kitchen to talk.

"Hi."

"Hi, yourself," she said, sounding happy. "I didn't think you were going to answer."

"I'm at Kara and Melissa's with Naomi so I wanted to go to another room before I answered."

"How's it going?"

"Quite well, actually." I told her about our non-breakfast and about Naomi opening up to the girls and how well they seemed to be getting along. "Your turn. How did the meeting with the superintendent go?"

"Quite well, actually," she parroted. We laughed as she went on to tell me about her interview. "He didn't ask me anything new. All the same old 'How will you be more of an asset as principal than as head of the English department?' type questions. Hopefully he liked my answers. I'll know in the next ten days to two weeks."

We talked for a while longer, each sentiment we exchanged serving to remind me how much I missed her. Kara stuck her head in the door and shook her head in mock dismay when I shooed her out. I realized I was being rude to my friends.

"Lovely lady, I really need to get back to the girls," I said.

"I know. I just hate to hang up. I miss you so much."

My heart hop scotched its way to my throat. She had once again put into words what I was feeling. No one else I ever dated was able to read my mind, say what I was thinking before I did.

"I miss you, too," I whispered, knowing if I spoke aloud my voice would be husky with emotion I hadn't felt in a long time. "I'll try to call back later."

"Okay," Valerie whispered back. "Do you know when y'all will be home?"

"Probably Thursday," I said. "I have to go now."

"Bye. See you soon." She hung up. In what was becoming a habit for me, I held the phone to my chest and closed my eyes.

"Boo!"

I jumped and almost fell off the chair as Kara, Melissa, and Naomi burst into the kitchen. They laughed as I tried to recover my dignity.

"Whoever was on the phone must be the same person you were dreaming about last night," Naomi said, chortling. Turning to Kara and Melissa she said, "Y'all should have seen the smile on her face last night while she was sleeping."

"Ohhhh, do tell." Melissa laughed, poking me in the ribs. "Tell us about the dreams you were having."

"And about who," Naomi said.

Kara smiled slyly. "We know who."

"Well, tell me," Naomi demanded.

Suddenly, there was silence. I looked at her as Melissa and Kara watched me. I knew they were thinking the same thing I was: could Naomi be trusted with the knowledge of who my lady was? If Valerie was outed in Yancey, there was a strong possibility she would not get the job as principal. She could even lose the position she already held.

"I'm not that person anymore," Naomi said as she realized the reason for my silence. She sat down beside me and rested her head on the table. Her sobs made me feel guilty.

"Naomi, please don't cry." I put an arm across her thin shoulders. "I have to be careful; if the wrong people found out, my friend could lose her job."

"And you don't trust me not to tell, do you?" she said sadly. She looked up at me and I saw the pain and the guilt in her eyes. "I don't blame you, Shelby. It's got to be hard to trust me again after what I did to y'all. It's okay if you don't tell me. I'm just glad you're happy."

I hugged her, but I still didn't tell her about Valerie. I knew I had to protect Valerie at all costs, and rebuilding my trust in Naomi would take time.

We stayed and visited with Melissa and Kara a little while longer, but Naomi was clearly tired and in a lot of pain. I got her into the car and took her back to the hotel. We promised Melissa and Kara we would visit them again the next day.

Some promises aren't meant to be kept and that turned out to be one of them. Naomi woke up in severe pain late Tuesday night and asked me to take her to the hospital. I called Kara and Melissa from the emergency room and they joined me in the long night of waiting. Finally, about six o'clock Wednesday morning, one of Naomi's attending physicians approached me.

"Mrs. Livingston?" he asked.

I decided to ignore the "Mrs." "Yes, sir," I said as I rose. He motioned for me to sit down and he took a seat beside me.

"Mrs. Jasper has given me permission to speak to you about her condition. As you know, she's in late stage lung cancer." I nodded so he continued. "She's very weak and in a lot of pain, and yet she is adamant about returning home to Yancey. I'm in touch with her doctor in Beaufort and we're arranging for her to be transported by ambulance or helicopter later today. She doesn't have much longer."

"Can we see her?" I asked.

"She's heavily medicated right now, but you may see her for a few minutes. Follow me."

I tried to rise, but swayed under the weight of the news he had delivered. He caught me and helped me sit back down.

"Mrs. Livingston, are you okay?"

"Just very tired and very sad," I said. "I'd like to see Naomi now, please."

This time I was able to stay steady on my feet as I followed him, accompanied by Melissa and Kara, through the double doors into the small room where Naomi lay. Machines beeped all around her and an IV in her port was delivering fluids and medication directly to her bloodstream. I moved to the side of her bed and took her hand while Kara and Melissa circled to the other side. Naomi opened her eyes and smiled weakly at us.

"I'm sorry I put a damper on things," she whispered.

I tried to tease. "If I'd known you wanted to go home so badly, I would have taken you." But imminent tears could be heard in my voice.

"Maybe so, but this will get me there faster," she teased in return, trying to squeeze my hand playfully.

I smiled at her through the haze of tears. I suddenly understood what Melissa meant by getting past the anger and learning from the experience. I realized I loved Naomi deeply: the love a sister has for a sister. As my tears spilled over, Naomi reached up and cradled my face in her hand.

"Go home, Shelby," she said. "I'll see you there."

I bent down and kissed her cheek; Melissa and Kara did the same. I stood there another moment before Kara came around the bed and led me out of the room. Out in the lobby, I broke down. My dear friends sat on either side of me and the three of us cried together. So many memories flooded my mind, my heart, my soul. Except for me, Howie was alone when he died. I didn't want that for Naomi.

"Y'all come back to Yancey with me," I said. "We can't let Naomi die alone."

"We'll follow you home, okay?" Kara rubbed my back soothingly. "We'll all be with Naomi."

When I was able to compose myself, I returned to the hotel, packed our things, and checked out. I drove to the girls' house where Kara was loading their bags and two huge crates into the back of their SUV.

"Hi, Shel. We'll be ready soon," she said. "Melissa's on the phone asking our neighbor if she'll babysit Charisma for us. She doesn't do road trips well."

"Okay," I said. "So Dick and Jane are coming with y'all?"

"Absolutely." She smiled. "The two grandmas would be beside themselves if we left their grand-dogs behind."

Melissa joined us on the sidewalk. She had Charisma, a small kitty bed, and a bag of Kitty Kibble in her hands. "Mrs. Johnson is going to watch the baby," she told us. "I'll be back in a minute."

While we waited for Melissa, I called the hospital. The doctor I'd talked to that morning wasn't available, but one of the nurses told me a helicopter would be taking Naomi from Columbia to the hospital in Beaufort at about eleven o'clock. From there an ambulance would transport her home.

Next I called Earl. I knew the doctor would have spoken to him, but I wanted to touch base.

"Thanks so much for getting Mom to the hospital. She's been in severe pain for so long, I've been expecting this day for a while. I've been in touch with the hospice in Beaufort and they're making arrangements for a hospital bed to be delivered before Mom gets here. They're also helping me arrange twenty-four hour care for her."

Lastly, I called Valerie. It was barely eight in the morning, but I desperately needed to talk to her. She didn't answer her phone, so I left her a voice mail telling her it was important that I talk to her as soon as possible. I hung up, sorry I hadn't been able to hear her voice. I felt a hand on my back and turned.

Kara gave me a quick, comforting hug. "She'll call back and you can tell her you're on the way home," she reassured me.

"Have y'all told Mrs. Ballard y'all are coming down?" I asked.

"Not yet," Kara said. "I'm sure Melissa will get around to calling them as we turn off Main Street."

I laughed. Melissa had always been notorious for waiting until the last minute to tell people she was on the way over. Sometimes I found out when she knocked on the door or just bounded in.

"Have y'all told them you've seen Naomi?" I asked.

"Melissa called her mom yesterday after you and Naomi went back to the hotel. They talked for a long time," Kara said. "Melissa gets her forgiving nature from her mom, you know. They agreed it was about time all of us put this behind us and moved on."

"So, Mrs. Ballard and Sue Ellen know how sick Naomi is?" I asked.

"Yes, they do," Melissa said. I jumped at her sudden unexpected reappearance, and she laughed. "You wouldn't be so jumpy if you didn't have a guilty conscience. I know y'all were talking about me. Let's get the dogs and hit the road."

Ten minutes later we were on our way out of Columbia, on our way home to Yancey.

Chapter Fifteen

Thirty minutes into our drive home, Valerie called me back. I was ready with my Bluetooth-connected earpiece in place. I related all that had happened and that I was on my way home. "As much as I'd like to see you, I don't know if I'll get to today. I think I should stay with Earl, at least until the ambulance arrives with Naomi."

She was sympathetic and understanding, and again I was surprised at the intensity of the feelings I felt for her. I wanted to reach through the phone and stroke her hair and kiss her full lips. I suddenly realized she hadn't finished speaking.

"I can't wait to hold you and kiss you. We'll see each other as soon as possible, I promise."

"I'll call you as soon as Naomi gets home. Bye."

Almost as soon as I hung up, my phone rang again. It was Melissa.

"Did you have a good conversation with your lady?"

"How did you know I was on the phone?"

"Oh, Shel, don't you know you talk with your hands, even in the car? Kara knew immediately you were on the phone when it started looking like you were leading a choir. And who else would you talk to for fifty miles?"

I laughed. "Yes, I did have a good conversation with Valerie, thank you."

We talked for a few more miles before hanging up. The rest of the drive was quiet and uneventful. When we got close to Yancey, the girls drove on into town and I took the road to Naomi's farm. Earl was waiting at the door as I parked the car.

I gave him a hug and asked, "How are you holding up?"

"As well as can be expected, I guess," he said with a shrug.

He showed me the hospital bed that hospice had delivered shortly before I arrived. They'd put it in Naomi's bedroom, close to the window so she could look out and watch her beloved horses. A cat had already made itself at home in the center of the bed. Earl picked up the tabby and hugged it.

"Momma will be home soon," he crooned. To me, he said, "This is Showman, Mom's baby boy."

As Earl buried his face in the cat's fur, I reached out and rested my hand on his head, his hair the color of his mother's but much tamer. I took him by the elbow and led him to the kitchen table. He sank down in one of the chairs, looking so much older than his twenty-eight years. I got him a cup of coffee from the pot on the stove. He took it gratefully. I looked at the clock and saw it was still half an hour before Naomi would leave Columbia. I could have gotten her home sooner, but probably not as comfortably.

"What can I do to help?" I asked.

Earl shook his head, clearly overwhelmed and exhausted. "I can't think of a thing," he said. "Mom is well prepared. She'd already made arrangements for the bed with hospice, so that was just a matter of a phone call. The funeral, her cremation, all of that is already paid for."

His voice caught as he listed all Naomi had done to make a difficult time easier on him. I was impressed with how prepared she was and wondered whether I would have been able to think as clearly as she obviously had if I were in her shoes. Not able to think of one thing to say to comfort him, I patted his arm. We sat in silence for a while before he excused himself.

"I might as well work on the books while we wait for Mom," he said.

"Have you eaten," I asked, "or can I fix something for you?"

"I'm fine," he said as he left the kitchen.

I went out to the car and grabbed the novel I'd been reading in Columbia. I didn't know if I would be able to concentrate, but at least it gave me something to do. I sat in the Carolina room off the kitchen, the overhead fan combating the heat coming through the windows. After staring at the same page for five minutes, I decided to call Valerie instead.

"Hi," she said. "How are you doing?"

I could hear the concern in her voice and I broke into tears. For a long moment, I couldn't speak.

"Oh, babe," she cried, "where are you? Can I come to you?"

"I'm afraid not," I said, snuffling. "I'm at Naomi's. We're waiting for the ambulance to bring her home. I don't think it would be a good idea for you to be here."

"I understand. I just hate to know that you're sad and there isn't anything I can do."

"Thanks, hon." It was hard not to start crying again. "I just needed to hear your voice. I'll try to call you when I get home this evening."

"Why don't you come here and let me fix you dinner instead of being in your big ol' house alone?"

"I don't know what time I'll be leaving here, but I'll call and let you know, okay? I'd love to come over, but please don't plan on it."

We talked a few minutes longer and hung up. I called Melissa next.

"Is she there yet?" Melissa asked without even saying hello.

"No." I checked my watch. "If they left on time, she just left Columbia about fifteen minutes ago. I don't know how long the flight will take. I expect someone will call Earl when they arrive in Beaufort."

"You'll let us know, right?"

"Of course. Was your mom surprised when y'all drove up?"

"I called her just as you turned off to go to Naomi's. She's glad we came down. I think she wishes we would get jobs down here, but I can't desert my students up in Columbia."

I laughed. I could just hear Mrs. Ballard begging them to come home — extolling the virtues of the Yancey schools, and resorting to bribery if necessary.

"She wants you and Valerie to come to dinner when y'all get a chance," she added.

"You told your mom about Valerie?"

"Of course I did. You know it's okay."

I did know. But it still worried me, especially since Valerie's job was in flux. She badly wanted to be principal at Yancey High, and I didn't want anything, especially our fledgling relationship, to jeopardize her chances.

"I know. I'm sorry. I just don't want her outed to the community unless and until she's ready."

"Mom won't tell," Melissa assured me. "You know a secret told Mom is as safe as gold at Fort Knox. Valerie is safe, I promise."

"Thank you, Melissa," I said. "Tell your mom I'll let her know when we can come. I doubt it will be in the next few days, but we'll see."

I heard the phone ring inside the house and Earl answered it. I went in, still talking to Melissa, to see if it was the hospital calling. Earl nodded and I told Melissa I would call her right back and disconnected our call. I leaned on the doorjamb of the study listening to Earl. He hung up and turned to me.

"The helicopter left Columbia just after 10:30 and arrived in Beaufort about twenty minutes ago. Mom is sedated and they're making sure she's stable before bringing her home. If all goes well, the ambulance should be here in about half an hour."

"Do you want me to hang around until she's here and settled, or would you prefer I came back later?"

"Oh, please, Ms. Livingston. Stay!"

Earl's voice had an edge of panic in it. I crossed the room and hugged him. "I'll stay as long as you need me."

"Thank you," he said. "I need to call hospice now and let them know when we expect her. They want one of their caregivers here when she arrives."

I went back to the kitchen and started foraging in the cabinets and refrigerator. I was sure Earl hadn't eaten breakfast and I wanted to be sure he at least had a bite to eat before his mom got home. I found bread and sandwich fixings and proceeded to make sandwiches for both of us. A pitcher of lemonade was in the refrigerator. I found a tray and glasses and took them and his sandwich to him.

He was sitting at the big oak desk that had been his grandfather's, then his mother's, and was now his. The pen in his right hand was poised above a large ledger book, but his eyes were a million miles away. I set the tray down on the desk and he looked up, startled.

"Ms. Livingston, you didn't have to do that."

"Yes, I did. We both need to eat before your mom gets here," I told him. I eyed the paperwork spread out on the desk. "Don't y'all have a computer to keep your records on?"

"I have my laptop," he said, "but Mom never could get the hang of it, so she just kept doing things the old-fashioned way. I guess it's good she's shown me how to do it manually, in case my computer ever crashes. Helps pass the time, too."

"I need to call Melissa and Kara and let them know what's going on," I told him. "I'll let you get back to dreaming or doing your books or whatever it was you were doing."

Laughing, he waved me out of the room. As I left, he picked up his sandwich and bit into it.

I called Melissa, then Valerie, and let them know what little I knew so far. While I talked to Valerie, a small brown car pulled up beside mine and a woman in purple scrubs climbed out. Her face was vaguely familiar. She removed a box from the back seat and moved toward the porch. I told Valerie I would talk to her later and went to meet the visitor.

"Hi," I called. "Can I help you?"

The woman looked up at me and we both stopped in our tracks. Our mouths fell open and in unison we exclaimed, "Oh my Gawd!"

Howie's little sister, Emma, and I had lost touch shortly after his death. The last time I had seen her was when I escorted Howie's body back to Yancey. Twelve years his junior, Emma was barely fifteen when he died. She worshipped him in life and was heartbroken by his death. Their parents wouldn't let her attend his funeral, but she sneaked up to the cemetery afterward and found me there. We talked a long time that long ago day. She tried to stay in touch with me, but like Melissa and Kara, she eventually stopped emailing when I never responded. Now, twenty-one years later, here she stood at the foot of Naomi's porch.

"What are you doing here?" I asked.

"I'm the hospice nurse who's been assigned to Ms. Jasper," she said. "I never expected to see you of all people out here."

"Naomi and I are working through a reconciliation," I told her. "She sought me out and I helped her connect with Melissa and Kara. We've been working on putting the past where it belongs, in the past."

"Good," she said. "When I saw Ms. Jasper's name on the list of patients, I specifically requested to be assigned to her. It's what Howie would have wanted."

Tears welling in my eyes, I hugged her. I was proud of the person Howie's little sister had become. He would have been proud of her, too.

We went inside where I introduced her to Earl. His eyes got big when we told him she was Howie's sister. Earl was well aware of Naomi's past. She'd been honest with him, hoping he would learn from her mistakes and be a more tolerant person than she had been. He knew she regretted not being able to make things right with Howie and Carolyn.

"Mr. Jasper, if you think my presence will cause your mother undue emotional pain, I'll understand and call for someone else to take my place," Emma said.

"I think we should let Mom decide," he said. "Personally, I think it'll be good for her to have you take care of her."

We heard a vehicle in the driveway and went to the door. The ambulance was backing up to the porch. Emma waited on the porch while Earl rushed down the steps to meet them. I stayed just inside the door, not wanting to get in the way.

I watched as the medics unloaded the gurney with Naomi on it. She had an oxygen tube in her nose and an IV in her left arm in addition to the one in her port. Her eyes fluttered briefly as they gently carried the gurney up the steps and then rolled it inside, but she didn't wake up.

Emma and the medics efficiently moved Naomi from the gurney to the hospital bed, arranging tubes and bottles and bags as they went. In a matter of minutes, the medics were pulling out of the driveway and Emma had taken charge. She looked over the records one of the medics had her sign just before they left and then turned to us.

"Ms. Jasper is heavily sedated," she told us. "They did that to help her handle the trip with as little pain as possible. I'm going to stop the IV with the sedative and I'll start another one that will help her begin to wake up. As much pain medicine as she's on, though, I doubt she'll be fully awake for a while. Why don't y'all find something to do and I'll call y'all when she's awake."

I left Emma my cell phone number and accompanied Earl back to his office. He sat down at his desk and put his head in his hands. I sat down across from him, waiting for him to compose himself. After a few minutes he looked up at me.

"She's so pale," he whispered.

"I know, hon," I said. "I wish I could do something to make this easier."

"You being here is so important to her," he said. "Her biggest worry when she found out she wasn't going to beat this was that she wouldn't be able to get in touch with y'all, and even if she did, that y'all wouldn't forgive her. Knowing y'all are at least willing to try has helped her so much. I think she hung on as long as she did just to be able to talk to y'all. Now that she has had that chance, I think she's ready to go."

Tears flowed down his face and I went around the desk and hugged him. He sobbed on my shoulder and I sobbed along with him. At length, we were able to stop.

"I've been up since just before midnight and the lack of sleep is catching up with me. I'm going to go home and take a nap."

"You could stay here and sleep in our guestroom, if you like," Earl offered.

"Thanks, but I think I'll sleep better in my own bed." I wanted to go home to my comfort zone. "You call me if you need me to come back." I hugged him again, then went to find Emma.

"Please call me immediately if there's any change, or if Naomi needs anything," I requested.

"Of course I will, Shelby," Emma said. We hugged one another and I drove home.

Once there, I barely made it up the stairs and into my bed before I fell asleep. The stress of the past two days and the realization that another dear friend was dying took their toll, sapping me of my last remaining energy. Sleep, while it came quickly, was not restful. Dark dreams plagued me, dreams I knew — even while I was dreaming them — I wouldn't be able to remember when I awoke. Howie danced along the periphery of my subconscious, as did Carolyn. Naomi's face hovered somewhere beyond my reach. All of them mouthed words at me I couldn't make out.

When I woke up, the room was dark. I thought I must have slept late into the night, but when I sat up I realized the darkness was a result of my heavy drapes being drawn across the bay window. I couldn't remember the last time the curtains had been closed. I was pretty sure I hadn't closed them, but I'd been in such a state of exhaustion I wasn't sure. I felt more than saw a presence in the room. A figure rose from my chair and approached the bed. My heart leapt into my throat but before I could react, the voice of an angel spoke.

"Feeling better, sleepyhead?" Valerie asked as she sat on the edge of the bed.

"Valerie," I said, afraid this too was a dream. I reached out for her and she came into my arms. My lips found hers, hungry for the taste of her. After a few minutes, she leaned back and caressed my cheek.

"I missed you," she said quietly.

"I missed you, too," I said. "How did you get in? How long have you been here?"

"A couple of hours," she said. "You left the back door open. It's a good thing you don't still live in Atlanta. I came over to put some food in your 'fridge and I saw your car in the driveway. When you weren't anywhere to be found downstairs, I came up here. You didn't even move when I came in."

"You're kidding. Shoot, I barely remember driving home from Naomi's much less anything else. What time is it anyway?"

I looked at the clock and was surprised to see it was just after five p.m. Valerie went to the window and pulled the drapes open. I shaded my eyes against the sudden light.

Once my eyes adjusted, I let them feast on Valerie. She stood with her back to the window, her body in silhouette. Her beauty struck me once again. She was just a bit taller than me, but her body was fuller. Her breasts were ample without being heavy. When she heard me gasp, she looked at me. Her smile told me she knew I was admiring her.

She strolled back to the bed and I quickly stood up. I knew if she sat down beside me, I wouldn't be able to restrain myself, and now was not a good time. I held my arms open and she slipped into my embrace.

"Let's go downstairs and you can show me what food you brought," I said, wishing I could ask her to show me something else altogether. She sighed, disappointed, I think. Together we descended the staircase.

Valerie pulled seafood lasagna and garlic bread out of the refrigerator. I reached in behind her to get the things to toss together a salad.

"Oh no you don't," she said, taking the greens from me. "You sit down at the table and relax. I'll fix the salad while the lasagna and garlic bread heat."

I didn't argue. I still felt numbingly tired and more than a little concerned that Emma hadn't called me yet.

"It seems like Naomi should have woke up by now," I said as I reached into my pocket for my cell phone. "I wonder why Emma hasn't called."

"Call her after you eat. I'm sure she would have called you if there was anything wrong."

I agreed and dug in as soon as she set the food in front of me. She enjoyed her food in a much more ladylike fashion, putting her napkin in her lap first and keeping her elbows off the table while she ate. I suddenly started to laugh.

"What's so funny?" she asked, startled by my outburst.

"I was just noticing what good manners you have."

"And that's funny, how?"

"No." I laughed again. "Your good manners aren't funny. I was just thinking how mine have suffered over the years of having to eat on the fly all the time. You're going to have to retrain me, I think."

Now she laughed with me. "I just thought you ate like that cuz you're a butch," she teased.

I threw a crust of garlic bread at her and she gasped in feigned shock. She rose from the table and came around to me, I thought for a hug, but then she dumped a glass of water over my head. I jumped up and chased her out of the house and down the steps. She beat me to the water spigot and before I knew it, I was being soaked with the garden hose. I wrestled it out of her hands and returned the favor.

We were both squealing like teenagers and didn't hear the car pull into the driveway until we heard laughter from the porch. We turned and looked toward the house. Melissa and Kara were standing on the top step, holding their sides and laughing. Valerie and I looked at each other and immediately turned the hose on them. A full-fledged water fight ensued. Suddenly, Melissa stopped and looked at me.

"Your cell phone is ringing!" she yelled, sprinting for the house, her wet shoes sloshing.

The rest of us ran in behind her. She grabbed it off the table and tossed it to me. How I caught it, I'll never know.

"Hello?" I said breathlessly.

"Ms. Livingston?" Earl's voice questioned. "Are you okay?"

"I'm fine. I just had to run to answer the phone and this old body isn't used to that kind of workout. Is your mom awake?"

"Yes, she is, and she is asking for you and Melissa and Kara. Can y'all come out?"

"You tell Naomi we'll be out there within an hour or so, okay?"

"Thanks, Ms. Livingston. I appreciate it. See you in a bit."

I hung up and we looked at each other in silence. I felt strangely guilty for having fun while our friend lay dying. I could see Melissa felt the same way. Valerie once again read my mind.

"Y'all have a right to have fun," she said. "Naomi would want you to. She's dying, which is even more reason for y'all to continue living."

Kara wrapped her arms around Melissa. "She's right, you know," she said. "And by the way, good to see you again, Ms. Gilmore."

We all laughed. It had been a strange reunion for them, after all. I'm sure Kara and Melissa had not expected to be greeted by a water fight when they drove up to my house. Valerie walked over and hugged both of them.

"I think y'all can get away with calling me Valerie," she said. She pointed to me. "After all, that big lug does."

We laughed again. The girls borrowed towels and then went home to change their clothes. We agreed they would come back to my house and we would ride out to Naomi's together. After Melissa and Kara left, I pulled Valerie in close and kissed her long and hard. Her playfulness had revived me and her wisdom was keeping me going.

"Can I go with you?" she asked when I finally stopped kissing her.

I held her at arm's length and looked searchingly into her eyes. I could see she truly wanted to.

"Hon, if you want to come with us, you're welcome to. Just be aware that by doing so, certain people might put two and two together. I don't want your job to be put in jeopardy because of me."

"I'll handle that issue if it arises but I want to be with you right now. I think you need me to be with you."

I kissed her softly and walked her out to her car. "Go home and change clothes. I'll see you in a little while."

Chapter Sixteen

Thirty minutes later the four of us pulled into Naomi's driveway, Melissa and Kara in their SUV and Valerie and me in my car. Earl met us on the porch where I introduced him to the others.

"Mom is awake, but groggy," he told us as we went inside. "She'll be talking and then just drift away. A few minutes later she'll wake up and pick up right where she left off. Emma said that's normal for someone on so much pain medication."

We thanked him for the warning. Just as we were about to go into Naomi's room, Emma came out. I'd forgotten to tell Melissa and Kara who Naomi's nurse was. The look of shock on their faces when they saw her caused me to laugh as I turned to them.

"Oh, yeah," I said, giggling. "I should tell y'all that Naomi's nurse is Howie's little sister."

"It's a little late now," Kara groused as she hugged Emma. "How are you? I remember when you were just a tiny baby. Howie couldn't put you down. He actually brought you to school for Show and Tell."

We laughed at the memory as Emma hugged each of us. I introduced her to Valerie, but Emma already knew who she was.

"I had you for eleventh grade English; you were tough. I hear you may be the new principal."

"That is a possibility," Valerie said. "It looks like you made your dreams come true. I remember the end of the year essay I assigned asking the class to tell me what y'all's goals were. Yours stood out because you were so sure you'd be a hospice nurse and help people die with dignity."

Emma's eyes filled with tears. "I can't believe you remember that. That was the year after Howie died. Shelby told me that except for her, he died alone, ostracized, and I was determined no one in this community would ever have that happen. When I finished nursing school, I knew exactly where I wanted to work and what I wanted to do, and here I am."

I gulped. "Thank you, Emma. Howie would be so proud of you."

"Y'all go in and see Naomi," Emma said, holding the door open for us. "She's been asking for you."

Melissa and Kara went on in, but I hung back for a moment. "Emma," I touched her arm, "does Naomi know you're Howie's sister?"

"I don't know; I haven't told her, but she does keep looking at me like she's trying to figure out how she knows me. Do you want to tell her?"

"If you like," I said.

She nodded and turned her attention to Naomi's medical chart.

When I entered the room, Naomi's eyes were closed but her face was turned toward the window. I approached her bed but didn't touch her; I didn't want to wake her. She must have felt my presence because she opened her eyes and turned to look at me.

"'Bout time you got here," she whispered hoarsely. I picked up the glass of water next to the bed and offered her the straw. She sipped a tiny bit and nodded.

"Sorry I wasn't here when you woke up. I went home and took a nap myself."

She grinned weakly. "Lazy bones. Are Melissa and Kara with you?"

"We're right here," Melissa said from the foot of the bed. Naomi smiled and closed her eyes. I could tell by her breathing she had gone back to sleep. We all sat down in the chairs Earl had thoughtfully brought in. We talked quietly until Kara noticed Naomi stirring again. I moved my chair close to the side of her bed and took her hand.

The next few hours were spent in sporadic conversation. Emma would periodically come in and check on Naomi. Earl also came in several times to see if we needed anything and to let Naomi know he was there if she needed him. As night fell, Emma finally came and told us we needed to leave so Naomi could get some uninterrupted rest. Melissa and Kara kissed Naomi's cheek as they left and promised they'd be back the next day. Valerie also let Naomi know she would be back and squeezed her hand. I stayed for a few more minutes.

"I'll be back early tomorrow," I told her. "What can I bring you?"

She smiled tiredly. "Just you, Shel; I'm so glad y'all are here. And I'm glad you found Ms. Gilmore and brought her, too. I always liked and respected her."

"Hon, I need to tell you something about Emma."

"She looks so familiar to me," she said, "but I can't figure out why."

I took her hand and she looked at me questioningly. "Sweetie, Emma is Howie's little sister. She specifically requested to be your hospice nurse."

Naomi's eyes widened. She looked away from me, out into the dark yard.

"Naomi, it's okay. She wants you to know she doesn't hold anything against you. She knows it's not your fault her parents disowned Howie. And she told me she knows Howie would forgive you if he were here. I should have told you this sooner, but Naomi, Howie did forgive you. He told me he did just before he died."

Naomi turned back to me, tears silently falling from her sunken eyes. I got a tissue and dried her face. She grimaced and a moan of pain escaped her. I went to the door and signaled Emma. She came in and administered pain medicine to Naomi's IV.

"You'll feel better in a few minutes, Ms. Jasper," she said. "I'm going to be going home in about half an hour, but the night nurse, Sara, is here if you need anything, okay? And I'll be back at seven tomorrow morning."

Naomi managed a nod as she reached out and lightly touched Emma's sleeve. "Emma, would you please call me Naomi?" she asked. "I think Howie would like that."

Emma looked at me and I gave her a slight nod. She leaned down and kissed Naomi's wet cheek. "I'm proud to call you Naomi," she said, a catch in her voice. "I'll see you in the morning."

Sara came in then, efficiency personified in brightly colored scrubs. She shooed us out and turned to Naomi.

"Thank you, Shelby," Emma said. "Thank you for telling her who I am."

"You're welcome, Emma. I think she's grateful you're her nurse. It will help her know there are no grudges."

Emma looked around at the four of us. "Y'all go on home. You look exhausted. Come back tomorrow morning, anytime after eight. That will give me time to bathe Naomi and try to get some breakfast in her. I'll see y'all then."

Earl walked us out to our vehicles. I hugged him and thanked him for letting us be with Naomi.

"I'm glad y'all were able to be here, for Mom and for me. I promise to call you if anything happens during the night, so please get some rest and try not to worry."

I hugged him again and we left.

Melissa and Kara drove straight from Naomi's to Mrs. Ballard's house. Valerie and I drove in silence back to my house, her hand on my knee. Once home, we walked down to the dock and sat for a while. The moon was almost full and its reflection on the mirror-like surface of the marsh was mesmerizing.

I lay back on the warm wood of the deck. Valerie stretched out beside me on her side, kissing my ears and neck.

"You're making it extraordinarily difficult for me to stick to my resolution not to make love to you until we know each other better," I said halfheartedly.

"That's the idea," she said. She kept kissing and licking, her hand lightly caressing my stomach where my shirt met my shorts.

I turned on my side and caught her lips with mine. We kissed hungrily and caressed. I knew I was going to forget my resolution if I didn't put a quick stop to our physical contact. I leapt to my feet and offered her a hand up, then hugged her before leading her to her car.

"Valerie, go home," I said huskily, opening the car door for her. "I want you so badly, but I also want to wait. I don't want to hurt you and I'm afraid in the state of mind I'm in right now, that might happen."

"You're a hard woman," she said, a note of frustration in her voice. "I want you too, and to tell you the truth, I'm not sure I understand why we're waiting."

I hung my head. I wasn't sure I knew how to explain. Finally, I looked her in the eye.

"Valerie, I'm falling in love with you. In fact, I've been in love with you for thirty years and just didn't know it. But I am hard. I've gotten terribly hard over the course of my life, starting in August of '75. I've hurt so many women, and I'm scared to death I'm going to hurt you, too. I want to wait to make love to you until... I'm not sure. Feeling like this is unfamiliar territory for me."

I turned away from her, knowing I hadn't made myself clear. I never was good at verbalizing how I felt; that was why I became a writer. I could put my thoughts on paper and have them make sense, but speaking my thoughts was a painful chore. Valerie put her hand on my shoulder and turned me back to her. She lightly brushed her lips over mine.

"I still don't understand," she said quietly, "but while you were in Columbia, I realized that I love you. And because of that, I'll wait as long as you need me to."

I kissed her then, long and gently. Our tongues danced from one mouth to the other, licking and tasting. At length she moved away and sat down in her car.

"But that doesn't mean I'm not going to continue to try to seduce you." She laughed as she started the engine.

I closed the door, leaned through the open window, and kissed her again. "I'll see you in the morning."

Over the course of the following week, we fell into a routine. Valerie and I would go to Naomi's in the morning, and Melissa and Kara would join us shortly after lunch. The four of us would visit Naomi together until mid-afternoon, when Valerie and I would leave so Melissa and Kara could have some private time with her. Earl slept on a cot next to Naomi's bed every night so he would hear her if she needed anything. Sara and Emma assured him it wasn't necessary, they would get him if Naomi needed him, but he couldn't be dissuaded, so they let him do what made him feel comfortable.

Mrs. Ballard and Sue Ellen also came to visit. They wanted Naomi to know she had their complete forgiveness. Naomi became progressively weaker and slept more and more. I don't think Naomi even knew we were there during some of our visits. Other times, she could carry on nearly normal conversations. I had been through a similar time with Howie and knew our time with Naomi was coming to an end. I was glad she'd had the courage to come to my house so few weeks before. So much time had been wasted hating and holding grudges. Now I wanted to become reacquainted with my old friend, to know how she lived her life before the cancer took over. I was sorry we'd lost so much time and there was now so little left.

The morning of my birthday dawned overcast and gray. Clouds touched the marsh and the calls of the water birds echoed off the fog. I sat in my kitchen nursing a cup of coffee, waiting for Valerie so we could go to Naomi's. I was remembering past birthdays in this kitchen. Mom always baked me a yellow cake with yellow butter cream frosting. Each year it was decorated according to my interests at the time. The last cake she decorated for me had a toy camera and a toy typewriter on it. My reverie was interrupted by the sound of my phone.

"Hello?" I said, still thinking of the past.

"Happy birthday, sister of mine."

I hadn't seen Kyle since the day he and Paula and the boys drove down from Charleston. He was working the day I was in Charleston for my interview and spent time with Paula, and his schedule hadn't allowed him the freedom to come back to Yancey.

"Thanks, Kyle. How are y'all?"

"We're fine. How are you doing?" Even though Kyle and I hadn't had a chance to visit face to face, we'd talked on the phone many times and he knew about our vigil at Naomi's bedside.

"Frankly, I'm tired," I said. "I haven't slept well since Naomi came home from Columbia."

"This has to be really hard on you, Shelby. Can't you skip a day and spend your birthday doing something special for yourself?"

"I appreciate your concern, but I really can't. I'll have other birthdays; Naomi won't."

"You're a stronger person than I am. I don't think I could do what you're doing. Call me and let me know how things are going, okay?"

"Thanks for calling, Kyle. I love you."

"I love you, too, Sis. Happy birthday!"

After we hung up, I washed my few breakfast dishes and started getting ready to go to Naomi's. Valerie drove up as I was putting a bag of fruit from the farmer's market into the car. I walked over to meet her. As soon as she was out of the car, she grabbed me and kissed me long and sensuously. Even as she was kissing me, I was thinking it was a good thing my house was well back from the road and we were parked behind the house. Otherwise our secret would be out.

"Wow," I said when she let me go. "What was that for?"

"Happy birthday!"

I laughed. "Ummmm, if you're going to kiss me like that, I'll have a birthday more often." She gave me a big hug and grabbed her bag from her car. It was bulkier than usual so I offered to carry it.

"You just keep your grubby hands off my bag," she said, holding it behind her.

I put my hands on my hips in feigned exasperation. "What do you have in that bag that's so important you don't want me to carry it?" I asked, stalking her around the car. With a big grin I lunged for her, but she was faster and moved away before I could grab the bag.

"Get in the car, Shelby," she said sternly. "Naomi's going to think we got lost."

She slid into the passenger seat of the car, protecting the bag between her feet on the floor. I slid in beside her and leaned over and kissed her on the cheek. She smiled that smile that made me melt like ice on a hot day.

Halfway to Naomi's, Melissa and Kara pulled up behind us, honking and waving. A moment later, my cell phone rang and a chorus of "Happy Birthday" wailed over it, off key and out of tune. Kara passed me, and on the back of the SUV was a huge sign that read "Today is Shelby Livingston's 48th Birthday!" in bright blue and red colors. I was ready to shoot them both. Valerie was laughing at my reaction to the song and sign so hard she had tears rolling down her face.

When we arrived at Naomi's, I immediately tried to remove the sign, but was forcibly restrained and taken into the house. Apparently the girls had told Emma and Earl it was my birthday, as the kitchen was decorated in streamers and balloons.

"She's awake and asking for you," Emma told me with a smile.

I tiptoed into Naomi's room and discovered it had been decorated as well. The head of Naomi's bed had been raised so she could lie and watch the horses. She was watching them as I entered the room.

"Aren't they beautiful?" she asked as I joined her at the window and took her hand.

A roan and a gray were chasing each other around the closest paddock, enjoying the cool air that came with the overcast skies. Suddenly they stopped and approached the nearest fence, their ears forward, alert. I couldn't see what caught their attention, but Naomi smiled, the brightest smile I'd seen on her face in a while.

"What are they looking at?"

"My angels," she said.

I thought she was talking about the horses themselves, but then she turned to me and explained.

"For the past three days, angels have been around the house. The horses see them before I do most of the time."

I knew she was dying, but my heart didn't want to accept it. I squeezed her hand.

Seeing I was uncomfortable, she asked, "Where's everyone else?"

"In the kitchen," I said. "Melissa and Kara came out this morning instead of waiting until this afternoon."

"I know. I asked them to. I wanted to give you a birthday party."

I laughed, looking around. "I can see that."

"I ruined your eighteenth birthday so I wanted to make it up this year."

"Oh, Naomi," I said, hugging her. "You didn't ruin my eighteenth birthday. I left before it came, so it just didn't get celebrated the traditional way."

"Go get everyone else, okay?" she asked, her eyes bright.

I opened the door to summon the others but it wasn't necessary. They all stood huddled outside the door, everyone holding balloons and gifts, except Melissa. She held a yellow butter cream cake decorated with the *Charleston Magazine* logo.

"Surprise!" they said, and then broke into song, singing "Happy Birthday" and "She's a Jolly Good Fellow".

I stood aside so they could come in, laughing and crying at the same time. I hadn't had a birthday party in thirty-one years, not since I turned seventeen. And knowing Naomi had planned it made it extra special.

The morning passed quickly. We ate the cake and I opened the gifts. Naomi gave me one of her favorite paperweights. It was heavy glass with horses etched on each side. When the light caught it just right, rainbows formed inside. Melissa and Kara gave me two nice button down shirts to wear to my new job. I needed them. As a freelancer, I had always been able to dress as I pleased, but at the magazine, I needed to look a little more professional.

Valerie's gift made me turn to her in inquiry. It was a pair of stainless steel dog food bowls, a collar, and a leash.

"That's so she can keep you under her control," Kara quipped.

After the laughter faded, Valerie explained her real gift would be to take me to the animal shelter in Beaufort so I could adopt a dog. I had shared with Valerie that since I got the job at the magazine, I eventually wanted to get a dog. I was never allowed pets growing up and I'd always wanted one.

By noon Naomi was exhausted. Emma gave her a mild sedative and her pain medicine and the rest of us went to the Carolina room. We sat around and talked about nothing in particular, enjoying the sound of the rain on the tin roof. I didn't tell anyone about Naomi seeing angels.

Valerie and I left about four o'clock to go take care of her babies. Valerie had been spending more time at Naomi's with me than at home with her pets, and they were showing signs of rebellion. When we arrived at the house, Bella let us know in no uncertain terms that she felt neglected. She could clearly be heard letting the world know she wanted her mom. We entered the house to find two bed pillows on the floor in the living room, one with the corner chewed off. Valerie fussed at her, but Bella was unrepentant. We cleaned up the mess and spent some time playing ball with her before Valerie fed her and the cats.

After feeding the animals, Valerie prepared steaks with mushroom sauce, fresh broccoli, and corn on the cob for me. She served benne seed wafers and peach ice cream for dessert. Sweet ice tea accompanied my birthday dinner. After we cleaned the kitchen, we sat on the sofa and cuddled and kissed. Bella tried hard to insinuate herself between us, but Valerie firmly told her "down" and the little dog lay at her feet, pouting. Despite the pleasure of the company, I was exhausted and I left for my house about nine. Valerie walked me to the car.

"You don't have to drive home, you know," she teased. "I have a big, comfortable bed."

After looking around for nosy neighbors, I kissed her lightly on the lips, just a peck of a kiss although I would have preferred to kiss her long and hard. My resolve to wait got weaker each moment I spent with her.

At home I turned on my laptop, checked my email, and wrote in the journal I'd started when I found out how sick Naomi was. I had recorded each day's events ever since. My journalist's mind saw an article lurking in there somewhere. I knew I would soon be writing what other people wanted me to, so I was trying to write for myself as much as possible before that happened. I also wrote in a separate journal about my feelings for Valerie. In it I tried to help myself understand the love I felt growing for her and why it was so important for us to wait before consummating our relationship. I was usually able to articulate my feelings better on paper or computer screen than I could verbally, but in this case my writing seemed just as confused as my heart and head.

My computer still perched on my lap, I fell asleep in my chair; the chair that had been my father's favorite place to spend a rainy evening. I dreamed he stood at the foot of the chair, smiling at me. Behind him, Howie and Carolyn were chatting, smiling and laughing and occasionally waving at me. I tried to wave back, but my arms were too heavy to lift. A door formed in the wall beyond where they sat and I sensed rather than heard a knock at it. Howie rose and placed his hand on the doorknob. He looked over his shoulder at me and mouthed, "Should I open it?" I wanted to shout, "No, No, No!" but I couldn't make myself speak.

I awoke with a start, catching my laptop as it began to slide off my lap. I sat quietly for a moment, getting my bearings. I shut the computer and placed it on the desk, my hands shaking as I thought about the odd dream. I glanced at the clock. One a.m. I was going upstairs to my bedroom when my cell phone broke the silence. I dug it out of my pocket, knowing it was Earl without looking at the screen. I sat down on the step and hesitantly answered the phone.

"Hello?" I whispered.

"Ms. Livingston, y'all need to head on back out here if you want to see Mom before she passes," Earl said quietly. "She's slipping fast."

"Oh, Earl. I'm so sorry. I'll call the others and we'll be there as soon as we can."

"Thank you. Hurry, please."

We hung up and I sat for a moment, trying to collect my thoughts. Finally I called Melissa's cell phone. Kara answered on the second ring.

"It's time," I said simply.

"We'll meet you there," she said and hung up.

I called Valerie next and she also said she'd meet me at Naomi's. I went upstairs and washed my face and put on a clean shirt. I looked around my bedroom and wondered how many times Naomi had sat in that chair at my desk, leaning back on two legs; and how many times she'd climbed out my window and down the oak tree just because she could; and how many times the two of us had slept together in that bed — friends, sisters. I knew I couldn't afford to break down now, so I rushed down the stairs and out to my car.

It seemed every light in the house was on at Naomi's. I let myself in the back door and hurried straight for her bedroom. The night nurse, Sara, sat in a chair outside the room, tears streaking her face.

"Am I too late?" I asked in a panic.

"No, Ms. Livingston," she said. "I always cry when one of my patients is dying. Earl is in there with her now. He told me to tell you to go on in."

I patted her on the shoulder as I went through the door. Earl sat at the side of the bed, holding Naomi's hand. He looked up when I put my hand on his arm. He stood up, relinquishing his chair to me but not letting go of his mom's hand. I sat down and laid my head on the bed. Naomi's breathing was labored and the beeping of the heart monitor seemed quite slow. I felt a hand on my head and looked up.

"Hi," Naomi whispered, trying gallantly to smile at me. Her hand rested on my cheek. "Howie came to visit me a little earlier," she said, struggling for air as she spoke. "He told me to tell you hello and that you should try not to be sad."

I laughed nervously, sadly. "Howie and Carolyn and my dad came to visit me earlier," I told her. "They looked happy. I know they'll welcome you with open arms."

"I hope so," she gasped. "Lay down with me, please?"

I cautiously climbed onto the hospital bed beside her and gently laid my arm across her. I put my head next to hers on the pillow. The others came in, but I didn't acknowledge their presence. Naomi slept for a while and then woke again, gasping for air. Sara came in and adjusted Naomi's oxygen and Naomi rested again.

I lay there with her until the sun began to rise. Mist rose from the paddocks; fog shrouded the far outbuildings. Naomi opened her eyes and looked out the window toward her horses. I sat up and looked out with her. Suddenly I noticed every horse in sight was looking toward the house, their ears forward, alert, as though someone was talking to them. Naomi smiled and weakly raised her hand as though to wave at them. Her hand fell back to the bed just as the heart monitor sounded its alarm.

I looked down at Naomi. Her eyes were open, but I could tell she was gone. Emma came to the bed and checked her pulse while Sara shut off the alarm on the monitor. Emma looked at me and shook her head. She gently closed Naomi's eyes. I gathered Naomi in my arms in farewell.

I slipped off the bed and looked around the room. Kara held Melissa, both of them sobbing. Valerie stood next to them, tears also streaming down her face. Earl sat in the chair next to the bed, his face in his hands. Emma and Sara were just outside the door, hugging.

I left the room wordlessly, walked into the kitchen, and sat down at the table. I couldn't cry; the tears wouldn't come. I sat there, unseeing. Someone set a cup of coffee in front of me and I sipped it without tasting it. I vaguely heard people moving around me. Emma called the funeral home and made the necessary arrangements for Naomi's body to be picked up. I occasionally felt a hand on my shoulder. But I couldn't respond; I couldn't think; I couldn't even feel.

I left Naomi's house without a word to anyone. In the car, I turned off my cell phone and just drove aimlessly before finally stopping at Sheldon Church ruins where I wandered among the huge red brick columns. I sat on one of the old grave markers that had been used as an operating table during the Civil War and recalled the times the six of us wandered these ruins together, sharing a picnic lunch and secrets we kept from the rest of the world. I remembered the time Naomi found an injured squirrel at the base of one of the huge oak trees and insisted we take it home so she could nurse it back to health. I still couldn't cry.

When I finally went home, Valerie was sitting on my porch waiting for me. She met me at the car and hugged me. I was unable to return the hug. She led me up the steps into the kitchen, where she placed a plate of toast and apple butter in front of me. When I made no move to eat, she nudged me up and led me to my bedroom. She gently sat me on my bed, removed my shoes, and softly pushed me back onto my pillow. She covered me with the light blanket from the end of the bed. I watched as she crossed to the window and closed the heavy drapes.

Valerie came back to the bed and lay down beside me, just as I had lain beside Naomi that morning. I could feel her tears on my shoulder, but I couldn't move to hold her or to comfort her. She lay there until I finally fell asleep.

Chapter Seventeen

I woke up, arms and legs entwined with Valerie's. She was sleeping and I studied the lines of her eyes and mouth. Her face was streaked with dried tears. I brushed her brown hair off her forehead and kissed the spot between her eyebrows. Her eyes flitted open.

"Hi," she said, her voice thick with sleep. "Are you okay?"

I struggled with an answer. I was glad Naomi was out of pain, but I knew from experience my pain was just starting. I knew Earl's pain was just starting. I hoped he would continue to let us be a part of his life so we could help him get through the difficult times ahead.

"I don't know yet," I said truthfully.

She kissed the corner of my mouth, a comforting kiss. I turned my head and caught her lips with mine. I wanted more than a comforting kiss. I thrust my tongue into her mouth and she caught it with her teeth, flicking the end of it with her own tongue. I felt a fire growing, a flame that raced through my body as Valerie's hands caressed me.

"Stop," I pleaded.

"Why?" she moaned back.

Suddenly the tears that refused to come that morning were streaming down my cheeks. I buried my face against her shoulder and sobbed big choking sobs. Valerie sat up and cradled my head on her chest. She rubbed my back and stroked my hair and let me cry. When my sobs finally subsided into great heaving hiccups, she sat me up and got out of bed. She came back with a damp washcloth and bathed my burning face.

"Let's go downstairs and get something to eat," she said, offering me her hand. She led me to the kitchen as though I was a child. "You might want to turn your cell phone on," she said, as she took eggs and bread from the refrigerator.

"Oh, good grief. I forgot I turned it off." I had five voice mail messages.

"One of those is from me," Valerie said. I checked the list and saw one was from Emma and the other three were from Melissa and Kara. I called them back first. Sue Ellen answered Melissa's phone.

"Hi, sweetie," she said. "Are you okay?"

The second time in an hour I was asked that and I still didn't know. "I will be," I told her. "Are Melissa and Kara sleeping?"

"Yes," she said. "I'm the keeper of the cell phone and doggy babysitter until they wake up."

I chuckled. I could hear the dogs barking in the background. "I can hear Dick and Jane," I said. "Won't they wake the girls up, barking like that?"

"Oh, we're at the park letting them run. They wouldn't leave their mommas alone, so we had to get them out of the house."

"Would you have the girls call me when they're conscious again?"

"You got it, sugar. You sound awfully tired. Try to get some more rest, okay?"

"Yes, Momma Sue." I laughed as we hung up.

"It's good to hear you laugh, Shelby." Valerie set a plate with scrambled eggs and toast in front of me, then kissed me on the forehead before she took a seat on the other side of the table.

We ate in silence, each watching the other but thinking our own thoughts. I couldn't get Naomi's face out of my mind. The little wave she gave just before she died haunted me. Was she waving at her horses, or at the angels? Or maybe at Howie and Carolyn. I didn't realize I was crying again until tears dropped into my plate. Valerie reached across the table and held my hand.

My cell phone rang and we both jumped. It was Earl.

"Earl," I said. "How are you doing? What can we do for you?"

"I'm as well as can be expected," he said. I could tell from his voice he was exhausted. "I just wanted to let you know what the arrangements are. Mom made them last year when she found out she wasn't going to beat the cancer. It was just a matter of letting the funeral home know it was time."

I got up to get a notepad and ink pen. "I'm ready, hon."

"The service will be at Martin's Memorial Funeral Home, across from First Baptist Church, at ten on the twenty-third. Mom's being cremated, so there won't be a viewing. I thought I'd invite everyone back here after the service. If people keep bringing me food, I'll have enough to feed a large crowd several times over."

I wrote down the details and let him know I was available to help him get the house ready if he needed it.

"Thanks, Ms. Livingston. I may take you up on that. Hospice is coming for the hospital bed tomorrow. I haven't done a thorough house cleaning in a week or so and I could sure use the help."

"I'll be out around eleven, okay?"

A short time later, Valerie had to go home to take care of her babies, but she promised to come over the next day and go to Naomi's with me. We kissed a long time before she drove away.

The twenty-third dawned bright and beautiful. I dressed carefully in a crisp white button down shirt with black, sharply creased slacks and a black vest. I picked Valerie up at eight and we met Melissa and Kara, Mrs. Ballard and Sue Ellen at Robbie's for breakfast. Robbie was there, in her customary spot behind the register, dressed in a black dress with a large white collar.

At nine-thirty, we walked up Main Street to the funeral home. Earl met us at the door of the chapel. He kissed each of us on the cheek as we hugged him.

"Would y'all do me a favor?" he asked, tugging uncomfortably at his tie. "Would y'all sit up front in the family pew with me? I really don't want to sit there all alone and y'all were more family to her when she was growing up than Granny or Grandpa ever were."

"Oh, Earl, of course we will," I said, hugging him again.

Melissa and Kara and Mrs. Ballard and Sue Ellen and Valerie and I walked to the pew at the front of the chapel and sat down. It was hard to realize that Earl was all the family Naomi had left. Her mother was still alive, but Naomi had confided in me they hadn't spoken since her father passed away. When she found out she was terminally ill, Naomi tried to make her peace with her mother, but her mother brushed off her attempts.

I twisted in the pew and watched the other mourners arrive. Robbie came with her granddaughter. Lora Krantz Best and a few others from our class at Yancey High showed up, too. I was sure they were not there to mourn Naomi but to be seen. Lora's eyes got wide when she saw us in the family pew, and she and the others immediately began to whisper among themselves. I didn't know most of the other people in attendance. Naomi's equestrian training facility was well-known across the South, so many of the people were likely her clients.

The memorial service was short. A large picture of Naomi with one of her horses was on a table up front where a coffin would normally lie. The picture was surrounded by flowers.

The chaplain provided by the funeral home opened the service with a prayer, and then Earl approached the podium. He paused for a moment beside Naomi's picture. I had to bite my lip to keep from bursting into sobs when he ran his hand across it before mounting the steps to the dais.

"Thank you all so much for coming out today to honor my mother, Naomi Jasper. Many of you have been Mom's students at the farm and you know how much she loved her horses. All animals, in fact. Sometimes I think she got along with animals better than she did with people. She taught me that animals will love you unconditionally, even if they're mistreated, but they will rescue you, save your life if necessary if they are treated with respect and love. I would probably have been an animal lover even if I hadn't had the privilege of being raised on one of the largest horse farms in the South, but Mom instilled in me an even greater love. When I was quite young, she began teaching me how to run the farm, to manage the paperwork, to take care of things. She practically turned over the entire business to me when I turned eighteen, ten years ago.

"When I was twelve years old, I called a classmate a derogatory name I won't mention here. My teacher overheard me and sent a note home to Mom. I was scared to death I was going to be in so much trouble. Instead, Mom sat me down and told me the story of her senior year in high school, how she lost five wonderful friends because of hate she carried in her heart; because of ugly and nasty words that came from her mouth; and worse, because of actions she took with a wrong motive. She made me understand how a simple word can cause an unending cycle of pain. I've never forgotten the look in her eyes, the tears, the remorse in her voice. I learned my lesson that day and I also found out why my mother always looked sad, even when she was laughing.

"Mom was a fighter. She fought her own personal demons for nearly thirty years, but some dear friends came back into her life at just the right moment to help her rid herself of them before it was too late. The night before she died, we talked. She was more lucid than she'd been for a week. She told me that her friends Howie and Carolyn had come to visit her earlier that evening and that they assured her they had forgiven her for the pain she had caused them. She also told me that now she could die in peace — all five of her best friends knew she loved them and they were at least trying to forgive her."

Earl looked down at me and Melissa and Kara. "Thank you, from the bottom of my heart. Because you were willing to listen to her and were willing to forgive her, my mom was able to die with no lingering regrets. Bless you all."

I nodded up at him, my hand over my mouth to stifle my sobs, Valerie's hand holding tightly to my other one. Melissa's head was on Kara's shoulder, her sobs barely audible.

"Mom raised me alone — without the help of the man who fathered me, without the help of her parents. And, if I do say so myself, she did a pretty damn good job."

We laughed through our tears as Earl left the stage and stood in front of Naomi's picture.

"Thank you, Mom. Thank you for loving me, for taking such good care of me. I love you."

There wasn't a dry eye in the chapel when he sat down.

After the service, people mingled outside, chatting and reminiscing about Naomi. Earl went from group to group inviting them back to the farm. Just as Valerie and I started back to Robbie's to pick up our car, the owner of the funeral home approached me.

"Ms. Livingston, may I have a moment of your time?" Mr. Martin asked me quietly. "Or, if you prefer, may we make an appointment for you to come back to visit with me for a few minutes?"

I hesitated a moment before answering. I had no clue what he wanted to talk to me about. Valerie quietly urged me to go see what he needed. We stepped away from the crowd at the door, his hand gently on my elbow, his typically serious face even more so.

"Ms. Livingston, your mother made no arrangements for the disposal of her ashes. They're still here in our vault. I've attempted to contact your brother but he hasn't returned any of my telephone calls."

"My mother's ashes?" I asked, incredulous. The lawyer had told me her wishes were for the funeral home to dispose of them. Why would they still have them? I posed that question to Mr. Martin.

"We don't have the means to dispose of them," he said.

"What will happen to them if they aren't claimed?"

"Once a year we bury all unclaimed remains in a common grave," he said solemnly. "Surely you don't want that for your mother?"

My emotions were running the gamut from disgusted to sad to relieved and back again. I couldn't make an immediate decision. "May I think about this for a day or two?" I asked.

"Of course, Ms. Livingston," he said. "Take your time. Here's my card. Please let me know what you decide."

I rejoined Valerie, who waited in the shade of a huge oak tree. Melissa and Kara waited with her.

"What was that all about?" Valerie asked.

"Can you believe the funeral home still has Mom's ashes?" I asked after explaining the situation to them. "I thought they would have disposed of them by now. I don't know why Kyle hasn't done something with them before now."

"So, are you going to pick up the ashes?" Melissa asked.

"I don't know. What in the world would I do with them?"

"I think you should accept them," Valerie said. "It might help you achieve some closure."

"I hate that word," I said. "Closure. What exactly is that? Just because we said good-bye to Naomi doesn't mean I've closed the door on her."

"Of course it doesn't," Valerie said. "But doesn't it help you accept her death a little more? Didn't it help you accept Howie's death to bring him home and bury him?"

I stopped walking and turned to her. "I don't think I'll ever be able to accept their deaths. Neither of them should have died like they did, or when they did."

Valerie put a comforting hand on my arm. "Of course, they shouldn't have, Shelby, but they did. You have to admit that having a ceremony like the one we just left helps. And that's why I think you should take your Mom's ashes and figure out a way to honor her, honor them."

"But, Valerie," Kara said, "you don't know how horrible Shel's mom was to her. I understand why she doesn't want to take them. I'm not sure I'd want to if my mom had treated me like Mrs. Livingston treated Shel."

"It has to be Shel's decision," Melissa said. She looked up at me and then gave me a hug. "Whatever you decide is okay, Shelby, regardless of what anyone else thinks."

"Thanks, Melissa," I said, struggling to control my emotions.

"You're right, of course, Melissa," Valerie said. "I'm sorry, Shelby. You do what you need to do."

Later that evening, after spending the afternoon helping Earl and sharing the early evening with Valerie, I sat alone in my father's office. My conversations with Mr. Martin and with the girls replayed over and over in my head. I finally picked up my phone and called Kyle.

"Hey, Sis," he said when Paula called him to the phone.

"Hey, yourself."

"How was the memorial service?" he asked somberly.

"It was beautiful. Earl gave Naomi a wonderful eulogy. I wish we hadn't become estranged. I would've loved to have known the Naomi he described," I said sadly. "But that's not why I'm calling."

"Okay. What's up?"

"I spoke to Mr. Martin after the service. The funeral home still has Mom's ashes. He said you don't return his calls. I thought the lawyer was taking care of the disposal of her ashes and now I find out that hasn't happened. Do you know what's going on?"

An uncomfortable silence fell between us; the phone line hummed with tension. After a long moment, Kyle finally answered.

"Shelby, Mom and I were not exactly on good terms when she died," he said. "She got to a point as she aged where nothing anyone did was good enough. She disapproved of how Paula and I were raising the boys; she disapproved of me taking the job here in Charleston instead of taking a better paying job somewhere else. Nothing was ever right and I got sick and tired of it. I quit having much to do with her about a year or so before she died." Kyle's voice broke.

"I didn't even know she was sick until the lawyer called and told me she'd passed away. I was so ashamed I hadn't been with her. Mom left instructions that there be no funeral or memorial service, just that she be cremated. When Mr. Martin first called me about her ashes, I told him I'd get back to him, but I never did. I just couldn't take her ashes. I had no idea what to do with them."

I sat in stunned silence. I hadn't stayed in touch with my family any more than I had my friends, but when I did talk to them there was never a hint that Kyle and Mom weren't getting along. They were always close when we were growing up; I'd been jealous of their relationship.

"Shelby, are you still there?"

I could hear the tears in Kyle's voice. "I'm still here," I said. "Why haven't you told me this before?"

"You and Mom were never close and I didn't want to make things worse," he said. "Even when I wasn't speaking to her, I kept hoping you and she would be able to make things right between you."

"She never let me. She was so cold to me the few times I came home. I would try to talk to her, but she only wanted to tell me how wrong I was to be a lesbian, how I needed to settle down," I whispered. I had hoped Mom would accept me as I was, tell me she was proud of me just once, but it never happened. And now it was too late.

"Shelby, Mom talked about you to anyone who would listen. That was one of the things that drove Paula nuts. Mom was always talking about what a success you are, how brave you are, and asking Paula why she didn't take a page out of your book and make something of herself. Mom never could accept that Paula liked being a stay-at-home mom. Mom kept telling her, 'Don't let Kyle hold you back like his dad did me.'"

"Naomi told me Mom bragged about me, but I didn't realize she held me up like that. She never had a word of encouragement to say to me when we talked." Tears threatened.

"Shelby, let's think of some place Mom loved and let's go together to spread her ashes."

I had to digest all he had told me before I could make a decision. "Let me think about it, Kyle."

After we hung up, I sat in the dark for a long time. I felt as though I'd walked in the dark for so many years. I wanted to be close to Mom, but whenever I made the effort, she pushed me away with harsh words and cruel reminders. I would never understand how she could be so cold to me and at the same time brag on me to the people around her. The spirit of the little child inside of me ached. I wished I had known that part of Mom — the part that loved me, that was proud of me.

I put my head on the desk and let the tears fall. I longed for the people I had lost to come back and let me right the wrongs between us. I had worked long, hard, arduous hours to get a story so the public would know what was wrong in this world and maybe become indignant enough to do something about it. And all the while, I had never made the effort to fix the wrongs in my own private world.

Howie died wanting to reconnect with Naomi and I wouldn't let him. We would never know why Carolyn died, but I couldn't help but wonder if she would have taken her life if the Six had been able to overcome those events of our senior year and reconcile. Dad died sad and alone because he and Mom weren't able to resolve the differences between them. And Mom died alone, because she wouldn't let the people who loved her near.

My heart broke until I felt it could never be repaired. I sobbed like I never had before, soaking the desk blotter and the front of my shirt. I knew I had to let down the walls I had built around my heart and make sure the people I loved knew how much they meant to me.

Chapter Eighteen

I woke with a start. I had a terrible crick in my neck from sleeping with my head on the desk. Morning sunlight poured through the window, pooling on the desk in front of me. I stretched and gingerly turned my head from side to side, trying to relieve the pain. My face was tight with dried tears.

I went upstairs to shower and put on clean clothes. I let the hot water sluice over my body, soothing the aches from my unconventional sleeping position. I missed the fancy showerhead in my apartment in Atlanta. I knew I needed to go back to retrieve the rest of my belongings and close up the apartment. I had friends who could do it for me, but I decided I needed to do this myself and say my good-byes in person.

After breakfast, I called Kyle. "I thought about Mom and Dad and us and everything else," I told him. "I know where we should take Mom's ashes."

"Where?"

"Sea Pines Audubon Preserve on Hilton Head."

"Oh, Sis, that's perfect!"

I was flooded with memories and knew Kyle must be, too. "How many times did she disappear while Dad took us to the beach? And we always found her beside the lagoon at the Preserve, watching the birds and hoping to see a deer," I said.

"Remember that time we came up the path to find her and there were those two deer, one on either side of her bench?"

"She sat so still, so quiet, they just came right up to her. I do remember. That's why I know Sea Pines is where she'd want her final resting place to be."

"When do you want to do this?" Kyle asked.

"If I can get the ashes today, do you want to go tomorrow? And Kyle, do you think Paula would mind if it were just the two of us?"

"Tomorrow's fine, Shelby. I'll talk to Paula; I'm sure she'll understand. Call and let me know what time, okay?"

We hung up and I called Mr. Martin and made arrangements to take delivery of Mom's ashes later in the day. I called Valerie next.

"You sound tired," she said when she heard my voice.

"I am." I related my conversation with Kyle the night before and about falling asleep at the desk. I also told her about my decision concerning Mom's ashes and going to Hilton Head the following day.

"Do you want me to go with you?"

"Thank you, but no," I said. "Paula isn't even going. Kyle and I are going to do this ourselves. I need this to be just the two of us. I hope you understand."

"I understand, hon," she said. "I'll be here for you when you get home."

"I'm heading to Atlanta from Hilton Head," I told her.

"Whoa. Now I feel like you're running away from me. Promise you'll come back."

"I'll be back, silly." I laughed. "Probably on Tuesday or Wednesday, depending on how long it takes to tie up loose ends."

"At least come over this evening and let me fix you dinner," she said.

"Wouldn't miss it."

We hung up and I leaned back in my chair, my feet propped on the table. I laughed when I realized what I was doing. I could almost hear Mom yelling, "Shelby Louise! You get your feet off the table this minute!" I stood up and walked onto the back porch. The sun glinted off the marsh, the water rippled in the light breeze. *Good fishing weather*, I thought.

My hand on the door handle, I stood on the step of Martin's Memorial Funeral Home, unable to propel myself over the threshold. I had been in the funeral home many times over the years, but this time was different. It was hard to believe I was there to take possession of my mother's ashes. I finally entered the building and went to Mr. Martin's office.

"Come in, Ms. Livingston," he said. "Please have a seat. I'm so glad you've decided to accept your mother's ashes rather than having them buried in a common grave. I'll be glad to show you some urns in which she can rest."

"No, thank you, sir," I said, inwardly cringing. "My brother and I have already decided what we're going to do and we won't need an urn."

Schooling his features to hide any disappointment he might have felt, Mr. Martin left the room. I sat with my hands in my lap, trying hard not to fidget. I don't know why I was so nervous, but it felt as though I was waiting for Mom herself to come back into the office. I could hear her scolding me for not coming for her sooner and my palms began to sweat. It wasn't long before Mr. Martin was back, a nondescript white box held reverently in his hands. He set it on the desk in front of me.

"Ms. Livingston, I have some papers for you to sign. Once that's done, you're free to take your mother's cremains."

I cringed again and signed the papers in the places he indicated. We both stood up and he solemnly shook my hand, then handed me the box. I thanked him and left, gingerly carrying the box with both hands. I just knew I was going to trip between his office and the parking lot, scattering my mother's ashes over the lobby or lawn. I was relieved to get to the car and safely deposit the box on the passenger floor of the front seat.

I drove home carefully, avoiding bumps and potholes so Mom's ashes wouldn't be jarred. The last place I wanted them was in my car. I could see taking my car to the carwash and trying to explain why the upholstery and floorboards were covered in ash. Back at the house, I set the box in the middle of the kitchen table, sat down, and contemplated it. Inside that container was my mother, all that was left of her earthly body, anyway. Some part of me wanted to reach out and caress it, a caress I never gave her while she was living. Another part wanted to get as far away from it as possible. That part won out.

Feeling smothered indoors, I left the house and went down to the dock where I sprawled out across the weathered planks. I closed my eyes. I could smell the pluff mud, exposed by the outgoing tide. I listened carefully and heard fiddler crabs scurrying across the surface from one tunnel to the next. Sometimes I could even hear as the little crabs sparred with their oversized claws. I heard a fish jump far out in the marsh and remembered I had planned to go fishing. I decided to give the fish a reprieve for the day.

After a while, the sun became too warm for me to stay on the dock. I forced myself up and went back to the house. As I reached for the door handle, I could see the box still sitting on the kitchen table. I started to go around to the front door instead, but something stopped me. I stormed into the kitchen and confronted the box.

"Mom, this is my house now! I'm not going to let you stop me from enjoying it by sitting in the middle of the table like you own it."

Good grief, I thought. *I've finally lost my mind. I'm screaming at a box that Mr. Martin says contains my mother's ashes. It could be someone else's ashes, or even a box of sand, for that matter*. But now I couldn't stop. I sat down and drew the box closer.

"Listen to me," I said to the box. "You never once told me you loved me or that you were proud of me or anything like that. I have to find out those things from Naomi and from Kyle. I wonder if you realize how much that hurts."

I listened for an answer, but all I heard was the breeze through the branches of the oak. Far away I heard the afternoon birds calling to one another and insects buzzing through the flower beds, but I didn't hear my mother's spirit speaking to me. I only heard my heart pounding and my breath catching as I began to realize I actually missed her.

"I'm not going to cry over you. You didn't shed a tear over me, or at least you never let me see you cry. I don't really know why I'm wasting my energy taking you out to Hilton Head. But I promised Kyle, so that's where you're going, whether you like it or not."

I slammed my fist on the table so hard the box bounced dangerously close to the edge. I wasn't sure why I was so angry, but the pain of it tore through me like a hot poker. I stood up so fast my chair fell over backwards. I shook my finger at the box, reminiscent of the way Mom shook hers at me in anger and exasperation.

"How dare you die without talking to me first? How dare you tell everyone how proud of me you were and not tell me before you left? How dare you? How dare you!"

I jumped as I felt hands on my shoulders. I turned and found Valerie standing behind me.

"What are you doing here?" I snapped, stepping back, away from her touch.

"I had a feeling you might need a friend," she said quietly, circling to the opposite side of the table.

I studied her as she sat down and gently pulled the box away from the edge of the table. I could see I'd hurt her feelings. She sat quietly, one hand lingering on the box even though it was now safe from falling. Her face was serious, her eyes full of concern. Her brown hair was pulled off her face with silver barrettes. A simple silver necklace adorned her neck. She wore a pink tank top with pink madras shorts. Her beauty stunned me, even through the haze of anger. I wasn't sure whom or what I was angry about.

"Shelby, would you like to go for a walk, maybe a drive?" Valerie said. "Let's go somewhere away from here and talk."

I turned and walked mechanically to the back door. I stood leaning on the door frame, looking blindly out toward the marsh, my back to the table and to Valerie. My mind was reeling with memories flying through it like a movie on fast forward. I rubbed my temples; I had a splitting headache.

Valerie came to stand beside me. She leaned on the opposite side of the door and together we stood in silence for a long time. Finally she reached out a hand but didn't touch me.

"Come on, hon," she whispered, "let me help you. Tell me what you're feeling."

I took her hand and held it, stroking her palm with my thumb. "I'm sorry I snapped at you," I said, unable to look at her. "I don't know why I did that."

"Shelby, you've been through the mill this month. A lot has happened in such a short period of time. If anyone has a reason to snap, you certainly do."

Had it really only been a month since I returned to Yancey for my high school reunion? It felt like an eternity since I arrived back in town. Valerie was right — a lot had happened and I was on the verge of exhaustion. I let her lead me onto the porch where I collapsed into my favorite wicker chair. She disappeared back into the kitchen, reappearing with a pitcher of lemonade and a plate of graham crackers.

"You need to go grocery shopping," she said. "You're out of almost everything."

"I know," I said sheepishly. Grocery shopping was one of my least favorite chores. My itinerant lifestyle as a freelance reporter had saved me from having to go very often; I just ate out. I knew I would have to get used to shopping since I was going to be staying in one place, hopefully for a long time. "I'll go when I get back from Atlanta next week."

We talked for a little while about what I needed to accomplish on my trip. I told her I thought I had someone lined up to sublet the apartment, but we had to finalize the details on paper. I also had to pack up the few belongings I'd left there and say goodbye to friends in the area. "I won't be gone more than a few days, I promise."

"Shelby, are you going to be okay?" she asked. "You just lost Naomi and now you are dealing with disposing of your mom's ashes. Can't that wait for a while until you heal a bit?"

I shook my head and rested my face in my hands. I seldom lost control of my emotions the way I had in the kitchen. I knew I had to put all of the hurts of the past behind me if I was going to be successful in Charleston. I couldn't continue to run from my history and my life. I finally looked up at her. The concern on her face melted my heart.

"I have to do this now. I've been running for too long; it's time I faced my feelings and the things I left behind when I left here in '76. The time I spend with Naomi..." My voice caught in my throat as I realized I had spoken of her as though she were still alive. Valerie placed a hand on my shoulder, but stayed silent. "Spent with Naomi," I corrected. "The time I spent with Naomi helped a lot, but I think scattering Mom's ashes with Kyle tomorrow will be another step forward. I've learned more about Mom since I've been home than I knew the entire time she was alive."

I turned and looked Valerie in the eye. "She was proud of me, Valerie." I shook my head in disbelief. "She never once, not in my whole life, told me that. But she told Naomi; she told Kyle; apparently she told anyone who would listen. Why couldn't she tell me?"

Valerie knelt in front of me and wrapped her arms around me. She held me as if I were sobbing, even though my tears refused to fall. I hugged her back and we rocked in unison for a moment.

"I don't know why some people are unable to tell the ones they love the important things," she said. "If it were a perfect world, we'd all know exactly how everyone else feels about us, but unfortunately, that's not the way it is. So often we're left grasping for straws and coming up with precious little. I'm so sorry."

I took her face in my hands and kissed her deeply. She returned my kiss and my body melted. I stood up and held her in my arms. I resolved right then that she would always know how I felt about her.

"Valerie, I want to make love to you, but I want to wait just a little while longer. I want to be able to enjoy you, and right now I'm exhausted, mentally and physically."

She ran her hands up and down my back, and I shivered. "I know, babe," she whispered, her voice husky with desire. "I want you, too, but I know right now is not a good time. We'll both know when the time is right."

I stepped back from her so I could look her in the eyes. I saw something more there than just desire, something I could only hope was the same thing I felt for her.

"Valerie Gilmore," I said, my voice catching again, "I have to tell you something, something very important."

She cocked her head to one side, a smile playing at the corners of her mouth. I kissed her lightly, gently, first between the eyes, then the tip of her nose, then her lips.

"I have fallen head over heels in love with you. I've had a crush on you since the first day you set foot in my English Lit class, but it's so much more than that now."

"I should hope it's more than a crush," she said with a laugh. "Shelby, I love you, too. I have for a long time."

I crushed her into my arms again and kissed her passionately. We stayed locked in each other's arms for several minutes. A voice from the driveway made us both jump.

Kara laughed. "Y'all really should take it inside, you know."

I looked over Valerie's shoulder and stuck my tongue out at her and Melissa. Dick and Jane were in their crates in the back of the SUV. Suitcases were stacked on the backseat.

"Y'all are headed home, I see," I said, a sense of loss sweeping through me.

"Yes. Our kitty cat thinks we don't love her anymore," Melissa said. "How are you doing?"

I told them about my plans to meet Kyle on Hilton Head the next day and also about my trip back to Atlanta. I hugged them. I hated that they wouldn't be in Yancey when I got back and said so.

"When do you start working at the magazine?" Melissa asked.

"August first," I said. "I have a month to finish moving everything here and try to figure out how to stay in one place for more than a few weeks at a time."

"It's easier than you think," Valerie said, her arm protectively and possessively around my waist. "Especially when you know the people who love you need you nearby."

Melissa and Kara gave each other a knowing look and a wink.

"So, do people who love you live nearby?" Melissa teased. "Anyone specific?"

Valerie and I looked at each other and laughed. Melissa and Kara joined in, then it was time for them to go. We hugged each other again and they climbed into the SUV. Melissa leaned out the passenger window.

"Why don't y'all come up and spend the Fourth of July with us?" she said.

"We'll let you know, okay?" I said. "Y'all drive safely."

We waved them out of the driveway before going back to the porch. We sat in the wicker loveseat, each listening to our own thoughts. Valerie's head was on my shoulder, her leg thrown over mine, my arm around her shoulders.

My mind still raced with memories, wanted and unwanted. The girls leaving so soon after Naomi's funeral felt like another loss. I knew they had to return to Columbia, but my heart ached because they were no longer just a stone's throw away.

I don't know how much time passed, but I was suddenly aware of the rumbling of my empty stomach. Except for a few graham crackers, I hadn't eaten anything since early that morning. Valerie looked up at me and grinned.

"I'm going to go home and get us some dinner started, okay?" she said.

She stood up and I followed her out to her car. "I'm going to pack for Atlanta," I told her. "I'll see you in about an hour." I leaned through the window and kissed her lightly.

"I love you," she whispered, just before putting the car in drive.

I stood and watched as she turned the car out of the driveway toward Yancey. My heart followed her and I knew I no longer wanted my life to be without Valerie Gilmore in it.

Chapter Nineteen

The next morning I rose early, just as the sun was beginning to light the Spanish moss hanging from the oak tree. I had packed my bag and loaded the car the night before, so I spent a little while going through the house, closing windows and shutters, turning off the water, basically preparing the house to be empty for a while. As I finished, I stood in the kitchen staring at the box in the middle of the table. Suddenly I realized I hadn't needed to be so thorough closing up the house; I was only going to be gone a short time. *Old habits die hard,* I thought, laughing to myself. *You trained me well,* I told Mom's spirit as I picked up the box and went out the back door, placing the spare house key in its usual spot under the doormat.

Kyle and I met for breakfast at a diner on Hilton Head. I hadn't been to Hilton Head since the early '90s, and I was stunned by how much the place had changed. Traffic was much heavier than I remembered and we had to wait for a table at the diner.

Over breakfast we reminisced about the many times Dad had brought us to the island as children. Mom and Dad would set up an umbrella and blankets and unpack a picnic lunch. We brought our bicycles and cycled all over the island, stopping for ice cream or shaved ice. We played in the surf and sometimes fished as well. At the end of the day, we always ate at a popular café that served huge hamburgers. Sometimes Mom borrowed my bicycle and disappeared. We always found her at the nature preserve, spending quiet time with the birds.

"Remember the time we buried Dad in the sand?" Kyle asked.

"Which time, Kyle? We buried him in the sand almost every time we came out here."

"I think it was the year I was twelve. We got him all buried and Mom came back from wherever she had biked off to. She called us up to help her start getting ready to go and we completely forgot Dad."

"I do remember that. We were on our way to the car when we heard him calmly call, 'Anne Marie, do you plan on letting me come home with y'all?'"

"Mom jumped about a mile. She didn't even realize he hadn't been helping. The look on her face was priceless." Kyle shook his head. "Sometimes I wondered if her mind was really on her family.

She would be talking to me and I could tell she was really thinking about something else."

"I know. Dad said something like that while we were unburying him. 'She's here in body but not spirit' is what I think he said."

"Well now she's here in spirit, not body," Kyle said.

"Both of them are," I said. "We had a good childhood, didn't we, Kyle?"

"Yes, Shelby, we did. Each of our parents loved us in their own way and they made sure we always had everything we needed."

I reached across the table and squeezed his hand.

"Mom really did love it here," he said, wiping his eyes with his napkin. "I'm glad you thought of bringing her back."

At the preserve, Kyle placed a small sign at the trailhead, asking other visitors to respect our privacy for about twenty minutes. It didn't take long to reach the small lagoon and the bench Mom had so often occupied. We sat in silence for a few minutes, watching a cardinal flash its brilliant red in the foliage of the oak trees. A painted bunting appeared briefly in a tree to my side, its blue and green and yellow feathers bright against the green leaves. The pine trees towered toward a brilliant blue sky, wisps of white clouds just visible at the treetops. A breeze caressed my face and I realized my face was wet with tears. I glanced at Kyle; his face was tear-streaked. Silently taking the box from his lap, I stood and walked to the water's edge, opening the box. Kyle cut the bag holding the ashes open and I let the breeze catch the fine ash. Some of it fell on the water and some flew toward the trees. Kyle joined me and together we spilled the remaining ashes into the water, disturbing a dragonfly resting on a reed. We clasped each other tightly for a long time and then walked back to the parking area, not speaking a word.

I hugged Kyle again as we stood beside my car.

"I didn't realize it would be so hard." He laid his head on my shoulder and cried. "Oh, Shelby, I miss her and Dad so much. Why didn't I try harder to be the son they wanted me to be?"

I didn't have an answer for him. I was wondering why I couldn't have been the daughter they wanted me to be. I just held him and let him cry. As though I had already shed my quota of tears, I stood dry eyed. After a few minutes, he composed himself.

"Have a safe trip to Atlanta." He climbed into his SUV and sat looking at me over the roof of my car. "I'm really proud of you, Sis. I know you haven't heard those words from your family in a long time. But you are an awesome writer and photographer and the best sister a guy could want."

And then he drove off, leaving me standing beside the car with my mouth hanging open. Dad was the only person who had ever told me he was proud of me. I knew Mom told others, but neither she nor Kyle had ever told me before today. A big, silly grin on my face, I got into the car and left the island.

Four days later, it was late in the afternoon when I pulled off I-95 at the Yancey exit, glad to be through with the hustle and bustle of Atlanta. The month I spent in the quiet serenity of Yancey had spoiled me. The traffic and the noise of Atlanta gave me a headache I was still trying to get rid of.

I'd spent the time there sub-letting my apartment, collecting the rest of my belongings, and finalizing plans with the moving company to deliver the artifacts I had collected in my travels. Well-meaning friends had wined and dined me, trying to talk me out of moving away by reminding me of the fun we had and the open and welcoming community Atlanta supported. I visited my agent and reminded her I was no longer available for long trips, but urged her to stay in touch with short assignments in the area.

I was pleased with all I had accomplished, but I was anxious to get home. Though I spoke with Valerie daily, sometimes several times a day, I missed her. In the total of all my travels over all the years, I had never missed anyone as much as I missed Valerie during those four days. I craved her touch, her kiss. My drive home was spent in a six hour long erotic daydream involving the two of us.

The turn-off to my house was a welcome sight. I followed the long driveway to the rear of the house and was out of the car almost before it came to a complete stop. I raced to the dock and threw my arms wide, welcoming myself home. Birdsong and fiddler crab duels and rustling sea grass greeted me, and I plopped down, stripped off my sandals, and dangled my feet off the edge. I took a deep breath of the salty air, enjoying even the rancid smell of the pluff mud. I knew I never wanted to leave again, at least not for any length of time. I lay back on the warm wood and closed my eyes. I was glad I'd chosen to wear my five button jeans shorts and a tank top for the drive home. The sun beating down on my bare arms and legs and face felt like a golden hug. The smile on my face felt good. I was home and I was at peace.

After a while I went back up to the car and grabbed my bag and one of the boxes I'd brought back from Atlanta. I stopped short of the house when I saw the back door was open. Quietly setting down the baggage, I stepped inside. The sight that greeted me was a welcome one.

Valerie had taken advantage of knowing where I hid the house key. She stood at the sink, her back to me, wearing a simple white tank top over navy blue shorts that fit her figure like a glove. I let my eyes rove from her head to her toes. She must have felt my presence or heard my intake of breath, because she turned to me and smiled the smile that always melted my heart.

"Welcome home, Shelby," she said as she moved toward me.

I couldn't close the distance between us fast enough. I swept her into my arms and kissed her, first each eye, then the bridge of her nose, and finally that wonderful, welcoming mouth. Our tongues danced a *pas de deux* as our lips found their rhythm. I could feel my heart pounding in my chest, or was it her heart?

My hands explored her curves and this time I didn't stop myself. Hearing her rasping breaths, I stepped back, took her hand, and led her to the living room sofa. I tugged her tank top up over her head and admired her body. I ached to taste her, to touch her. I laid her back on the sofa and settled beside her, kissing, caressing. Her hands were busy, too, and my body responded to her touch, arching into her hands. I pulled my shirt over my head and we lay breast to breast.

After fevered moments of touching and kissing, I realized the bed would be more comfortable than the sofa. I stood up and offered her my hand. She silently took it and we went upstairs. The only other times Valerie had been in my room were to watch me sleep. She looked around before turning to me with a wry smile.

"Are you just going to stand there?" she asked, "or are you going to join me over here?"

She backed up to the bed as she spoke, motioning for me to follow. I quickly joined her and we nestled together on the bed, resuming the caressing we started downstairs. My hands traced down her body, stopping just short of the waistband of her shorts. She pressed against my hand and I fumbled with the button securing her shorts.

"Shelby, stop."

"What?" My body ached for her and now she was telling me to stop.

"I'm too old to fumble around like a teenager," she said with a laugh, standing up.

I watched as she unbuttoned and unzipped her shorts, then stepped out of them and out of her panties. She stood in front of me, naked and gorgeous, and all I could do was stare. She turned slowly, posing as she went.

"I take it you like what you see." She took my hands and, urging me to stand up, she unbuttoned each of the five buttons on the fly of my shorts and then pushed them down over my hips. In a flash, I stood naked before her.

We lay back on the bed and began to enjoy one another in earnest. As the evening sky darkened, sighs of pleasure and cries of ecstasy rose from my bed.

The next morning I woke with my face between Valerie's breasts and one leg thrown across her body. Her breath ruffled my hair and her hands rested on my back; a rush of desire rippled through my body. I leaned up and looked at her as she slept. A smile tugged at her lips and her eyelids twitched in a dream. I kissed them gently, watching as they began to flicker open.

"Good morning," I whispered in her ear as I kissed the tender spot just below it.

"Mmmmmm. Good morning to you, too."

I kissed her then, gently, as my hands caressed her, lingering on the spots that I knew would make her moan with anticipation and joy.

An hour later, we stood together under the flowing water in my shower. We laughed as we washed each other in the tiny space and then toweled off. As we started to dress, Valerie realized her shirt was still downstairs where I had stripped it off the night before. Ogling her bare back as she went down the stairs, I couldn't resist following her and slipping my arms around her, caressing her beautiful breasts.

"Stop it, Shelby," she said, even though she leaned into my touch. "I have to get home and feed the girls. I fed them before I came over yesterday but by now they're going to think I've deserted them."

"Hey. How did you get here yesterday? I didn't see your car in the drive when I came up from the dock."

She laughed. "I wanted to surprise you when you came in, so I parked in front of the house instead of in back. I saw you on the dock and thought about joining you there, but then decided it would be better if I waited for you inside."

"It was better. It was the best," I murmured as I kissed the side of her neck and let her go. I watched ruefully as she slipped into her tank top.

In the kitchen I started the coffeemaker. The back door was still open, my bag and box on the porch. I went to retrieve them and had to laugh when I saw my car door hanging open as well.

"What are you laughing at?" Valerie asked as she slipped her arms around my waist.

"My car is wide open. This is the second time since I got back that I've left it open. If we lived anywhere but Yancey, it would either be missing or stripped, but I bet not one thing has been disturbed."

As I finished speaking, a face peered at me through the windshield. "Out! Out! Out!" I yelled, sprinting for the car. A large raccoon sauntered out of the car and down to the marsh.

Valerie was right behind me, laughing. "Did he get into anything?" she asked as she caught up with me.

"Doesn't look like it," I said, inspecting the interior of the car.

The corner of one box was chewed on, but the four-legged bandit apparently hadn't had time to finish his breaking and entering before he was discovered. Valerie and I each grabbed a couple of boxes and lugged them into the kitchen.

"We didn't have much of a chance to talk last night," Valerie said, blushing at the memory of my welcome home. "I assume you got all your business in Atlanta taken care of."

I poured each of us a cup of coffee and popped some English muffins into the toaster oven. Valerie sat at the table and watched me.

"Yup," I said. "I sub-let the apartment to a reporter my agent recommended. He's young, just out of college, and as eager as I was when I first started. He wanted me out so badly he had all my things packed before I knew it."

I hesitated a moment before continuing. "I had the most awesome dream while I was there," I said. "I dreamed I was sitting on the dock, fishing, when a party boat floated by. It was decorated with streamers and balloons and I could hear music and laughter. The boat stopped for a moment in front of me and I could see inside. Mom and Dad were dancing together, and Naomi and Howie and Carolyn were watching. Suddenly they stopped, turned toward me, and waved. I could see how happy, how serene they were. When I woke up, I felt more at peace than I can remember being in decades."

Valerie joined me at the counter and hugged me. The nearness of her lips was tempting, and I kissed her. My heart was filled with a happiness I couldn't recall ever having felt before. I knew I wanted to share the rest of my life with this wonderful woman, but

I was afraid to say so. I didn't want to jeopardize what we already had.

After we ate our muffins, I walked Valerie out to her car. I didn't want her to leave, but I knew she had responsibilities she needed to tend to. I squeezed her tightly before releasing her to climb into the driver's seat.

"I love you," she whispered in my ear. "I love you more than I ever imagined possible."

My mind reeled, but my heart sang. "I love you too, Valerie."

"I'll see you later, okay?" she asked. "After you finish unpacking and doing whatever else you need to do, come over and I'll cook you dinner."

I kissed her again, glad that my house was on a private road, far from the main one. Shutting the car door, I waved to her as she drove out of the driveway. I stood there for a long time, even after she was out of sight.

At length I turned and looked at my house, studying it as though I'd never seen it before. It was a large two-story, Victorian style house with a wraparound porch along three sides. The blue-gray paint was peeling and a couple of shutters looked as if they could fall off at any time. The front door was a non-descript wood with three staggered rectangular windows. The porch was bare, the customary chairs and swing long since removed. The shrubs in the beds bordering the porch were overgrown and downright ugly.

I walked around the house, noting places repairs needed to be made. Since the driveway led around to the back, most visitors didn't even stop in front. Because of that, the back of the house was better taken care of. It needed to be painted, but the furniture on the back porch was in good condition and inviting. The caretaker had lovingly tended the rear flower beds. They were lush with hibiscus and lantana, daisies and zinnias.

Inside the house, my critical eye continued the examination. I already knew I wanted to turn the formal dining room into a library for Dad's books as well as my own, and also a showplace for my collections. Now I saw the kitchen through the eyes of a homeowner rather than a temporary boarder. The yellow cabinets were faded to a drab cream; the harvest gold appliances were all old, dating from the mid-Seventies when Mom last remodeled the room. The counter tops were chipped Formica, an ugly mustard yellow. The floor had potential; it was a checkerboard of one-foot square black and white tiles.

I moved to the living room. The large front window was hidden behind heavy drapes, designed to keep the summer sun from fading the furniture and carpet. I threw open the curtains and took a hard look around. The room was beautiful, in an aged sort of way. The walls were an eggshell white. Wainscoting and crown molding softened the room's edges. The current furnishings were circa mid-nineteen sixties. I decided almost all of it would go. I knew hardwood floors were hidden beneath the carpet; I would have the carpet pulled up and the floors refinished.

In the study, I sat down at Dad's old desk. The huge oak desk took up most of the room, but I knew I wouldn't part with it. I could remember playing hide-and-seek below the desk, even though I knew it was the first place anyone would look. With the exception of my bedroom, this was my favorite room in the house. This room was Dad's and my refuge when we needed to escape the stresses of our day or when it was too hot or too wet to be outdoors. The flocked red and gold wallpaper was the only thing in the room I truly disliked.

The staircase rising from the entrance foyer in the center of the house was a work of art. The banister was hand-carved oak. When Mom and Dad were alive, the wood shone, but now it was dull and needed to be refinished. Upstairs a long hallway bisected the house. To the left was the master suite. I hadn't entered it since returning home, afraid the ghosts and memories would overwhelm me. To the right and at a right angle to my room was the guest suite. The upstairs bathroom, Kyle's room, and my room faced the upstairs hallway.

I entered my bedroom and looked around, once again with a critical eye. What I saw brought a smile of dismay to my face. The bedroom hadn't changed since I left in 1976 at the ripe old age of seventeen. The décor was that of a Seventies teen who didn't know what she really wanted. The bed, bought when I was twelve, was a full-size canopy bed, without the canopy. The French Provincial bed was old and, as Valerie and I discovered the night before, rather rickety. The dresser and chest were from the same era, painted off-white with flowers stenciled on each drawer, rather juvenile for me now at forty-eight.

I sat in my rocking chair and looked around again. I definitely needed to make some changes to my living space. I took a notepad and pen from my desk and started a list. The exterior would be my first priority. I would call around and ask for recommendations for contractors. My job in Charleston didn't start for another month; I wondered if the work could be completed by then.

I stopped making my list and leaned back in the rocker and wondered why I was so interested in fixing this house up. I jumped when the ringing of my cell phone startled me out of my reverie.

"Hi, love." Valerie's voice made my heart pound. I felt weak with love and longing. "I just called to thank you again for last night and to tell you how much I love you."

"I love you, too," I said. "And last night was a gift I'll never forget." I could hear Bella yapping in the background and one of the cats mewling close by. "I'm making a list of renovations I want to have done on the house. I'd love to get your input on some of my ideas."

"I'd love to help you decorate," she said. "If I hadn't become a teacher, I would have gone into interior design. Tell me some of your ideas. I can listen while I feed these heathens."

I laughed and started telling her what I wanted to do to the house, both inside and out. She listened carefully, occasionally interjecting an idea which I would jot on my notepad. After an hour of chatting, I had filled several pages.

"I feel like I'm creating a home," I said.

"You are, Shelby." I could hear the smile in her voice. "And I'm glad it's in Yancey."

"Me, too."

"Oh, good grief!" Valerie yelped. "I completely forgot to tell you my news."

"What news?"

"The superintendent called me yesterday morning. I'm officially the new principal of Yancey High."

"Valerie. That's wonderful. We need to go celebrate. Tomorrow I'm taking you up to the fanciest restaurant in Charleston. In fact, if you can find someone to pet sit, why don't we just plan on staying the night up there?"

"Oh, Shelby, thank you. I'll let you know when you come over this evening, okay?"

"Okay. I'll be there about six. What can I bring?"

"Just your beautiful body. I love you."

"I love you too, Valerie. I'll see you later."

Chapter Twenty

The next month flew by in a flurry of activity. Valerie and I spent every possible moment together, most of it in her tiny house near the high school since my house was full of contractors and construction dust. We spent our first weekend as lovers in Charleston at a beautiful bed and breakfast. After that we went up to Columbia and spent three days visiting Melissa and Kara, where we watched the fireworks over the capitol on the Fourth of July. They were excited and pleased to see our relationship blossoming.

Shortly after we returned from Columbia, Valerie made good on her birthday promise to me. On a bright, beautiful day we drove over to the Beaufort animal shelter. I knew I wanted a medium sized dog, but other than that, I wasn't sure. The attendants at the shelter were wonderful. They allowed me to take several dogs and puppies out on the lawn to romp and play. I adopted a tall, slender dog that appeared to have some greyhound in her but otherwise was of indistinguishable breeding. The shelter workers had named her Shadow. A smoky gray, she tended to follow people around closely, thus her name.

Since my house was in shambles during the renovation, the first night Shadow was with me was spent at Valerie's. Bella quickly let the larger dog know that regardless of her size, she was queen of the household and would brook no interlopers. The cats, Victoria and Kelsey, hissed and disappeared into their respective hiding places. Poor Shadow stuck to my side like glue.

It took a little while, but before long Bella and Shadow learned to co-exist and, finally, to be friends. Both loved to retrieve balls and discovered tug-of-war was much more fun when played with a canine friend rather than a human one. Bella taught Shadow to beg and Shadow taught Bella that playing in the water could be great fun. The cats eventually accepted Shadow's presence and ceased to disappear when the two of us would show up on the doorstep.

My poor car, at fourteen years old and with well over 150,000 miles on the odometer, was finally giving up the ghost. It had served me well, but the time had come to retire the poor old thing. Valerie and I went to Charleston and another dream came true. I drove off the car lot in a bright red pickup truck, Valerie proudly riding shotgun.

The renovations on my house were completed the last Friday in July. I once again stood in front of my house, this time reveling in its beauty. It was freshly painted a rich butter yellow. The shutters were properly hung, repainted a striking forest green. The tin roof sparkled in the sunlight.

The porch was now inviting with its new white wicker furniture and cozy swing. The shrubs had been tamed and the flowerbeds overflowed with caladium and moss rose. Hanging baskets of ferns lent a formal air to an otherwise informal setting. The oval etched glass window in the new front door added a touch of sophistication.

Inside, the pegged hardwood floors had been refinished throughout the house. The mirror shine on them reflected the light from new fixtures in the entryway, living room, and my new library. Dad's study had been re-paneled in a pale, whitewashed pine.

The masterpiece downstairs was my new kitchen. Bright birch cabinets replaced the dull yellow ones. Light brown speckled granite countertops surrounded the deep custom sink and butted up against the new turquoise tile backsplash. A stainless steel dishwasher, refrigerator, and stove completed my up-to-date kitchen. I had kept the old red Formica and stainless breakfast table and recovered the red vinyl kitchen chairs to add a retro touch to the room.

I started up the newly refurbished staircase, trailing my hand along the smooth, shining banister. Not one step creaked, a phenomenon I didn't know was possible.

Upstairs, I had combined my bedroom with the guest suite, making the two rooms the new master suite. My new king size bed barely took up any space in the huge area. Valerie helped me choose a bed with delicate iron work on the headboard and a low, almost non-existent footboard. A bench upholstered in rich gold-on-gold brocade sat at the end of the bed. The new dresser and chest were of a rich, dark mahogany, while the bedside tables were glass with delicate iron legs.

My original bedroom area became a cozy reading nook that was open to the rest of the room. A floor lamp angled over the back of a deep red chaise lounge. My beloved rocking chair, stripped and refinished, sat across from the lounge next to a small round table covered in a fringed tablecloth. A bookcase with my favorite books graced one wall. The opposite wall was my family wall. I hung the picture Mom took of me at graduation along with other photos I'd taken of my family. I also found old sepia and black and white portraits that I framed and hung with pride. In a place of honor were pictures of the Six: Howie, Carolyn, Naomi, Kara,

Melissa, and I looked out at the world beyond the picture frames, forever young.

The suite also included a large cedar-lined walk-in closet, and a master bathroom that was decorated to appear old. It included a claw foot tub that on closer inspection was actually a Jacuzzi. The magnificent shower had one showerhead hanging from the ceiling as well as several others at different levels. A large old enamel bowl I'd found stashed in the back of one of the kitchen cabinets was now my sink.

The original upstairs bathroom was upgraded with new fixtures and a new shower stall. Except for a thorough cleaning, fresh paint, and new mattresses on the beds, I left the original master suite and Kyle's room alone. I planned on using those two rooms for guests. I was often reminded what blessings good friends were, and I hoped my house would be filled with their company and their laughter.

I was sitting in my rocking chair, basking in the satisfaction that all the work had been completed when I heard a car horn sound in my driveway. I looked out the window and was pleased to see Valerie's car on the newly graveled parking area. Shadow and I raced down the stairs to greet her as she entered the back door. I grabbed her up and swung her around, laughing as Shadow barked her approval.

"Put me down, silly."

I lowered her feet to the floor and silenced her laughter with a deep kiss. Her arms snaked around my neck and we stood toe to toe, breast to breast. My hands found their way under her shirt and caressed her bare back. She moaned in contentment and let her hands drop from my neck to my sides, brushing my breasts as they went. When we finally came up for breath, we were both flushed with desire.

I sat down in one of the kitchen chairs, pulled her down on my lap and resumed kissing her until she put her hands on my shoulders and pushed away from me.

"I feel like a teenager again," she said, breathless. "I just can't get enough of you, but stop for now and show me the house. It looks great outside and I love the way the kitchen turned out. You've kept me in the dark the past week and I want to see the finished product."

"Did you notice I even had the dock re-surfaced and the boathouse painted?" I asked.

"I did. They both look great." She laughed at my enthusiasm. "I also saw Shadow's new kennel and that the bare spots in the yard have been re-sod. But I already knew about all that; I want to see the inside."

I took her hand and gave her a guided tour of the house. We spent a lot of time in my new library, where I showed her my prized artifacts and told her where I had acquired each one and the story behind it. Many of the items were from people I had interviewed and I had the gift displayed with the corresponding article about the giver. Two walls were covered with photographs I had taken over the years, and the other two walls had floor to ceiling bookcases filled with books and keepsakes. Comfortable easy chairs and two reading tables completed the room, the floor graced with the only rug in the house, an oriental rug that was a gift from a friend in Thailand.

In the office, Valerie admired the new paneling and was amazed at how the oak desk reflected her image in its new finish. "What are these?" she asked, picking a ragged edged notebook off a stack on one corner of the desk.

"Those are Howie's journals. He started keeping them when he first moved to San Francisco. I've had them since he died, but I've never been able to read them before now. I started looking at them when I went to Atlanta last month. I never realized what a wonderful writer he was."

Valerie laughed. "He didn't show a lot of potential as a writer when I had him in English Comp. I bet I used up more red ink on his essays than anyone else's." She looked down at the notebook. "He was a special young man, wasn't he? I wish I'd had the chance to get to know him better."

"Howie was special, more special than many people know. But I hope to change that. I'm thinking of using his journals to write a book about him — his memoirs and biography all tied up together in one book."

"What a wonderful idea." Valerie laid the notebook back on the stack before coming around the desk to hug me. "Now show me the rest of the house."

The living room was still devoid of furniture. I'd had the heavy drapes replaced with light, airy panels in a rich gold. The walls were repainted the palest of yellows and the wainscoting and crown molding, a bright white.

"What are you going to put in here?" Valerie asked, her voice echoing off the bare floors.

I shrugged. "I don't know yet. I can't decide if I want to go with antiques or with more modern furniture. I thought we could hit some of the furniture stores in Charleston or Savannah some weekend soon."

"Oh, I'd love to help you decorate this space." Valerie clapped her hands like a child with a new toy. I laughed and hugged her before leading her upstairs.

"Wow!" she exclaimed as I opened the door to the new master suite. "This is huge. And beautiful."

"You like it?" I asked, sincerely hoping for her approval. She turned to me and pulled my face to hers. I kissed her, reveling in the taste and feel of her lips against mine.

"I love it. Almost as much as I love you," she whispered in my ear.

I led her to the bed and gently laid her back on it. I snuggled next to her, nuzzling her neck and ears and caressing her breasts. She arched her back to meet my hands, and before long we were both thoroughly enjoying my new bed.

Several hours later we were lounging on the chaise in my new sitting area. Shadow was curled in her dog bed, watching us with limpid eyes. I held Valerie close, gathering my courage. Finally, I decided I just had to say what was in my heart. I leaned forward and turned so I could look her in the eye.

"I have something really important I want to talk to you about," I said.

"This sounds serious. Is everything okay?"

"Everything is better than okay and I want it to be better yet. I want you and the girls to move in here with me."

Valerie's mouth dropped open, her eyes wide. She stared at me without saying anything. I waited, my heart pounding. I was so afraid she'd tell me I was crazy. She wrapped her arms around me and hugged me. I could feel her shoulders shaking and her tears dampened my shoulder.

"Valerie?" My voice shook with apprehension.

It took a few minutes for her to compose herself, but she finally sat back and looked at me. Her face, though tear-streaked, was still beautiful.

"Shelby, I'd love to move in here with you," she said, hiccupping. "I'm so honored you asked me."

I felt there was more; I was afraid there was more. "But?"

"But, nothing." She laughed. "I have to admit I was hoping you'd ask and I was afraid you wouldn't."

I gathered her into my arms, my own tears beginning. For the first time in a long time, I was crying tears of joy rather than of sorrow, anger, or frustration. My lips found Valerie's and we spent a long time snuggling and kissing before we were interrupted by Shadow's cold nose on my arm.

"I think someone thinks it's dinnertime," I said with a laugh.

August was a busy time for Valerie and me. I started my new job at *Charleston Magazine* and immediately fell in love with my position. I seldom stayed in the office, even though my official title was "in-house reporter", but traveled the Lowcountry of South Carolina, north to Myrtle Beach and south to Hilton Head and Daufauskie Island, interviewing people and photographing both people and places for the human interest stories that were the magazine's specialty. I discovered I could do most of the writing and editing of the articles I wrote from home, thanks to email and the internet. With my boss' permission, I worked more and more from the house, traveling to Charleston only for staff meetings and to help put the magazine to bed.

Valerie's position as principal at Yancey High proved to be extremely time consuming. Although classes didn't start until shortly before Labor Day, Valerie held teaching seminars for the teachers beginning the first week in August. She tried to be present at each band and football practice that began later the same week, even if only for a few minutes. The teachers and students loved her and whenever the two of us would go out to Robbie's or just stroll Main Street, we would be greeted by many students or their parents.

We worried about how our little town would accept our relationship and tried hard to keep it under wraps. It soon became obvious, however, that we were almost expected to be seen together. If one of us went to the supermarket or for a walk without the other one, we would be stopped by well-meaning citizens of Yancey and asked, "Where's your friend? She's not sick, is she?" It was refreshing to know we were loved by the townspeople and they were either tolerant of us or turned a benevolent blind eye.

We decided to put off moving Valerie into my house until after the first of September when the rush of my new job and the new school year had subsided. We gradually introduced Bella to my house, but discovered we had little to worry about. She and Shadow found that it was great fun to run up and down the staircase at top speed, sounding more like a herd of elephants than two dogs with dainty feet. They loved to fly down the dock and off the end into the water, startling the water birds into flight. Or if the tide was out, they'd stand and bark endlessly at the fiddler crabs that diligently ignored them as long as they remained on the dock.

As the days passed, our career responsibilities gave us less time to spend with each other, and still we found our love growing. When I was on the road driving to yet another interview or photo op, I found myself lost in daydreams of Valerie. I missed an exit off I-95 more than once thinking about her. When we were together, our time was sweet. Valerie was all I ever dreamed of in a partner and more.

Finally the day came for us to move Valerie's household. Kara and Melissa drove to Yancey on Friday. Saturday morning, they, Mrs. Ballard, and Sue Ellen met us at Robbie's for breakfast, then we caravanned to Valerie's to load furniture and boxes. With the six of us, it was short work emptying the house and cleaning it to the realtor's specifications.

At my house, we formed a human chain and conveyed box after box from the trucks into the still empty living room. By two o'clock in the afternoon, the room was wall to wall boxes and furniture. Valerie and I stood in the door and surveyed the controlled chaos.

"Now the fun really begins." She laughed. "I had no idea I had so much junk."

"Well, we don't have to find room for it all today," I said, snuggling into the crook of her neck. "We know where the important stuff like clothes and computer are; the rest can wait a few days."

"You're right," she said, turning to face me. I tightened my arms around her, kissing her lightly at first and then harder.

"Y'all are hotter than the grill." Melissa's laughter pulled us apart. We grinned at her, the silly grins we found on our faces more and more. "Y'all come out here and visit with us. You have the rest of your lives to snuggle and play kissy-kiss, but we have to go home tomorrow."

"Play kissy-kiss?" Valerie laughed as we followed Melissa through the kitchen to the backyard. "Is that what they call it these days?"

I laughed too, but my mind settled on the words "the rest of your lives". My heart soared at the sound of them. I stopped Valerie just before we went through the back door and hugged her again.

"Welcome home," I said, kissing her. "Welcome home."

"How long have you been writing?" is a question often asked of authors. Glenda Poulter's answer is, "As long as I can remember." Glenda was three or four years old when her mother, desperate for some peace and quiet, handed Glenda a piece of paper and some crayons and asked her to draw a picture. Instead, Glenda drew a story.

Glenda has been writing ever since. Her short stories and poetry were published in her high school magazine, where she dreamed of one day being a professional writer. But that dream was put on hold when she married a career Air Force man shortly out of high school. She had two children, Kaycee and Scott, during the twenty-two years she was married. Glenda's writing during that time was limited to prolific journal entries and short stories written to entertain the children.

In 2005, after her divorce from her husband, Glenda came bursting out of the closet to no surprise of most of the people who knew her. She met Lisa in March 2006, and they have been together ever since. Early in their relationship, Lisa asked Glenda what her dreams were. "I always wanted to be a writer" was Glenda's answer. "Write me a story" became Lisa's mantra. Glenda wrote *Welcome Home* (after several false starts) to shut Lisa up. It didn't work. Lisa still urges Glenda to write more and more.

Glenda and Lisa live in the Raleigh/Durham area of North Carolina with their three cats and two dogs. Glenda's day job as a Customer Service Representative helps keep the lights on and food on the table so she can keep on writing. Some of her hobbies include photography, painting, bird watching, and playing *Bejeweled Blitz* on Facebook.

If you would like to contact Glenda, you are welcome to email her at imtogfer@gmail.com; join her yahoogroup, GlendaPoulter@yahoogroups.com; or friend her at Facebook, where you are also welcome to try to beat her high score of 164,000+ at *Bejeweled Blitz*. If you would like to read more of Glenda's writing, you will find short stories and poetry at her website www.GlendaPoulter.com, where you can also view some of her photography.